DROP DEAD CHOCOLATE

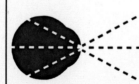

This Large Print Book carries the
Seal of Approval of N.A.V.H.

DROP DEAD CHOCOLATE

JESSICA BECK

WHEELER PUBLISHING
A part of Gale, Cengage Learning

GALE
CENGAGE Learning

Detroit • New York • San Francisco • New Haven, Conn • Waterville, Maine • London

GALE
CENGAGE Learning

LIBRARY OF CONGRESS CATALOGING-IN-PUBLICATION DATA

Beck, Jessica.
    Drop dead chocolate : a donut shop mystery / by Jessica Beck. — Large print ed.
        p. cm. — (Wheeler Publishing large print cozy mystery) (A donut shop mystery)
        ISBN 978-1-4104-5265-8 (softcover) — ISBN 1-4104-5265-4 (softcover) 1. Doughnuts—Fiction. 2. Coffee shops—North Carolina—Fiction. 3. Private investigators—Fiction. 4. Mayors—Election—Fiction. 5. Murder—Investigation—Fiction. 6. Large type books. I. Title.
PS3602.E2693D76 2012
813'.6—dc23   2012032699

Published in 2012 by arrangement with St. Martin's Press, LLC.

To my spouse,
for tasting all of the recipes with me,
the good ones I use,
and the bad ones I don't,
a true meaning of the phrase
"for better or for worse"

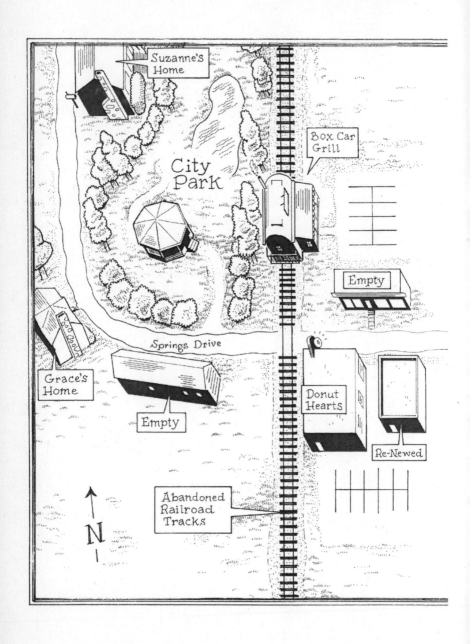

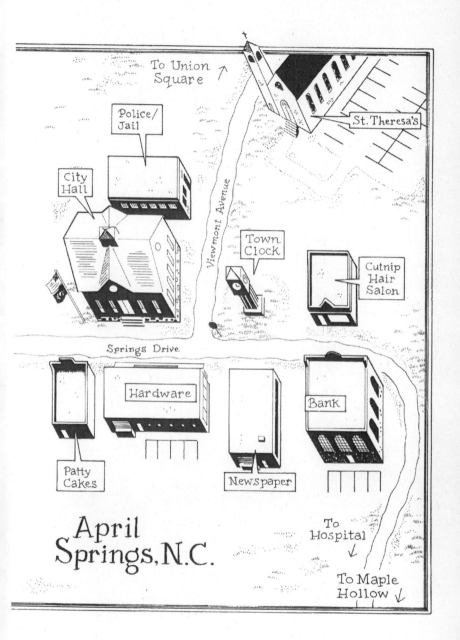

To Union Square ↑

Police/Jail

City Hall

St. Theresa's

Viewmont Avenue

Town Clock

Cutnip Hair Salon

Springs Drive

Hardware

Bank

Patty Cakes

Newspaper

To Hospital ↓

April Springs, N.C.

To Maple Hollow ↓

"An actor without a playwright is like a hole without a doughnut."

— George Jean Nathan

CHAPTER 1

I guess you could say that the murder was partly my fault. After all, I was the one who urged my mother to run for mayor of April Springs. If I'd had the slightest idea what that would lead to, I like to think that I would have kept my mouth shut when the subject first came up and stuck with making donuts, the thing that I did best in this world.

But then again, knowing me, I probably wouldn't have been able to stop myself, even with the foreknowledge of what was to come.

And one of our town's citizens would be dead because of it.

Worse yet, suspicion would turn its gaze onto me and my family once again, and I would be thrown into another murder investigation that I didn't ask for.

"This is outrageous," my mother said as she

stormed into the cottage we shared in April Springs, North Carolina, late one February afternoon.

"I agree wholeheartedly," I said as I sat up from the couch where I'd been napping. I worked some pretty brutal hours at the donut shop I owned, so I tried my best to grab some shut-eye whenever the opportunity afforded itself. As I stretched, I asked, "What exactly are we upset about this time?"

Momma gave me that look she'd honed since I'd been a kid, the one that said my humor was not exactly hers. "Suzanne, I'm not in the mood for your witty banter. Our mayor has finally gone off the deep end. Did you read the newspaper this morning?"

As the owner and head baker at Donut Hearts, I got to work every morning at three a.m., well before the newspaper was even printed, and I didn't exactly have time to sit around reading all morning. There were donuts and coffee to sell, tables to clean, and customers to greet. Emma Blake, my young assistant who worked with me, kept up with dishes in back while we were open, but the most important part of her day was helping me make the donuts six days a week. She got one day off to rest, but I was there every day that ended in *y.* I knew I could close one day, but I couldn't stand giving up the income. It was all part of the joy of being a small business owner.

I stood up and stretched again. "Sorry, I didn't have the time to look at it. What has Emma's dad been up to now? Is he trying to stir up trouble to increase his circulation again?" The *April Springs Sentinel* was barely more than an advertising machine for local businesses, but every now and then Ray Blake liked to write an editorial or post a controversial interview in an attempt to boost his readership. Ray was barely one step above a tabloid as far as most folks around town were concerned, though I knew that deep in his heart, he considered himself a true journalist.

"There's a story in here about our mayor," Momma said as she smacked the paper in her hand. "You need to read this."

As she handed me the paper, I said, "Why don't you save us both some time and give me the condensed version?"

"Suzanne, this is important."

I knew from her tone of voice that there was no escaping it, so I took the newspaper and unfolded it so that I could read the front page.

The banner headline blared out: MAYOR CAM HAMILTON AWARDED COUNTY JOB.

CAUSES BIG STINK.

"What's this about?" I asked Momma.

"Read on," she said, clearly too upset to add more until I'd read the entire article.

The story read, "This reporter has uncovered the carefully guarded secret that our mayor has submitted and won a contract to construct the new county waste disposal treatment plant on the edge of town. Normally happy to work on small jobs around our quaint fair city to leave more time for his mayoral duties, Hamilton has decided to go big time, and something doesn't smell quite right about our commander in chief going after a taxpayer-funded job while he's in office."

"Can he do that?" I asked, looking up from the newspaper. "It doesn't seem legal."

Momma's lips were pursed into a pair of thin lines before she spoke. "I checked, and there's nothing specific in our town charter that forbids it, but one of his cronies is on the committee that awarded him the job. For once, I think the *Sentinel* got it right. There *should* be a big stink about this, despite the clever play on words for a treatment plant. Cam Hamilton needs to walk away from this."

"Fat chance he'll ever do that," I said, remembering how self-important our mayor could be. He'd once told me that the police department worked for him, not the citizens of April Springs, and when I'd informed him that things didn't work like that in our part of North Carolina, he'd nearly thrown me out of his office. The man did not enjoy being challenged on any level.

Momma said, "If he doesn't withdraw, and I mean right now, I'll make him sorry that he ever made that bid."

"Why don't you run against him?" I suggested. "You'd make a great mayor, and the election's coming up soon. You'd do an excellent job."

She looked at me askance, another expression I was used to. "Suzanne, I'm not a politician."

"That's why it's so perfect," I said, beginning to really warm to the idea. "Think about all of the good you could do as mayor. There wouldn't be any of this nonsense, that's for sure."

Momma stood there for a second mulling it over, and then grabbed her coat and her purse as she headed for the door.

"Where are you going?" I asked.

"Where do you think? I'm going to have a word with Cam Hamilton," she said.

"Wait up, I'll go with you." I didn't want my mother rampaging around city hall by

15

herself. She was barely five feet tall and didn't weigh a hundred pounds soaking wet, but when she was on fire like this, there was no one in their right mind who wanted to go up against her. I was going not to protect her, but anyone who might be foolish enough to stand in her way.

"You don't have to babysit me, young lady," she said as I hurriedly put on my tennis shoes.

"Are you kidding? I wouldn't miss this for the world. I want a ringside seat for the fireworks."

She didn't seem to approve of me going with her, but then again, she didn't actively protest it, so I ended up tagging along.

As she drove to city hall, I said, "You know, there's a good chance that he may not even be there."

Momma frowned. "If he's not, I'll hunt him down like the mad dog he is."

"You might not want to open with that," I said, trying to take a little sting out of her mood.

It clearly didn't work. "If anything, I can only get angrier from here."

Momma pulled up in front of city hall and was half-way up the steps before I caught up with her. I put a hand on her shoulder, and somehow managed to slow her down,

16

at least momentarily. "Hang on a second."

"What for?"

I looked into her eyes and said, "Momma, you need to take a deep breath and count to ten before you go in there."

"Suzanne, I am in full control of my facilities," she said. "There is no need for a childish exercise."

"Humor me," I said.

She didn't want to, but I watched as Momma did as I asked. When she was finished, her breathing had slowed a little, and a touch of the fire had gone out of her eyes. "There. Are you satisfied?" she asked me.

"Absolutely. Thanks," I said, knowing that if I got in her way much more, her ire would shift toward me, something I had no interest in experiencing.

We got to the mayor's office, where Polly North, a retired librarian who worked the desk as the town hall secretary these days, was at her station. Like Momma, she was a woman of small stature, but she wasn't someone worth crossing, either.

"Hello, Dorothy," Polly said, not even acknowledging me by name, but offering me a quick glance before focusing on my mother.

"Is he in?" Momma asked as she looked

17

at the mayor's closed door.

Polly didn't skip a bit as she replied, "Why, I'm fine. And you?"

Momma got it, and I could see her expression soften for just a moment. "Sorry, Polly. I'm not mad at you. It's just that he's gone too far this time. I need to see him right now."

Polly pointed to the office door, smiled, and nodded, all the while saying, "I'm sorry. I'm afraid His Honor can't be disturbed right now."

Momma shot her a quick smile. "Got it. If anyone asks, I barged into the room uninvited."

Returning the grin, Polly said in a happy voice, "I really must ask you not to go in there," all the while nodding her head vigorously for us to go right in.

As Momma threw open the door, I saw that Cam was behind his desk, his feet propped up, a soda in one hand. There was a hot dog on his desk, and it wasn't too tough to see why he'd put on weight since he'd played high school football many years before. Only his hair had stayed the same, carefully styled and sprayed, with nothing out of place.

"Ladies," Cam said as he sat up in his chair. "Polly," he added, nearly bellowing,

18

"I told you I wasn't to be disturbed."

"Don't blame her," Momma said. "She tried to stop me, but I wouldn't allow it. What is this nonsense about you making a bid on a county project while you're mayor of April Springs?"

Cam dabbed at his lips with a napkin and said, "So, you've seen the newspaper."

I could see the steam start to build in Momma's eyes. "Everyone has. It's wrong, Cam, and you know it."

He looked as though that last bite of hot dog hadn't agreed with him. "Dorothy, if you please, I'm happy to be called Cam on the street, but when I'm at my desk here at city hall, I ask that you respect the office. It's Mr. Mayor."

I thought Momma might have a stroke just then, but she took a deep breath, and then said almost cordially, "You really enjoy having that title, don't you?"

He looked smugly at her as he replied, "Why shouldn't I? It's a perfect description of who I am."

Momma shook her head. "There you're wrong. It's a job description, not a personal one. Whoever is mayor at the moment owns that title."

He looked puzzled by her comment. "What's your point? I am the mayor."

"For now, perhaps."

That clearly got his attention. He sat up in his chair and put his soda on his desktop. "What do you mean by that?"

"This is an election year, Mr. Mayor, or have you forgotten that? I know you haven't bothered putting signs up yet, probably because you'd like folks to forget, but the filing deadline is tomorrow, and the election is in a week." Our local political races ran in February, an odd time compared to the state and national election cycles, though no one I knew understood why.

"No one's running against me," he said. "It's a safe bet that I'm going to retain my title as long as I care to have it." Wow, he was so smug, if Momma didn't run against him, I was considering it myself. That man needed to be taken down a few notches.

"Are you dead set on taking this project?" Momma asked in a soft voice that I knew meant that she was serious.

"It's a done deal, Dorothy. I don't know what the fuss is about. After all, I deserve the right to earn a living."

"I'm not saying you don't," Momma said. "But this smells bad to everyone who is going to hear about it. It doesn't just make *you* look bad. It's a poor reflection on all of us."

The mayor shook his head. "If you've got a problem with that, blame it on Blake and his catchy headline."

"I'm not kidding, Mr. Mayor," Momma said, managing to put a great deal of scorn into her words, especially his title.

"You put her up to this, didn't you?" Cam asked me as he looked at me, acknowledging me for the first time since I'd walked in.

"Don't try to blame me. I'm just along for the ride," I said, trying my best to smile brightly.

"I'll bet," he said.

"Mr. Mayor, I'm perfectly capable of acting on my own," Momma said. "I will ask you only once more. Will you walk away from this right here and now?"

"No, ma'am, respectfully, I won't. You can't tell me what to do, and I won't be bullied by a . . . citizen in my own office." I had a feeling he wanted to use a different word than "citizen," but even he wasn't that foolhardy.

Momma nodded curtly. "Then I'm going downstairs and filing my name as a candidate for mayor."

Cam didn't look happy about the news, but something must have suddenly occurred to him. He smiled broadly as he said, "Sorry, but you can't."

"What do you mean, she can't?" I asked. "Do you honestly think that you can stop her?"

The mayor drummed his fingers on the desktop. "The town charter clearly states that she needs a hundred signatures before she can file, and I doubt she can get them by tomorrow."

"I'd be glad to wager that you're wrong there," my mother said as she pivoted and headed for the door.

"Dorothy, you're biting off more than you can chew this time," Cam said as Momma reached the door.

She turned and gave him a withering stare. "Is that a threat, Cam?"

"It's Mr. Mayor, remember?"

Momma smiled, but there was no warmth in it. "For now," she said, and then I followed her out, carefully leaving the door open behind us.

Polly was standing just beside it, and it wouldn't have surprised me a bit to learn that she'd been eavesdropping on our conversation. She silently clapped a few times and smiled, but then Cam yelled for her, and she disappeared inside.

"What now?" I asked. "If the donut shop were open, I could get you the signatures you need in a heartbeat, but where are you going to find a hundred people right now? Are we going door-to-door begging for them?"

Momma shook her head. "We won't have to. We're going to start at the Boxcar Grill and move on from there until we've made our quota."

As soon as we walked into the diner, we told Trish Granger, the owner and one of my best friends, what we were up to. When she heard the news, she whooped with great joy. "Well, all I can say is that it's about time."

"I think so, too," I said.

Momma asked, "Do you mind helping us, Trish?"

"Are you kidding? I want to be the first one to sign it."

I looked at Momma and said, "We forgot to make up a sheet. Some campaign chair I turned out to be."

"Who said you could run my election?"

"Come on, I'm the logical choice," I said. "Who in the world believes in you more than I do?"

She softened for a just a moment, then said matter-of-factly, "Very well, but that means you need to take orders from me without resistance."

I wasn't sure I could abide by that. "I'll try."

Momma looked at me a second longer and then nodded. "I suppose that will have to do."

Trish reached into a drawer behind the register and brought out ten sheets of blank paper. She stapled them together, and then wrote in big letters on the front page: "Petition to Put Dorothy Hart on the Ballot for Mayor of April Springs."

She showed us and then asked, "How's that?"

"It's perfect," Momma said.

"Good." Trish signed her name bigger than John Hancock's, and then announced, "Let's go, folks. Dorothy Hart for mayor: Be one of the lucky ones who gets to sign the petition."

There was a rush up front, whether for my mother or against Cam Hamilton, but it really didn't matter what their motivation was. We needed signatures, and we needed them quickly.

As people signed, more came into the diner, and I found Trish working her telephone. When she hung up, I asked, "Where are they all coming from?"

"I dialed the ladies on the Disaster Alert call list, and they're phoning everyone in town. We'll have those signatures before the clerk's office closes."

"Should you be doing that?" I asked.

"Why shouldn't I? The list is strictly done on a volunteer basis, and it's not associated with any government agency at all."

I still wasn't sure this was the best way to start our campaign. "But it's not really a disaster, is it?"

Trish nodded. "You bet it is. Cam Hamilton has been mayor long enough. If getting your mother elected isn't a number one priority for this community, I don't know what is."

More folks were signing, most likely more than we needed.

"On second thought, you should be the one running her campaign," I said. "You've got a lot of ties to the community, and folks around here clearly respond to you."

"They respond to you, too," she replied.

"Maybe if they're craving donuts," I said. "But you're a natural leader."

"Don't sell yourself short. I wouldn't know how to run a mayoral campaign." She looked around the crowded restaurant and added, "I wouldn't mind being head of PR, though. I can spread the word like nobody's business."

I nodded. "As soon as I get my mother's

approval, you've got the job."

Trish looked pleased by the honor when my best friend, Grace Gauge, walked into the diner. "Hey, why didn't anyone call me? I didn't know we were having a party."

"It's better than that," I said. "Momma's running for mayor."

"It's about time," she said. "How can I help?"

"There's a petition right over there," I said, pointing to a crowd midway through the diner. "You'd better hurry, though. Slots are filling up fast."

"Not without me," she said as she pushed her way into the mess.

A few minutes later Momma rejoined us, with Grace close behind her. My mother looked a little surprised by the outpouring.

"Are you okay?" I asked.

"We've already got one hundred twenty-seven signatures," she said, clearly a little dumbfounded. "I kept telling them we had enough, but people kept insisting that the have the right to sign. It's all a bit over-whelming."

"You can be stunned tomorrow," I said. "Right now, we need to get these signatures to the courthouse so we can get you regis-tered." I pulled her aside and asked softly, "Are you sure you want to do this? It's still not too late to back out."

She looked at me for a second before she answered. "Is that what you want, Suzanne?"

I laughed. "Are you kidding me? I'd love to see you wipe the floor up with that windbag."

"Even if it makes life a little harder for you?"

"Momma, you need to be mayor of April Springs, and no one else. I'm voting for you twice if I can figure out how to get away with it."

Grace said, "It's not that tough. The first thing you need to do is —"

"I don't want to hear it," Momma said. "Suzanne, let's go to the courthouse before I change my mind."

Grace stayed behind to grab a bite at Trish's, but she promised to catch up with us later at the house.

As Momma and I walked back to the city hall building, I said, "I didn't push you into this, did I? You're sure you want to do this, right?"

Momma frowned a moment. "There is one thing I'm concerned about. I have my fingers in a great many pies around town," she said. "It might not be appropriate for me to run for public office. After all, I just chastised Cam for something some might justifiably accuse me of doing myself."

Even I didn't have any idea what kind of businesses my mother owned a part of in and around April Springs, and I was her only child, not to mention her roommate, since my divorce from Max. She played her cards close to the vest, and I had a hunch she liked it that way. "The difference is, folks already know that about you. No one expects you to stop what you're doing and sell all of your stakes, but your contacts could make life around here a lot easier for everyone involved. Are you planning on bidding on any jobs that involve city or county government while you're in office?"

"Of course not," she said.

"Then I don't see a problem."

"There's something else to consider as well. The job comes with a great many headaches, I'm sure," Momma said, though I could see that she was beginning to like the idea of being mayor.

"But just think: you'll be Grand Marshal of the Pageant Parade, and you get to give away keys to the city whenever you feel like it, too."

She laughed shortly. "Leave it to you to name those two functions of the position. If

I were to do this, I would be intent on allowing folks a voice in how they are governed, instead of just bullying them the way Cam does."

I met her smile with one of my own. "I agree, but just picture his expression when we walk in and he sees how fast you got those signatures," I said. "It's nearly worth it just to watch his face."

"I shouldn't admit it, but you're right," she said, waving the sheets filled with signatures in the air. As though she couldn't believe it herself, Momma said, "I'm running for mayor!"

"I couldn't be happier about it. I'm backing you a thousand percent. You've got a campaign manager, and Trish has already volunteered to run your PR, which is huge," I said, getting into the spirit of her declaration.

Momma looked at me warily. "Are you sure you'll be able to take orders from me?"

"About the campaign, sure," I conceded. "Everything else is off-limits, though."

Momma nodded, bit her lower lip, took a deep breath, and then said, "I suppose that makes it official. I'm running."

"Let me get out my jogging shoes, because I'm going to be right beside you."

CHAPTER 2

To my delight, Cam was downstairs in the clerk's office at the Board of Elections when we walked in. He didn't look all that pleased to see us. "You've made your point, Dorothy. There's no need to keep hammering it home. I get it."

"I don't know what you're talking about," Momma said. She turned to the clerk, a woman named Hillary Mast, who loved my donuts. "Hillary," my mother said, "I'd like to file my papers for the mayoral election."

If Hillary was surprised by the announcement, she didn't show it. "Good, you've come to the right place. I need just two things from you: the signatures of one hundred registered voters, and a fifty-dollar fee. I can vouch for your proof of residency myself."

"Here are the names," Momma said, "and I have the money in my purse."

"Let me see those," Cam said, not being

particularly nice about it at all. He tried to grab them as they changed hands, but Hillary was much too quick for him.

"If you touch those papers, I will go directly to the police station and swear out a warrant for your arrest for tampering with an election," Hillary said.

"You've got to be joking," Cam replied.

To my delight, Hillary didn't bat an eye. "If you think I'm bluffing, try it. Truth be told, there would be nothing that would give me greater pleasure."

"Are you on her side, too?" he asked her, clearly incredulous. "Do you think that's wise, given the fact that I'm your boss?"

"You don't scare me. I'm an elected official, too," Hillary said. "I work for the people of the town of April Springs in the state of North Carolina, and there's nothing in my job description that says you're my employer. Now, if you don't have any more official business here, I'll ask you to leave."

Cam stared wickedly at Hillary, at me, and then longer at my mother before he finally left the room and walked up the stairs.

"I've been wanting to do that for three years," Hillary said with a smile after he was gone.

"You didn't get into trouble on my account, did you?" Momma asked.

"Trust me, I meant what I said. He can't touch me."

Hillary scanned the signatures and then said, "I'll have to check these against our voter registration logs, but they look good for me. All I need from you now is your fee and I'll enter your name on the rolls."

Momma looked inside her purse, growing more and more frantic, and said, "I can't believe this. My wallet must be at home."

Hillary looked upset as she said, "I'm really sorry, but without a fee, you can't file. I can't bend the rules for anyone, Dorothy, not even you."

"Hang on a second. I've got it," I said. I suddenly remembered the two twenties and a ten I'd put in my pants pocket that afternoon. I'd been planning to spend it on something completely unnecessary, but I was delighted to use it for this opportunity. As I unfolded the bills and handed them to Hillary, I said to Momma, "This is on me."

"Nonsense, I'll pay you back as soon as we get home."

I wasn't about to argue with her. "It's your call, but I want you to know that I'm supporting you with everything I've got."

"I should certainly hope so," Momma said.

Hillary looked around to make sure no

one was close enough to hear her, and then said, "You've got my vote as well, though I'd appreciate if you wouldn't tell anyone. I don't want a whisper of voting irregularities, if you know what I mean."

Momma looked touched by the declarations. "Thank you both for your support."

Hillary wrote out a receipt and handed it to Momma. "Good luck."

"Thank you."

As we left the courthouse, Polly was waiting outside for us. "What exactly did you do to that man?"

"Whatever do you mean?" Momma asked.

"He came up to his office, stayed less than a minute, and then stormed out of here as though he were on fire."

"If I had to guess, I suppose he was displeased when he found out that I was serious about running for mayor," Momma said, as though she were trying the words out for the first time.

Polly laughed. "You've got my vote, and if you need any campaign workers, let me know."

I knew Polly didn't have Hillary's protected status. "Hang on a second. Won't he fire you?"

"He can't," Polly said with a grin. "I just decided to quit. I took the job as a volunteer to fill some empty hours, but I'm good at what I do. Dorothy, I'd like to formally ask you for my old job back the day you take over the mayor's office."

"Of course, but I can't be certain I'll win."

"Trust me, Cam Hamilton's support is not what it used to be. He's double-crossed too many folks in this town to keep getting away with it."

"We'll see," Momma said. She glanced at her watch and then said, "Suzanne, you must be starving. Let's go home and I'll whip something up for us."

"Tell you what, Momma. I'll take you out to eat tonight. This is a cause for celebration, don't you think? Should we call Chief Martin? He can come, too." I'd slowly grown to accept the fact that my mother was dating our chief of police.

"Thank you for the offer, but he's working the desk tonight," Momma said. "I probably should have told him before I did this, but it was a time that called for quick action."

"You don't have to ask his permission, do you?" I asked. My mother and the chief of police had been dating for a while, but I hadn't realized they'd gotten that serious yet. Of course, he'd been pining over her ever since they dated in grade school, but they'd both married other people. Momma hadn't even been able to think about another man for years after my dad's death, but then Chief Martin's marriage had fallen apart and he'd finally summoned the nerve to ask her for a date.

"Don't be silly, but he should find out what I'm doing before he hears the rumors around town. If you don't mind, I believe I'll go tell him right now."

As she trailed off to the police annex, Polly commented, "I didn't know they were that close. I knew they were dating, but she sounded serious."

"I'm sure she's just touching base as a courtesy," I said.

"Tell that to Evelyn," Polly said.

"Excuse me?"

"I'm sorry, I shouldn't have said anything."

"What are you talking about, Polly?" I didn't like the way she'd said that last bit, and I wasn't afraid to let her know it.

"The chief's ex-wife has been making some snide comments about your mother breaking up her marriage. I told Evelyn that she'd lost him long ago, but she wouldn't listen to me."

"But they've been divorced for over a year," I said, amazed that I was defending a man I'd butted heads with several times in the past.

"She thought he'd get tired of being single and come back to her, but when it was clear he wasn't just getting your mother out of his system, she finally started to realize that it was over."

This was all news to me. "I can't believe this. Does Momma know?"

"Not as far as I can tell," Polly said. "Maybe you should tell her to keep her eyes open. Evelyn looks all sweet and timid to the outside world, but I know that woman, and she's got a mean streak."

"I'll talk to Momma," I said, wondering how in the world I was going to bring that particular topic up.

As Momma made her way back across the grass, I asked Polly, "Care to join us for dinner? You're most welcome, and that way you can tell Momma about Evelyn yourself."

"Sorry. I'd love to, but I have plans tonight," Polly said.

"Coward," I said with a grin.

"You've got that right," she answered, returning my smile.

"What were you two talking about?" Momma asked me as she neared.

"Nothing much."

"Suzanne, I know better than that. I saw

36

the expression on your face."

I took her hands in mine and said, "Momma, we can talk about it tomorrow. Tonight, let's just celebrate. What did the chief say?"

"He asked me what took me so long," Momma said with a grin. "Jake's more than welcome to come along, you know that, don't you?"

Jake was my steady boyfriend, if you can call a man in his forties that. I'd met him on a case, which was natural enough, since he was a state police inspector, going where the crime dictated. He wasn't often in town for very large chunks at a time, but we managed to make it work for us. "I'm sure he'd love to, but he can't. He's in Hickory right now," I said.

"Is there a case? I hadn't heard anything was going on there."

"For once it's not a murder. It seems a wealthy businessman is being blackmailed, and the man asked the governor specifically for Jake's help."

"My, your young man has friends in high places, doesn't he?"

I shrugged. "Sometimes I wish he weren't quite so good at his job."

Momma put an arm around me. "That's what we face when we both see lawmen.

So, what do you say to a girls' night out? We can ask Grace as well."

"She's most likely busy," I said. "This new boyfriend of hers is tying her up most nights."

"Is she happy with him?" Momma asked as we walked toward the Boxcar Grill. It was one of the nicest things about living in a small town. We could usually walk just about anywhere we needed to go.

"She seems to be," I admitted, "but I miss her company."

"Then tell her that," Momma said. "I'm sure that she'll make time for you if let her know that you're feeling neglected."

I had to laugh at the thought of that particular conversation. "Maybe. I've got an idea. Instead of the Boxcar, let's go to Napoli's."

"What a delightful idea," Momma said. "That sounds like great fun."

"Then let's do it."

Momma took in my jeans and T-shirt as we neared the car. "Don't you want to change first?"

Normally I might fight her on it, but it was her night, after all. "Okay. Let's swing by the house so I can grab a quick shower and change, and then I'll be ready."

"Thank you," Momma said.

"Hey, it's not every night your mom decides to run for mayor," I said with a laugh.

"Let's just hope neither one of us has any reason to regret it."

Angelica DeAngelis met us when we walked into the restaurant. Usually, the mother of three girls and the main chef there was working in the kitchen, but not tonight.

"Angelica? You aren't cooking?" I asked after I hugged her briefly.

"Suzanne," my mother said sharply.

"No, it's a fair question, Dorothy." She turned to me and said, "There's been a coup tonight. They threw me out of my kitchen."

"What happened?" I knew it had to be dire for Angelica's daughters to gang up on her like that.

"They want to prove themselves to me," Angelica said. "They've worked shifts alone before, but never an entire night without me." In a lower voice, she added, "I'm proud of them. Honestly, I've taught Antonia all I can, and Maria is not far behind."

"But you've still got Sophia, right?" I asked. I knew the youngest DeAngelis was still almost completely under her mother's wing.

"She's running the dining room," Angelica said.

"It's amazing how quickly they stop needing us, isn't it?" Momma asked.

Angelica nodded. "Sometimes it's difficult to accept, isn't it?"

"It can be," Momma said as she took my hand. "But they can be rather nice all grown-up, too."

I wasn't about to say anything to that. After all, it was one of the sweetest things my mother had ever said about me in my presence.

"What's the real reason they're doing this?" I asked Angelica.

"They want me to go on a cruise," she admitted.

"What a wonderful idea," I said. "You work so hard, you deserve a real vacation. Are you going to take them up on it?"

"We'll see how tonight goes first," she said. "At least they're allowing me to hostess. Come this way."

We followed her from the ornately decorated lobby into the restaurant. There was a good crowd there already, but Angelica found us one of their best tables. As we were seated, Angelica handed us our menus. "Enjoy, ladies."

"We will," I said.

40

As Momma and I scanned our menus, I said, "Angelica runs this place with an iron hand. They've got guts, I'll give them that."

Momma laughed, and I asked, "What's so funny?"

"There are folks in April Springs who say the same thing about you. It's well-known that I don't suffer insolence lightly, and yet you continue to get away with things others would suffer direly for."

"I suppose no child is ever in awe of their parents, no matter how tough they may look to the outside world." I glanced back at the menu, then set it aside. "What are you going to have?"

"I was thinking about a small salad."

I looked at her in disbelief. "Don't you trust Angelica's daughters? They're great cooks in their own right."

"I'm sure they are. I just thought I'd eat light tonight."

"Momma, you have to order some kind of pasta, even if it's just a small side of spaghetti. There's more than dining at stake here. These girls need us to show that we believe in them."

"Very well," she agreed. "And you?"

"I'm having the lasagna-and-ravioli combo plate," I said.

"Can you actually eat all of that?"

I grinned at her. "If there's anything left on my plate, I'll take it home for later."

When Sophia came to take our order, I said with a gentle grin, "Congratulations on the revolution."

Sophia smiled broadly, making her look more beautiful than she already did. All of Angelica's daughters were visions of loveliness, and I wouldn't be surprised if many of the single men who came into the restaurant hoped to catch their attention, but Sophia was the loveliest of them all. "We're still amazed we managed it."

"Just make it good," I said.

She nodded. "Believe me, my sisters are living and dying with every dish they prepare. It's one thing to assist Momma, but it's something else entirely trying to replace her. I'll get your drinks, and then I'll get your order into the kitchen."

Momma and I were enjoying ourselves when I looked up to see our mayor entering the restaurant.

I pointed him out to Momma. "Did he actually have the nerve to follow us here?"

"I don't see how he could have," Momma said dismissively. "We didn't even know we'd be dining here until an hour ago."

"What should we do?" I asked.

Momma looked at me with a slight smile.

"We continue to enjoy ourselves. I won't let him run me out of my favorite restaurant."

"That's the spirit," I said.

I was hoping Cam would avoid us, but instead of following Angela to a table, he came straight toward us. "Hello, ladies. We meet again."

"Hello, Cam," Momma said. "I assume it's okay to call you by your given name now that you're out of your office."

"That's fine with me," he said. "Just don't get used to it. I'll be back there tomorrow, bright and early."

"Enjoy it while you can," Momma said.

"For years to come," Cam agreed.

"Your table is ready," I said, staring pointedly at him.

"So it is," Cam said, and then turned and followed Angelica the rest of the way.

"Do you want to know something, Suzanne? I'm going to really enjoy grinding him into the dust," Momma said.

"Wow, you surely sound motivated," I admitted.

"Just wait. This is going to be fun." She snapped her fingers and then added, "It just occurred to me. I've got the perfect place for campaign headquarters."

"Where, the donut shop?" I asked.

"No, but nearby. Suzanne, there's too

much activity at your place, and not enough room. I was thinking more along the lines of Hannah's Notions." Before it had gone out of business as a sewing shop, Hannah's had been a place next door to mine on the opposite side of ReNEWed and across the railroad tracks. It had been empty for years, and I had no idea who even owned the building.

"Can you get them to lend it to you?"

"I shouldn't have any problems," she said. "Wouldn't it make a great headquarters?"

"It's probably filthy with dust," I said, "but I'll help you clean it up. When do you want to do it? Tonight?"

She laughed. "As much as I appreciate your enthusiasm, I believe tomorrow will do nicely. We can meet there after you close the donut shop. How does eleven fifteen sound to you?"

"You've got a date. I'll bring some volunteers with me, too."

Momma smiled. "The more the merrier. This is going to be such great fun."

"Cleaning, or going after the mayor?"

She smiled at me. "Guess."

As we ate, I tried my best to ignore our mayor, but it was difficult. His date had arrived, late, but for all of the attention Cam paid her, I was amazed she bothered showing up at all. He stayed on his cell phone throughout most of the meal, and he was still talking on it as we left.

"That's pretty rude," I said. "Did he even acknowledge that woman's presence?"

"Cam has always been more focused on himself than anyone else," Momma said.

Angelica had clearly been waiting for us at the register. "How were your meals tonight, ladies?"

"Marvelous," I said as I handed her my money. "You don't have anything to worry about."

"Their food was as good as mine?" she asked. Was she actually a little disappointed by our response?

Momma spoke up. "I'd have to say that they were extremely close to being as good as your usual offerings. After all, they've had an excellent teacher. Your daughters are wonderful chefs. You have nothing to worry about."

"Good," Angelica said. "I'm happy to hear that."

"So, you'll book your cruise now?" I asked with a grin.

"We'll see," Angelica said with a smile of her own.

She gave me my change, and Momma and I walked out into the evening air. It was a

45

lovely night, cold and crisp, with the stars shining clear and bright above us. Not even the mayor's appearance had managed to dampen our evening, and as we drove back home I said, "That was fun. We should do it more often."

"When do we get the chance, now that we both have men in our lives?"

I shrugged. "I'm not sure how frequent a visitor Jake is most of the time," I said. "But at least you can count on Chief Martin."

"Phillip *is* rather attentive these days, isn't he?" Momma said.

"I'm amazed you get a night to yourself now and then," I said.

Momma laughed, a rich and lovely sound I cherished. "He wants to make up for lost time."

"Well, that's one thing I have to give him credit for."

"What's that?" my mother asked.

"He has excellent taste in women."

She grinned and patted my arm lightly. "I could say the same thing about Jake."

I'd managed not to bring up Chief Martin's ex-wife during the entire evening, and I'd planned on waiting until tomorrow to broach the subject, but driving back was a perfect time to do it. There was a dark silence in the world around us, and we were isolated within it.

I took a deep breath, and then said, "I need to tell you something, but I don't want to ruin the nice mood we're both in."

"Are you and Jake getting married?" she asked expectantly.

I couldn't have been more surprised by her question. "What? No. Of course not. What gave you that idea?"

"I'm sorry. Perhaps I've been waiting for an announcement for some time."

"Well, I wouldn't hold my breath if I were you. Jake and I are both just fine with the way things are now."

"You haven't even discussed the possibility?" she asked softly.

"Not a whisper," I said. "You know as well as I do that my marriage to Max was mostly a nightmare, and Jake lost his wife and child in a car crash. I know it happened a long time ago, but the wound is still fresh in his heart. Jake loves me, and he even tells me so now, but his wife was on a whole other level. I couldn't begin to replace her in his eyes, and I know it."

There was silence for some time before Momma finally broke it. "Of course you can never replace her, but you don't have to. It doesn't mean that Jake still can't marry you."

I couldn't believe we were having this particular conversation. It was miles from where I wanted to be. "Momma, I can say with all certainty that if Jake were on our porch on bended knee with a ring in his hand when we got home tonight, I would run away into the woods screaming."

"Was it honestly that bad being with Max?" she asked.

"There's a reason I call him the Great Impersonator," I said. "I never knew when to believe him. The funny thing is, though, I was still surprised when I caught him with Darlene. That's something that's not easily forgotten."

"Jake is a better man than Max, though."

"Of course he is," I said. "But that doesn't mean I want to exchange vows with him."

We were silent for a few miles, and then Momma asked, "Ever?"

"I won't rule it out forever," I admitted. "But neither one of us is in any hurry to expedite things, and I hope you can say the same thing about you and our police chief."

"He asked me, I turned him down, and things are finally getting back to normal," she said with a smile. "I'm making him court me until further notice."

"Good for you. In a roundabout way, the chief is what I want to talk to you about."

I looked over and saw Momma's lips press firmly against each other. "Suzanne, you're still not happy about me seeing him, are you?"

I laughed softly. "You know what? It turns out that it's not nearly as bad as I feared it would be."

"Then what is it?"

"It's Evelyn," I said simply.

I saw Momma stiffen. "So, you've heard the rumors, too."

"You know what she's been saying about you?" I asked.

"Of course I do. I have excellent connections in April Springs, and it would be impossible not to know that she's been trashing me in public."

"What are you going to do about it?" I asked as we entered April Springs.

"Nothing," she said simply.

"Nothing? Seriously?"

"What can I do? I didn't steal her husband, and everyone knows it. Evelyn assumed he'd come running back to her sooner or later, but she was wrong. I firmly believe that whether Phillip and I continue to see each other is irrelevant. That marriage is dead, a stake driven through its heart long ago."

"So you're not concerned about it?"

She shook her head as we pulled into our driveway. The cottage looked lovely bathed in moonlight, nestled beside the park. "I try not to worry about things I cannot change, and one thing is certain: Evelyn Martin is never going to stop believing that I broke up her marriage."

Baked Chocolate Sugar Bombs

This donut is a true chocolate sensation! I created this one day when my family was craving something chocolate, and everyone loved the finished product. Using chocolate milk made a big difference in this recipe, and adds a special zing! For those less adventurous, 1/4 cup whole milk and 1/4 cup light cream may be substituted.

Ingredients

Wet
- 1 egg, beaten
- 1/2 cup chocolate milk (2% or whole preferred)
- 3 tablespoons butter, melted (I use unsalted; salted can be used, but cut the added salt by half.)
- 1/2 cup granulated sugar
- 1 teaspoon vanilla extract

Dry
- 1 cup bread flour (Unbleached all-purpose flour can be used as well.)
- 1/4 cup cocoa (unsweetened)
- 1 teaspoon baking powder
- 1/4 teaspoon baking soda
- 1/4 teaspoon nutmeg

- 1/4 teaspoon cinnamon
- 1/8 teaspoon of salt

Directions

Combine the dry ingredients (flour, cocoa, baking powder, baking soda, nutmeg, cinnamon, and salt) in a bowl and sift together. In another bowl, combine the wet ingredients (beaten egg, chocolate milk, butter, sugar, and vanilla extract). Slowly add the wet mix to the dry mix, stirring until it's incorporated. Don't overmix.

The donuts can be baked in the oven at 350 degrees for 10–15 minutes in cupcake trays or small donut molds, but I bought a dedicated donut baker that sits on my countertop. It's easy to use, reliable, not expensive at all, and makes perfect donuts every time. These donuts usually take 6–7 minutes.

Once the donuts are finished, remove them to a cooling rack. These can be covered with chocolate icing or a chocolate glaze with chocolate sprinkles for an extra jolt, but actually, they are good enough to eat as they come out of the oven.

Makes 5–9 donuts, depending on baking method

1/2 teaspoon peppermint extract may be added for a change of pace, and has a nice bounce off the chocolate when added to the wet ingredients.

CHAPTER 3

"Your mom is an absolute rock star," Emma said the next morning when she came into the donut shop. It was three thirty, and I'd already been there half an hour prepping the dough for our cake donuts. We'd been on our new schedule for a while now, and we hadn't had any problems adjusting to a little more sleep. These days we worked until six a.m. making donuts, sold them until eleven, and then closed for the day. It was amazing how getting to Donut Hearts a little late and leaving a little early every day managed to still feel like a vacation.

As I rolled out the apple spice donuts on the stainless steel counter, I asked, "I doubt she's ever been called that before. Why do you say that?"

Emma looked at me and laughed. "You're kidding, right? Everybody's buzzing about her running for office. To be honest with you, my dad's even taking some of the credit."

"He should," I said. "The article he wrote about Cam's shady deal was the last straw for Momma. It's what made her decide that we need a change around here."

Emma looked proud enough to burst. "May I tell him that?"

What harm could it do? Then again, I'd been bitten before by overstepping my bounds with my mother, so it might be wise to be careful. "I don't see why not, but maybe we should clear it with Momma first. Now that she's a politician, I'm probably going to have to start watching what I say about her, at least in public."

Emma grinned. "I can't see her losing the race for mayor, can you? Everyone loves her, and the best Cam Hamilton can muster is ambivalence."

"I hope Momma wins, there's no doubt about it. After all, it would look bad on me too, if she didn't, since I'm her campaign manager."

"Can I volunteer?" she asked eagerly, her voice bursting with enthusiasm. "I just love politics."

"I'm sure we can find a place for you." I started cutting out the donut and hole shapes with my rolling donut cutter. I'd found this particular cutter locally, and at a price I liked, though every time I used it I was reminded of a time when I'd been a murder suspect, which was not exactly the best memory I had. "We're cleaning up Hannah's, so we can use it as our headquarters after work this morning, and you're more than welcome to join us." I took a deep breath, knowing that I was on shaky ground, and then asked, "But don't you have a new boyfriend taking up all of your time these days?"

"Do you mean Chad? He's history," she said.

That was news to me. "Since when?"

Emma shrugged as she replied, "We broke up yesterday."

I frowned at the news. I hated when Emma's heart was broken. "I'm so sorry."

She started cleaning up my mess as she answered, "Don't be. He didn't turn out to be the guy I thought he was."

"You'll find someone," I said. "You're too special not to."

"I just hope I find someone as perfect as Grace did," Emma said with a sigh. "I saw them out last night, and they looked like they were really in love."

That was pushing it; at least I hope that it was. To my mind, Grace had gone from be-

ing extremely picky to being overly accepting lately, though I'd never say that to her.
"It might be too soon to say that, but I know
that she's awfully fond of him."

Emma laughed as I finished rolling the
cutter over the last bit of dough, producing
perfectly shaped donuts and holes and leaving only scraps behind. She said, "You
sound like my grandmother. Is anyone really
still fond of the person they're dating in this
day and age?"

I swatted her with my towel. "Don't make
fun of me, young lady. After all, I'm still
your boss."

With a big grin, Emma saluted and said,
"Yes, ma'am. I mean, no, ma'am. I wouldn't
dream of it."

I handed her the cutter. "Would you mind
washing this while you're cleaning up?"

"I'm on it," she said.

As Emma filled the sink with warm water,
she said, "I don't care what you say, Suzanne, you've got to admit it, Peter Morgan
is kind of dreamy."

"He's handsome, I'll give you that." I'd
spent some time with Peter twice, and the
three of us had even had dinner together as
Grace kept staring at us both, willing us to
get along. It made for a long meal, and I'd
begged off the next time she asked. It was

almost painful watching Grace hope for my approval, and while I didn't have anything against the man, he didn't bowl me over as he had Emma. Maybe his charm reminded me a little too much of my ex, Max.

"Come on, he's awesome," Emma said.

"Fine, he's awesome." I didn't want to argue with her, so it was time to change the subject. "How is your father going to manage to wait a week before he can put out his next newspaper?"

Emma laughed. "You're kidding, right? He's in his office now getting ready to put out a special edition. The headline's going to be trumpeting your mother's candidacy."

That was news to me, and I had to wonder if Momma had heard yet. "Funny, he didn't even interview her about it, at least not that I heard."

Emma grinned. "When I went to bed last night, he was talking to your mother on the phone. I'm sure he got enough quotes to run the story."

"Good. Maybe he'll even endorse her," I said, half in jest.

Emma looked pleased to be able to tell me, "He already did. My dad and Cam Hamilton have had a blood feud going on for years. They legitimately hate each other, and it's got nothing to do with the fact that they are natural enemies because of their jobs."

"That's interesting," I said as I started on the dough for my new strawberry and cream cake donut. It was a classic combination that used real cream in the batter, and I had high hopes for it. I felt that I needed to keep adding new offerings to my menu to keep my customers coming back, and besides, it was fun for me. Adding real cream made the donut a little more expensive to create, but the taste was phenomenal. "What started it all?"

"My mother," Emma said with a grin. "Can you imagine two men fighting over her?"

I knew Emma's mother to be a pretty and intelligent woman with a gentle heart. "The only problem I have is imagining it just being limited to two of them."

"Well, evidently they fought pretty hard for her attention in high school," Emma said.

"And your dad won," I said as I worked on the dough.

"Nope," Emma said. "You'd think so, but that's not the way it happened at all."

"Hang on a second," I said as I stopped what I was doing. "She ended up marrying your father, right?"

"Not for a while. Mom dated Cam for two years, but something happened between them, and they broke up. I have to give my father credit: he didn't waste any time moving in on her. He finally managed to win her heart, and Cam never forgave either one of them, truth be told."

"It's amazing how the things that happen when we're young affect our lives for so many years," I said.

Emma nodded. "I don't care what happens in the future. I'm living my life right now, with no regrets."

"It's probably a little easier doing that when you're younger," I said.

She looked at me earnestly, and then asked, "Do you have many regrets, Suzanne?"

I thought about it for nearly a minute. "Marrying Max wasn't the smartest thing I ever did in my life," I admitted. "You might easily say that it was my biggest mistake, but I'm not sure I regret it, because look what happened after our divorce: I moved back in with Momma, and we've reconnected in a way we never had before. And don't forget, I bought this place with my settlement, so in the end, it all came out nicely. I could probably come up with some real regrets, if you're all that interested," I added with a smile.

"No," she said, laughing, as she handed me the clean cutter back. "I don't think we need to travel down that particular road, do you?"

"I'd rather not, if it's all the same to you," I answered. "Tell you what: Why don't we focus on the donuts instead?"

"Sounds good to me."

Emma and I were going outside for our normal break between making the cake donuts and the raised ones, and as I opened the door, I saw something on one of the outdoor tables we offered our customers. I wrapped my coat around me, since the end of February was still in winter's grip in our part of North Carolina.

"What's this?" I asked. "Since when did we start getting the newspaper delivered here at the donut shop this time of morning?"

Emma grinned. "Dad said he was going to leave us a couple of extras to read. Should we go back inside to check them out?"

"It can wait," I said. "I want to enjoy the cold, fresh air out here."

Emma took a deep breath, and then said, "I'm freezing, but it's worth it to be outside for a change." She looked at me, realizing how that must sound, and then quickly added, "Not that I'm complaining, but it is sort of nice not to smell donuts in the air."

I had to laugh. "Emma, I hate to break it to you, but we both smell like donuts all of the time."

Emma grinned as she wrapped her coat closer around her. "That was one of the things Chad said he liked most about me. He was an awfully good kisser, I'll give him that."

The wistful sound of her voice made me realize that Emma might not be ready to say good-bye to this particular beau. "It sounds to me as though you might not mind a chance to reconcile with him sometime."

"Maybe," she said with a shrug. "I don't know. Dating someone again seems like I'm repeating myself, you know? Besides, I'm not so sure he should get a second chance when there are so many guys who haven't gotten their first shot at being with me yet."

I had to laugh at her attitude. "You're a nut; you know that, don't you?"

"I like to think that it's part of my charm," she said.

"I'd say that you're right." I hadn't wanted to cut our break short, but I had to admit, I was curious about Ray Blake's article about my mother.

"Okay, I can't stand the suspense. Let's go in early and read these," I said.

"I thought you'd never suggest it," Emma said.

We walked in and took a table near the kitchen where we could read from the light spilling out of the other room. I liked to keep it dark out front until it was close to six and we were ready to open. That kept most folks from pounding on our front door asking when we opened, though the sign was right there in front of them.

In bold headlines, Ray had written, MAYOR GETS TOUGH COMPETITION. After reading the entire article, it sounded more like a love letter to my mother than hard news, and I wondered if Ray's wife might be jealous from all of the glowing praise he had heaped upon another woman.

"He's a real fan, isn't he?" I asked as I put the paper aside.

"Suzanne, I'm sure he likes your mother, but I don't think I realized just how much my dad hated Cam until just now," Emma said. "This is a little over-the-top, even for him."

"I hope there's no backlash from it," I said.

"What do you mean?"

I tapped the paper and said, "This makes

63

it sound as though the newspaper is in my mother's hip pocket. Don't you think people will notice it and talk about it?"

"If they do, Dad will be happy," Emma said. "He feels like any attention is good attention."

The timer in back went off, and Emma gathered the newspapers together. "Time to get going," she said.

"The donuts rest, but we never do," I said with a grin.

As the shop opened at six, there was actually a line waiting for our donuts. I'd opened at five not that long ago, but the sleep I got was well worth any business I might have lost at the donut shop. "Come on in," I said as I held the door open.

"Hey, look at that. It's the mayor's daughter," Penny Parsons said as she walked in, still in scrubs and clearly fresh off her shift at the hospital.

"Don't say it yet or you might jinx it," I said with a smile.

Penny shook her head. "Come on, Suzanne, I've been waiting for someone to run against Cam since he first took office."

"Why didn't you run yourself?" I asked her.

She laughed at the suggestion. "Are you kidding? I don't have the talent, or the temperament, or the time, either."

"That disqualifies me, too, then," I said as George Morris, a dear friend and retired cop who helped me with my criminal inquiries from time to time, walked in. "What are we all talking about this morning?"

"My mother is running for mayor of April Springs," I said.

"You're joking, right?" George asked.

"No, I don't see anything funny about it," I answered. With a smile, I asked, "What part of the job do you think my mother isn't qualified for, George?"

He knew better than to walk into that bear trap. "Are you kidding? I know she can do the job, and a lot better than Cam. I just figured she was too smart to take it. No offense intended."

"None taken," I said. "If you want to know the truth, she was so steamed about Cam taking that sanitation plant contract, she wanted to put him in his place."

George looked puzzled. "What are you talking about?"

I brought him up to speed, and he said, "I've been out of town for three days, and the world's gone crazy since I've been gone. When did this all happen?"

I handed him a newspaper. "Extra, extra, read all about it. Can I get you coffee and a donut?"

"Sure thing. I'm willing to take dealer's choice this morning," he answered.

"On the coffee or the donut?" George loved my donuts, but he wasn't all that fond of some of Emma's coffee blends.

"Go ahead and surprise me," he said, sounding more than a little unsure about what he might be getting. "I'm game to try just about anything."

I laughed and poured him a regular cup of coffee and got him a plain glazed donut. "You're in luck. I'm taking it easy on you today."

He looked delighted with my selections for him. "I greatly appreciate that." George took a sip of coffee, and then sighed. "Now that's good stuff."

"If you think that's good, wait until you taste the donut."

He took a bite, nodded his approval, and then said, "Since I retired from the force, I've got some time on my hands. Suzanne, if your mother is looking for volunteers for her campaign, put my name on the list."

"I'll do that," I said, and patted his hand lightly. "We're cleaning up Hannah's at eleven fifteen today, and you're more than welcome to join us."

"I'll be there," George said.

After I waited on the first rush of customers in the shop, Emma poked her head out through the kitchen door, giving me a quizzical look.

"What?" I asked.

She pulled the earbuds from her ears and asked, "Did you call me?"

"Not me. You should probably turn the volume on that down, Emma. You're going to go deaf."

"What did you say?" she asked as she cupped a hand behind one ear, pretending she couldn't hear me.

"Go back to work," I said with a laugh.

A little past eight, my best friend, Grace, came into the donut shop, with her boyfriend, Peter, trailing close behind her.

"Hey, stranger," I said. "Glad you could come by this morning."

Instead of letting Grace answer, Peter replied with a smile, "It's probably my fault that she's been gone so much lately. I've been taking up quite a bit of her free time."

"I'm not complaining," Grace said as she gave him a quick kiss. Peter was ruggedly handsome, with chiseled features, thick black hair, and clear blue eyes. I could easily see why Grace liked him, but I still wasn't sure about him. It wasn't out of jealousy, since I had a boyfriend of my own. If I was being honest about it, I would have to say that there was a good chance I didn't think anyone was good enough for my best friend.

I squelched this line of thinking and gave her my best smile. "What are you two up to today?"

"We're going antiquing," Grace said.

"And you're okay with that?" I asked Peter. I'd asked Jake to go with me once, but he'd clearly been so unhappy about the thought of going that I never asked again.

"I love it," Peter said. "I'm a nut for old tools, so it's fun for me, too."

"You might want to hold on to this one," I told Grace, knowing how much she loved looking at antiques.

"I plan to," she said with a smile. "Could we get two coffees and two glazed donuts to go, Suzanne?"

I poured two cups to go and grabbed a few donuts, throwing in some strawberry-and-cream donut holes on the house.

"I put a surprise in the bag," I said as I took Peter's money.

"Oooh, I love surprises," Grace said.

"Really? I didn't know that," Peter replied.

"Well, donut surprises, anyway," Grace said.

68

"I'll file that away for future reference," Peter said.

As they walked out, Penny said, "Why are all of the good ones taken?"

"I'm not at all sure that they are," I said.

"Easy for you to say," she answered. "I haven't been able to find any on my own."

"How can you say that, when there's one sitting right down here all by himself," George said out of the blue with a grin.

"Why, George, you old dog, I didn't know you had it in you," Penny said as she moved down to join him.

He was clearly startled by her reaction. "I didn't mean . . . er, what I was trying to say was . . . well . . ."

Penny let him squirm a little more, and then said with a smile, "Don't worry, handsome, you're safe with me. But you'd better believe that if I were twenty years older, I'd be chasing you all around town."

"If you were twenty years older, you wouldn't have to run far to catch me," George answered with a laugh.

"I don't know. You two might be perfect for each other," I said.

"You never know," Penny replied. She stood, then gave George a peck on the cheek on her way out the door.

To my vast amusement, George actually

69

blushed.

"She called your bluff, didn't she?" I asked with a smile.

"Who said I was bluffing?" George asked as he threw a five down on the counter. The attention had clearly stoked his ego a little.

"That's too big a tip for a coffee and one donut," I protested.

"Let's just say you helped make my day," George replied. "See you a little after eleven, Suzanne."

"See you then," I said.

The next hour flew by, with customers coming in and out at a really steady rate. It seemed that my mother's candidacy for mayor was doing great things for my bottom line. If I'd realized it sooner, I would have urged her to run a long time ago.

I looked up expectantly when the door opened again, but I doubted that this really was a customer.

From the expression on Evelyn Martin's face, she wasn't there looking for donuts and coffee.

CHAPTER 4

"Where is she, Suzanne?" Evelyn asked me as she stormed into my shop. Although Evelyn was younger than my mother, it was clear that the years had not been as kind to her. Her eyes were lined with wrinkles, and she'd put on more weight than she should have since her divorce. From the redness in her eyes and the bags under them, I had a feeling that the woman hadn't been getting much sleep lately, but that didn't excuse the way that she was acting.

"I'm not exactly sure who you're looking for," I said, trying to keep my voice neutral.

"Your mother," she said, snapping out the words as though they burned her throat. "Is she hiding out back there?" Evelyn asked as she pointed to the kitchen.

"I haven't seen my mother all morning, and that's the truth," I said. "Why are you looking for her?"

"Is that really any of your business?" she

asked harshly.

"You're here in my place of business," I said. "I didn't seek you out. You've clearly got a chip on your shoulder, and you're looking for my mother. Yeah, I think I have a few reasons to think it's my business."

"She's not going to get away with it," Evelyn said. "I don't care who she thinks she is."

"My mother did not steal your husband," I said, letting some steel come out in my voice. "He left you before he ever called her."

Evelyn looked as though she were about to cry. I could see the anger start to melt into pain, and her words were almost a whimper as she said, "He never would have left me if she hadn't encouraged him."

I didn't want to kick the woman when she was clearly down, but there were a few things that needed to be said. "Boy, do you have that wrong. I know you feel like you've been wronged here, but my mother practically slammed the door in his face whenever Chief Martin came around. She didn't try to get him; she made it clear that she wasn't interested in pursuing a relationship with him, no matter what his marital status was."

Evelyn started to get a little of her spunk back as she asked, "So, are you telling me that you never used reverse psychology on someone?"

"She wasn't goading him into anything, Evelyn," I said, hoping that my mother didn't choose that particular time to come into the shop for a visit.

"So you say." The vulnerability she'd just shown a minute ago was now gone, replaced again by anger. "We'll see how she likes things when the shoe's on the other foot."

"What are you talking about?" I asked her.

Evelyn's gaze narrowed. "She's not the only one who can run for mayor. I just filed my papers myself. It's going to be a three-way race."

"You actually found a hundred people to sign your petition?" I asked, not caring how it sounded to her. I was honestly stunned to think that a hundred of my fellow townspeople thought that her being mayor was a good idea. Then again, maybe they'd signed the petition to see a good fight. That I wouldn't put past some of the people of April Springs.

"Don't kid yourself: people were glad to sign my sheet. We'll see how your mother likes me being on that debate stage with her. She won't be able to duck me then, and she will have to finally face me and tell the truth."

I'd had about enough of that. It was clear that I wasn't going to be able to change her mind about anything. "Evelyn, if you're not here for coffee or for donuts, you probably should just move along."

"Are you trying to throw me out?" she asked, shouting now. My last two customers quietly slipped out through the front door, and we were now alone, with the exception of Emma in back.

"I'm asking you to make a selection or leave," I said, letting a little sting into my own voice. There was no reason to hold back now. I'd kept my temper in check so far, but that was about to end.

"There's nothing here I'd eat," she said, and then stormed out, trying to slam the door behind her. Fortunately, it was on slow-closing hinges, so her dramatic exit was ruined by technology.

Emma chose that moment to come out front, her earbuds dangling from their cords. "I could swear I heard voices again. Maybe you're right. I probably should turn the volume down."

I just shook my head. "If nothing else, at least you'd be able to hear when someone is threatening me."

She looked at me oddly. "Seriously? Some-one came in here and tried to scare you?

74

How crazy is that?"

"Just about as crazy as it sounds," I said.

After I told her what had happened, Emma collected the dirty dishes and mugs and took them to the back with her.

Two minutes later, Chief Martin came in.

"Did I just see Evelyn leaving here?" he asked. It was clear that he wasn't happy, but I was tired of appeasing crazy Martins.

"I wish I could say that you were wrong, but then I'd be lying. She's out of control, Chief. Somebody better stop her before she goes too far."

He looked stunned by my statement. "What do you mean? Did she threaten Dorothy?"

Okay, on second thought, most of what his ex-wife had said was implied, but that didn't make it any less inflammatory. "Let's just say she didn't wish her well. Did you know that Evelyn's running for mayor just to make Momma look bad? She's planning to ambush her at the debate, and from the sound of it, she thinks she's got a bombshell to drop."

The chief scratched the top of his head, bewilderment clear on his face. "I heard she might file to run for mayor, but I never thought she'd actually follow through with it."

75

"Trust me, she means business." As I reached for my telephone, I said, "Sorry, but I have to call Momma."

He looked hopefully at me as he said, "Why don't you let me tell her? After all, it's my fault this is all happening."

"You weren't under any obligation to stay married to Evelyn if you didn't love her anymore," I said, surprising myself by taking the chief's side. Maybe there was a little bit of my relationship with Max coloring my point of view, but I knew what it could be like having an ex who made life harder than it had to be.

"No, but Dorothy didn't sign up for this, either. As soon as I talk to your mother, I'll hunt Evelyn down and we'll have a chat."

"Good luck with that. Can I get you a donut?" I knew his policy of no donuts, but I thought he might make an exception this time.

He looked at the case, clearly tempted, but then shook his head. "I'd better not." Since his divorce over a year ago, he'd transformed himself into a new man, eating healthier, losing weight, and doing his best to convince my mother that she couldn't live without him. So far, at least to some degree, he'd succeeded; the man was persistent, I had to give him that.

"Do you happen to know where your mother is at the moment?"

"No, but I know that she'll be over at Hannah's a little after eleven. You can catch up with her there if you want to talk to her in person."

"I'll do that," he said. "It's crazy. The mayor made a big fuss over his plans to file for reelection this morning, but he never showed up. My ex-wife decides to run for his office, gets a hundred signatures and files, and now I can't find Cam for the life of me. This entire town has lost its collective mind." He shook his head and walked out, looking wistfully back at my donut case one last time before he got out the door.

The man had willpower, more than I had, that was for sure.

I knew in my heart that Evelyn didn't really want to be mayor. She just wanted an opportunity to hurt my mother, and I wasn't going to let her, not if I could help it.

I just wasn't sure what I could do about it. And now Cam was missing? What on earth was going on in April Springs?

I expected Momma to already be at Hannah's when Emma and I walked over to the empty store after we closed the shop, but we did find George waiting for her at the door.

"She's not here yet?" I asked as I pulled my coat closer. A chilly wind had kicked up since I'd been out last, and I was regretting not grabbing a hat before I left the shop.

George said, "If she is, she hasn't heard me pounding. I tried both doors, but no luck, they're both locked."

"I'm sure she'll be right along," Emma said, rubbing her hands together.

This was unacceptable, not a way to start a campaign. "We have volunteers ready to work, but we can't get in. I don't like making you two wait on the sidewalk like this."

As I pulled out my phone, George said, "Don't worry about it, Suzanne. It's no big deal."

"It is to me," I said.

I got Momma on the first ring.

"You're late," I said.

"I know. I'm almost there," Momma replied, nearly out of breath.

"What's the holdup? We have two volunteers I recruited today to help us get the shop ready. Did you have trouble getting the key?"

"No, I've got it. I just got into a conversation with Phillip that ran longer than I expected."

Shocker: my mother's boyfriend was at the heart of it. So, he'd decided to call her instead of facing her. I wasn't sure I could blame him for that.

"Momma, should we wait, or just come back later?"

"That won't be necessary," Momma said. "Look across the street."

I glanced up from my phone and saw my mother walking toward the shop from the direction of the cottage we shared.

I hung up, and as she approached, Momma turned to our volunteers and said, "I'm so sorry. Please forgive me for being late."

George and Emma were gracious enough about it that I decided that I could be, too. "What did the chief have to say?" As if I didn't know. I was just fishing to get Momma's reaction to the news that she now had two opponents instead of one.

Momma didn't answer; she just shook her head as she dove into her bag for a key. "Nothing in particular. It appears that our mayor is missing, and he wanted to know if I'd seen him."

Had he chickened out entirely? I was about to ask when Emma piped up. "What happened? Did he run away? Maybe he was afraid of the competition."

Momma fumbled with the key in the lock; she was having a little trouble opening it. "Well, that's just it. He has another sixteen minutes to file, or by the rules he won't be able to run for mayor again."

"Is that such a bad thing?" I asked Momma with a grin.

"It would be tragic," she said, clearly sincere, as she finally managed to open the door. "I want to trounce him fair and square, and the only way I can do that is if he runs against me."

I took the first step in the doorway and then stopped in my tracks.

Momma was impatient. I could hear it in her voice as she said, "Suzanne, you need to move so we can all get in."

"Call your boyfriend, Momma. I just found the mayor, and it's not good."

Inside, Cam Hamilton was on the floor of the shop, a halo of blood spreading out from the back of his head. Someone had taken a baseball bat and had killed him. His face was ashen, and there was no doubt in my mind that he was dead.

"Oh no," Momma said as she started toward the body.

George put a restraining arm on her.

"Don't go in there, Dorothy."

"It's my store," she said. "He might need our help."

"He's beyond anything we can do for him," George said after looking at the body.

Emma had glanced in for a moment, then stepped back outside. I noticed that she was on her cell phone, no doubt calling the tip in to her father. She'd become a reporter in the field for him lately, giving him anything he might be able to use for the newspaper. Emma and I had clashed over it once when she crossed the line, but since then, she'd been careful not to let it interfere with her work at Donut Hearts. I couldn't blame her for calling him. This, for once, was legitimate news that he could report.

And then something my mother had said sunk in. "You own this place?"

"Yes, along with several other pieces of real estate in town," she said dismissively. She'd called the chief, no doubt, because within a minute, he was there on the scene.

He touched Momma's shoulder gently, and then turned to George.

"Report."

At the moment, I wasn't at all certain that either one of them remembered that George had retired from the force years ago. He gave a succinct but pertinent report, and the chief nodded afterwards. "Thanks."

Only after leaning over the body and checking for a pulse we all knew he wouldn't find did he turn back to us. "We all need to step away now." After we complied and were on the sidewalk in front of the shop, the chief said, "I'll need statements from each of you." He looked at Momma and said, "The door was locked when you got here, correct?"

George had just told him that, but Momma nodded. I had a feeling the police chief was going out of his way not to show her any preferential treatment.

"Where did you get the key?"

"I own this building," she said, repeating something I still had a hard time believing. I had to wonder what else my mother hadn't told me over the years.

"Did you have the only key?" he asked, though it was clear that asking that particular question was killing him a little.

"I sincerely doubt it. The store has been empty for years, but it was pretty active in its day."

"Have you changed the locks since Hannah moved out?" the chief asked.

"No, of course not. Why would I?"

He looked a little exasperated as he explained, "Dorothy, practically anyone could have an old key to the place. There have to be a dozen folks in town who worked at Hannah's at one time or another, including my ex, two of Hannah's sisters, William Benson's late wife, and Trish's cousin, Louise, and that's just off the top of my head." As he named folks who might have keys as well, the relief in his voice was plain to hear. "I'm not sure how much good it will do, but I'll get Hannah to make up a list."

"Hannah herself would still have a key, wouldn't she?" I asked.

"I would imagine," the chief said.

I wasn't a huge fan of gossip, but there was something the chief of police needed to know. "Well, I hate to talk out of school, especially with what just happened, but Cam and Hannah hated each other."

That got the chief's interest. "How do you know that?"

"I saw them arguing in front of Donut Hearts not a week ago," I admitted. I'd been looking out the window when they'd bumped into each other, and though I hadn't been able to hear what they'd been saying, it was clear that they weren't exchanging recipes. There was raw anger there.

"I'll look into it," Chief Martin said as he pulled out a notebook and started taking notes. "Anything else?"

83

It was no time to hold back. "Well, I hate to bring it up, but you just said that your wife used to work for Hannah, right?"

"Ex," the chief corrected. "But yes, she did."

"Well, she wasn't exactly a fan of Cam's, either, was she?"

Chief Martin looked at me briefly, and it was pretty obvious that he wasn't pleased. "Are you saying that Evelyn murdered him? She might not have liked him, but she had no reason to kill him. That's insane."

"I'm just saying, she needs to be a suspect, too."

"As do I," Momma said softly.

"Dorothy, I know you didn't kill Cam Hamilton," the chief of police said.

"You can't know that though, can you?" Momma asked. "It's no secret the man and I couldn't stand each other, and he was killed in a locked building that I clearly have access to. How can I not be at the head of your list?"

The chief frowned at that but then said, "You were with me, though. I'm your alibi."

"Chief, maybe you should wait for the coroner's report before you say that," George said from behind him. "We don't have an exact time of death at the moment."

The police chief started to turn on George

when Momma said, "He's right. I'm afraid you might have to ask for some outside help on this one, Phillip. You're too close to it to investigate the crime. It might be best if you recuse yourself now."

"This is my town," he said. "I can put my feelings aside long enough to investigate a murder."

"I appreciate the sentiment, but I don't see how you can," Momma said softly. It was clear she was trying to be as gentle with him as she could manage.

The chief was scowling when I had a sudden idea. "I know. You could call Jake," I said.

Chief Martin wasn't all that excited by the prospect. "Do you think your boyfriend can be any more neutral than I can?"

"I know without much doubt that he'd lock me up in a heartbeat if he had evidence that I'd killed someone," I said, sure that I was telling the truth. Jake had two modes that I'd seen since we'd started dating: the sweet boyfriend, and the cop working a case. There was clear demarcation between the two sides of him, as apparent as if he had separate faces he wore. I'd seen him in full cop mode before, and it was almost as though I couldn't recognize him when he had his teeth into something. He would ar-

rest Momma, no matter what the consequences to his personal life, no matter how
much it might kill him to do it. Honestly, it
was one of the things I admired most about
him.

"I doubt that," the chief said.

"Then you'd be wrong. What can it hurt?"

"I thought he was working a case in
Hickory," the chief asked.

"He might be able to get out of it to
investigate a murder. Wouldn't you rather
have Jake here than some stranger looking
over your shoulder?"

The chief nodded. "I'll call him."

Two of April Springs' other police officers
had shown up and were now intent on
securing the crime scene as Chief Martin
made his telephone call. It was clear that
George wanted to help them, but somehow
he managed to restrain himself.

I looked up to see Emma's father, Ray
Blake, come racing up the street on foot, a
camera slung around his neck.

He tried to get a picture of the mayor's
body, but the chief hung up his phone and
closed the shop door before Ray could get a
shot.

"Come on, Chief, give me a break," Ray
said plaintively.

"I don't want to see a dead body on the

front page of your newspaper tomorrow," Martin said.

Ray shrugged, then stepped back and took a photo of our group. "Fine, I'll use this one. Care to comment?"

"No," the chief said.

"I already know it's the mayor," Ray said. "Give me something."

The chief glanced at Emma, who just smiled at him. He shook his head. "You won't be getting anything out of me, so you might as well go back to that cramped little office of yours and wait for another hot tip."

"If it's all the same to you, I think I'll stick around."

Ray winked at his daughter, and I saw her return it. I had a feeling that tomorrow's story would be full of quotes from an anonymous witness, but at least that way maybe Ray would get things right. I knew that for Emma, getting her father's approval about anything meant a great deal, so I couldn't really blame her.

"What happens now?" Momma asked.

"I need to speak with each of you alone," he said.

"What did Jake say?" I asked.

"He couldn't talk, but he said he'd call me right back," Chief Martin said. He then turned to my mother and suggested, "Doro-

87

thy, why don't we go first?"

"Are you sure someone else shouldn't conduct the interviews?" George asked.

"I can handle it fine on my own. Why, are you volunteering?" The last bit was said with a bite, and I saw George flinch a little.

He didn't back down, though. "Chief, you really should let Grant do it."

The chief looked at George as though he wanted to swat him, but again, Momma intervened. "You know, that might be for the best."

"Grant!" the chief barked out, and the young officer appeared quickly. Stephen Grant had become a friend of mine over the past few years, coming in for donuts when he was off duty, but no outsider would have been able to tell that at the moment.

"Sir," he said.

"Take this group to the squad room and interview them individually about what happened this morning. I expect you to be thorough and show no favoritism. Is that understood?"

The officer nodded, looked surprised for a split second, and then said to us, "If you'll all follow me, please."

As we walked away, I glanced back at the chief of police for one quick second. There was a look of helplessness on his face that I hadn't seen before, a vulnerability that made me like him more than I ever had. He was clearly torn between his love for my mother and his duty, and I didn't envy him that one bit. He was decent at what he did, but he wasn't on a level with Jake, and somehow that conflict made him a little more human to me.

I was waiting to speak with Officer Grant next when my phone rang. "What's going on, Suzanne?" Jake asked.

"Did you talk to the chief yet?" I asked.

"Yes," he admitted. "He asked me to take the mayor's murder case, but I'm not sure that's such a good idea."

I couldn't believe that Jake would back down from a case like that. "Why not? You know all of the people involved."

"That's the problem," he said. "It could really complicate things."

"Have you at least considered it?" I asked him.

He paused, and I could almost see him running his hand through his hair. "Suzanne, think about it. Do you really want to put me in a position where I might have to arrest your mother for murder?"

The thought chilled me, but I knew in my heart that at least if Jake were involved, he'd do everything in his power to be sure he had the facts before he acted. "I'm not worried about it at all, because I know in my heart that she didn't do it."

"That's exactly what I'm talking about. Whoops, sorry, I've got to go. Call you later."

With that, he hung up on me. Did Jake really have to go, or was he just unwilling to finish that conversation? I was still thinking about calling him back when Momma walked out of the conference room and motioned to me. "He's ready for you now."

I stopped when I got to her and gave Momma a hard and long hug. "How are you holding up?" I asked.

"I'm managing fine," she said. "Thanks for asking."

"I just asked Jake to come," I said as I pulled away.

"What did he say?" she asked, a glimmer of hope in her eyes. My mother was a big fan of Jake's, and I knew how much faith she had in him.

"We're still discussing it," I said.

She deflated a little just then, and I wanted to say more, but Officer Grant stepped out of the room and looked pointedly at me. "Suzanne, I need to see you right now."

There was an edge of steel in his voice as he said it, and I knew better than to do anything but comply.

"Stay strong," I said as I squeezed Momma's hand.

Inside, there was a video camera set up, as well as a microphone attached to a tape recorder. It was all rather intimidating, but I took a deep breath and sat down in the chair that he indicated. After I'd gone over my story three times and answered every question Officer Grant had, he reached over and shut off all of the equipment.

"Thanks," he said, easing his stern demeanor at last. "Suzanne, don't take offense by the way I acted."

I patted his hand. "Don't worry about me. I know that you're just doing your job."

"I appreciate that," he answered with a smile.

As I stood, I asked, "Who would you like next?"

"Send in George," he said. "I probably won't even have to prompt him."

I did as I was asked, and after George was inside, I sat down beside Emma on the bench in front of the interrogation room.

It was clear that the excitement had worn off and the ramifications of what we had seen were beginning to sink in. "I had to call Dad when I saw the mayor's body, Suzanne. Don't be mad at me."

I patted her hand. "I understand. Just don't let him stiff you on the fifty bucks." Ray Blake offered a crime dog reward to anyone who reported a major crime to him.

"Don't worry, he'll pay," she said.

"Listen," I said gently, "I know your father is going to interview you as soon as you get home, and I understand it's something you're going to have to do, but take it easy on Momma, okay?"

Emma looked taken aback by my request. "Suzanne, I don't think your mother's involved in this. I would never say anything like that, especially not to my dad."

I stepped carefully here. "Your father might have a way of bringing it out of you."

"If he tries to, Mom and I will make sure he never stops regretting it. I've got your back on this, trust me."

I nodded, but I knew Ray Blake, too. By tomorrow morning, all of April Springs might just be under the impression that my mother was a murderer.

I had no choice but to make sure they didn't believe it very long. Whether Jake worked the case or not, I was going to get Grace and George together, and we were going to find out what really happened to Cam Hamilton.

It was really the only thing that I could do.

CHAPTER 5

Outside of the police station, I looked around for Momma, hoping that she'd stayed close by, but she must have gone off on her own as soon as Officer Grant finished questioning her. I wasn't sure what to do with myself, but my growling stomach answered the question. It was nearly two and I hadn't had lunch yet. First things first.

I walked over to the Boxcar and found Trish standing up front at the register. Things had been buzzing inside until I showed up, but they'd suddenly gotten awfully quiet when folks realized that I'd walked in.

"Suzanne, are you all right?" Trish asked. She was a dear friend of mine, second only to Grace, and we'd been pals forever. She still wore the same ponytail she'd had all through school, and had somehow managed to stay fit and trim enough to fit into her prom dress, something that I would never be able to do again.

"I'm fine," I said, loud enough to give the customers eating at the restaurant a chance to hear. "Everything's good."

"It's just terrible about the mayor, isn't it?"

I had to agree. I hadn't been a big fan of the man, but he hadn't deserved to come to an end that way. "Murder is never an easy thing to take, no matter who the victim is."

"Do they have any idea who might have done it?" Trish asked.

"Not a clue yet," I said. I looked around the dining room, and most folks had the decency to at least look like they weren't watching and listening to us.

"If there's anything I can do — and I mean anything — all you have to do is ask. I'm on your side." She said it loud enough so that folks all the way over in Union Square could hear it. It meant a lot to me, having Trish's very public support.

I smiled at her as I said, "Thanks, but I'm good. Any chance I could get a table?"

"I've got one right here," she said, and seated me close to the register. "Is Grace coming, or is she working today?"

As a corporate sales rep for a cosmetics firm, my best friend's hours were pretty much her own, so it was a legitimate question. "She's off today, but she and her boyfriend are antiquing."

Trish hadn't had much luck finding someone to date over the past few years, so she said with a wistful air, "Peter's a real looker, isn't he? I can't believe he goes shopping with her, too."

I decided to let that go with a nod.

Trish got it immediately, dropped it on the spot, and then asked, "What can I get for you?"

I was in the mood for something different. "Let's shake things up today. How about a turkey sandwich on wheat bread with a side of coleslaw and a glass of sweet tea?"

"You've got it," she said.

I was sitting there, trying not to notice that folks were still staring at me, when my phone rang. I was happy for the distraction, and doubly pleased that it was Jake.

"I wasn't sure you were going to call me back," I said with a slight laugh. "I had a feeling you were finished with that particular conversation by the way you ended it."

"Sorry, my boss was on the line. When he calls, I answer."

"I didn't know he intimidated you," I said with a smile.

"He doesn't, but if I cross him, he has the

power to make me write parking tickets instead of investigating murder."

I got it. Jake loved the excitement of what he did, and if he had to do something far below his detecting abilities, it would drive him crazy. "Was he asking you for an update on the blackmail case? How is it going, by the way?"

"Actually, he called to congratulate me. I solved it this morning," Jake said matter-of-factly.

"Really? That's great. Whodunnit?"

"It wasn't that hard to figure out that it was his mistress," Jake said. "When the man refused to leave his wife, she decided to give him a little incentive. It wasn't the crime of the century; the local cops here would have solved it soon enough."

"Are you getting any time off?" I asked, perhaps a little too eagerly. Having Jake as close as he was and not being able to see him at least for one date would be torture. "I probably don't even have to say it, but if you have a spare hour or two, I'd love to see you."

"Be careful what you wish for, Suzanne," he said, his voice solemn.

"What does that mean?"

I heard Jake take a deep breath on the other end of the line, and then he said, "You got what you were hoping for. I've been officially assigned to Cam Hamilton's murder investigation."

"That's just great," I said, a little louder than I'd intended. "I can't believe it."

Jake sounded less than enthusiastic as he explained, "Suzanne, I tried to talk my boss out of the assignment, but he wouldn't budge. The mayor's murder is bound to get headlines, and he wants it solved quickly. 'Hard and fast' were his exact words. I'm afraid this is going to get intense."

"I'm not worried. I know that you'll do a good job," I said.

"I always give it my all, but we need to talk. It's important that we get one thing straight up front. I can't play favorites for you, your mother, or any of your friends. This is going to be strictly by the book. Do you understand?"

"Yes, sir," I replied.

After a moment's hesitation, he asked, "Are you being sarcastic?"

I knew better. As much as I liked to joke around, this was not the time for it. "Not a chance. I know you have a job to do, and there's no doubt in my mind that you're going to find the killer."

Jake paused long enough so that I wondered if he was still on the line. When he did speak, he said, "Suzanne, you're not digging into this yourself."

When I didn't respond, he asked, "Aren't you going to answer me?"

"Funny, I didn't hear a question," I replied.

"I mean it. This is serious. I won't have you meddling in something I've been ordered to investigate."

Again, I didn't answer.

He finally sighed and said, "You're going to do what you think is best no matter what I say, aren't you?"

"Finally, a real question. Yes, I am. Jake, there are folks who will talk to me who wouldn't dream of saying a word to you. I'll do my best not to get in your way, but I won't stay out of this. It's too important to me."

I could hear a weary edge to his voice as he said, "You could have just lied to me, you know."

I laughed. "I won't do that, so be careful about what questions you ask."

"Got it. Just be careful, okay? You're too important to me to lose you."

How sweet was that? There was a reason I loved this man. "When will you be here? Would you like to have dinner with us?"

"I wish I could, but until this case is over,

I'm not going to be able to socialize with you or your mother. Trust me, I don't want it to be that way, but there can't be the slightest hint that I'm being unduly influenced. I love you, and I want to spend every minute I can with you, but I'm afraid it's not going to happen this time."

"You're forgiven," I said, "only because I understand what you're saying, and you added that you loved me. I love you, too, by the way."

"It's not going to be easy, is it?" he asked, and I could almost hear the grin as he said it.

"No, but what fun would that be?" Getting serious again for a moment, I said, "Jake, do whatever you have to do, and when this is all over, we'll be a couple again."

"No matter what?"

"No matter what," I said, trying my best not to think about just how much ground that statement covered.

By the time I got home, I was feeling kind of blue. Having Jake in April Springs and not being able to see him was going to be tough, and I knew it. Every point he made was a good one, though, and I knew in my heart that he was right. We'd find a way to get through this.

I knew my mother couldn't be feeling all that great, so I did my best to put on a smile when I walked into the cottage.

I found her on the couch, crying.

I moved to her quickly and put my arms around her. "Are you okay?"

"I'm fine," she said, all evidence to the contrary. "This has turned into a horrible nightmare, and I keep hoping that I'm going to wake up and find it was all in my imagination. Seeing Cam dead like that was just so surreal."

"It wasn't your fault," I said. "Just because you filed to run against him doesn't mean that you had anything to do with his murder."

"I'm dropping out, of course," she said as she dabbed at her cheeks with a tissue.

I had to walk softly here. "Momma, you're a grown woman, and I can't tell you what you should do," I said softly, "but think about it for a second. If you quit, who's going to be our next mayor?"

"Evelyn Martin," Momma said, a hint of distaste in her voice. "I don't care. If she wants the job, she can have it."

"I understand your reaction, but there's no need to make a decision right now. Let's take a few days and think about it."

"Suzanne," she said, looking hard at me, "I'm not going to change my mind."

"The filing deadline has already passed," I said, "so there's nothing to be gained by quitting now. Just don't say anything to anyone about what you're going to do. Would you do that as a favor to me?"

"I don't see the point, but very well," Momma said. "Everyone in town must think I killed him. Why did it have to happen in my building?"

"I didn't even know you owned it until today," I said as I settled down on the couch beside her. "Who else knew?"

"It's a matter of public record for anyone who wants to dig through the county books, but offhand I'd probably say that just Hannah knew for sure, since I bought it from her. Anyone else is strictly a matter of speculation." Momma stood and began pacing. "Suzanne, you know I don't usually approve of you meddling into police investigations, but I'm afraid you don't have any choice this time. You need to find out who killed the mayor."

"I will, but there's some good news, too: Jake's coming to town," I said. "He's been assigned the case."

"How does that affect the two of you?" she asked. Leave it to Momma to worry more about my personal relationship than any of her own difficulties.

"We aren't going to see each other while he's investigating," I explained. "It's going to be tough, but there's really nothing we can do about. I trust him, Momma."

"As do I, but we both know full well that many of our fellow citizens won't cooperate with his investigation. You need to get Grace and George and start poking around behind the scenes. Folks around here will talk to you."

"Even if you're a suspect in their minds?" I hated to say it like that, but I didn't really have any choice. Momma and I weren't big on tiptoeing around things, and it wasn't the time to start now.

"Don't you see? Because of that, you'll have an easier time asking questions. You have a stake in the matter, after all."

"I can't believe you're suggesting it, but I like it. What do you think Chief Martin is going to say about it?"

"It's not his investigation anymore, is it? You worry about Jake and leave Phillip to me."

"With pleasure," I said. I shook my head and added, "I'll tell you the truth: I really don't want to see Evelyn Martin running April Springs. I'm not sure how you could do that to all of us. Let's face it, she'd make a lousy mayor, and you know it. You could do better just by showing up once in a while."

Momma nodded. "Perhaps you're right, but if I do keep my name on the ballot, I won't campaign. That means no signs, no badges, no ads. If folks want me, they'll have to decide for themselves."

It was a concession on her part, and I knew how hard it must have been for her to say it, but I couldn't let it go at that. "Even Evelyn might beat you if she campaigns and you don't. Folks have to know that you're running, and you need to remind them that they have a choice."

"That's final, Suzanne. If you agree to no campaigning, then I won't withdraw from the election. But if I see one flyer, one poster, or one yard sign with my name on it, I'm dropping out. Is that clear?"

"Hang on. I can't stop other folks from campaigning for you if they decide to. It would be impossible to police all of April Springs looking for unauthorized campaign materials." She was being unreasonable, but I could only push her so far.

"Perhaps, but I'm putting you in charge of it." She touched my cheek gently and said, "Thank you. I wasn't sure I could feel better, but you've managed to cheer me up a little. What do you say to some lemon chicken for dinner?"

"Do you really feel like cooking?" I asked as I got off the couch and moved over by the fireplace.

"What's the alternative? Can you imagine me going anywhere out to eat without someone whispering behind my back?"

"You've got a point," I said.

"Besides, cooking might help me take my mind off my troubles. You can . . . Never mind."

"What were you going to say?" I asked.

"I was about to add that you could invite Jake, but that's not within the rules, is it?"

"Don't worry. We'll have fun with just the two of us," I said. "Do you need any help in the kitchen?"

"I'm fine. Why don't you grab a quick nap if you can, and I'll wake you when dinner is ready."

"What makes you think I'm sleepy?" I asked as I fought off a yawn.

"Dear daughter, with your working hours, how can you not be? Now, go on and leave dinner to me."

I wasn't about to fight her, especially since I knew that if I kept talking, I might find a way to make it worse instead of better. I stretched out on the couch, and the next thing I realized, someone was knocking on our front door. For a split second I hoped that it was Jake, but I knew that he wouldn't be paying me any surprise visits until this case was solved.

"I'll get it," I said as I stood and stretched for a second.

"That woke you, didn't it?" Momma asked, coming out of the kitchen wearing her favorite apron.

"I needed to get up anyway," I said.

She stayed long enough to see who it was, but the second she saw that it was Grace on the porch, she waved and then headed back into the kitchen.

When I motioned Grace inside, she asked, "Hey, got a second?" Grace clearly realized that I'd been taking a nap, most likely from my disheveled hair. "I woke you, didn't I?"

"No, it's fine. I had to get up anyway. What's up? I thought you and Peter were spending the day together."

"He left," she said, looking sad as she admitted it.

"For good?" I asked.

"No, of course not. He was supposed to be on vacation, but his boss called him in to work. There's some kind of business emergency and he'll be gone at least a week, maybe more."

I did my best not to smile too broadly at the news. "His loss is my gain, then." I stepped aside and invited her in. "Would you like to stay for dinner?"

She took a deep breath, and I knew she was taking in the enticing aroma of Momma's famous lemon chicken. "I shouldn't," she said.

Ignoring her, I yelled out, "Momma, can Grace stay for dinner?"

"Suzanne," she said reprovingly as Momma came out.

"Of course she can. How are you, dear?" Momma asked.

"I'm fine. Sorry about what happened today."

"As are we all," Momma said. "Wash up, ladies. We'll be eating in three minutes."

Momma vanished back into the kitchen, and Grace turned to me. "Did I say the wrong thing just now?"

"With my mother, I doubt you could. She seems to cut you a great deal more slack than she ever did me," I said with a smile. "You're always welcome here, and you know it."

"I know I haven't been that great a friend lately," she said as we took turns washing our hands in the hall powder room. "You know how I am when there's someone new in my life. I tend to get a little tunnel vision."

"I understand," I said. "If I had a boyfriend who lived in town, I might be the same way."

"Thanks for saying that, but we both know that's not true. When you were married to Max, you still always managed to find time for me."

"Well, I was married to Max, after all," I said with a smile. "There were times when a little of him went a long way. You were my relief outlet."

She smiled. "Still, I'll try to do better from now on."

"No worries, Grace. We're good," I said.

She lowered her voice as she asked her next question. "Has your mother said much about the murder?"

"She wanted to drop out of the race, but I think I talked her out of it," I said softly enough so that Momma wouldn't hear me.

"That would have been disastrous," Grace said.

"Tell me about it. Can you imagine Evelyn Martin running our fair city? I'm already having nightmares about it."

"I'm talking about her image," Grace said. "If she quit now, it would look like she's abandoning April Springs just when the town needs her."

"Like I said, she's agreed to run, but there's one catch, and it's a whopper."

"What is it?" Grace asked.

"There is to be no campaigning for her of any sort," I replied. "I told her that it's not going to be easy keeping folks from spontaneously putting signs up, but she expects me to keep the town in check."

"Good luck with that," Grace said.

"I know."

"Ladies," Momma called out from the kitchen, "the food is on the table."

Grace and I joined her, and after we sat down, we said a blessing, then prepared to eat. There was enough food on the table to feed half of April Springs, with two kinds of potatoes, yams, green beans, cranberry sauce, and, of course, Momma's justifiably famous lemon chicken.

"This all looks so lovely," Grace said. "Thanks so much for inviting me."

"We're pleased to have you," Momma said.

As I filled my plate, I said, "You know, Jake would have really loved this."

"You could always take him a plate," Momma said.

"No, ma'am. They are his rules, and I'm

going to make him live by them," I said with a grin.

I'd had maybe three bites when there was a knock at the door. "Momma, did you invite anyone else to dinner?"

"Of course not," she said. "Perhaps Jake changed his mind."

"I doubt it. If I had to guess, I'm betting it's the police chief. He probably smelled your chicken from the station," I said as I got up and headed to the door.

It was neither man, though.

"George, come in," I said as I saw my old friend.

"You're eating," he said. "I'll come back later."

"Who is it?" Momma called out from the dining room.

"George," I said.

"Invite him in, Suzanne."

I grinned at him. "You heard her. Come in."

"I don't want to impose," he said, though I noticed that his attention was drawn to the delightful aroma coming from the other room.

"Please," I said. "We have enough food to feed an army. Grace is here too, so come on. The more the merrier."

He nodded. "If you're sure."

"You don't want to offend Momma, do you?"

"Not a chance of that," George said.

We walked into the dining room together.

"Hello, Dorothy," he said, doffing a hat he wasn't even wearing. I'd seen Southern men repeat that gesture all my life, and it never ceased to make me smile.

"George, come in. I'll get you a plate."

"No need, ma'am. I just wanted to have a word with Suzanne. I can come back after you're finished."

"George," my mother said sternly. "I won't ask you again. Sit."

He did as he was told, a broad smile on his face. "Yes, ma'am. I won't say no to you in your own house."

As we ate, we discussed many things, but two topics were tacitly off the table: the upcoming election and the murder of our mayor.

After we were finished, Momma said, "I wish I'd baked a fresh pie."

"I for one wouldn't know where to put it," I said.

She frowned as she studied the table. "I have some apple crisp in the refrigerator. I can warm it up and serve it with coffee and ice cream. Grace, would you or George like any?"

After they both declined, Momma stood and said, "Then I'll just get started on the dishes."

"We'll help," Grace said, and George and I echoed it.

"Ordinarily, I might take you up on it, but why don't the three of you retire to the front porch? I'd like to keep busy, and I'm sure you've got things to discuss."

"What do you mean?" Grace asked.

Momma smiled. "Don't try to sound innocent to me, young lady. I've already told Suzanne that I approve of the three of you investigating Cam's murder, and I expect that you have some planning to do."

I kissed her on the cheek. "Thanks, Momma. It was fantastic."

"Truly wonderful," George said, and Grace added her own thanks for dinner.

Once we were outside, George said, "Your mother's not as happy as she would like us to think."

"It's completely understandable," I said. "She's between a rock and a hard place right now. After having a pretty public fight with the mayor, he's found murdered in a building she just happens to own. We need to clear this up, and fast."

"Is Jake coming to give us a hand?" George asked. He'd worked with my boyfriend in the past on some of our impromptu investigations, and I knew how much he enjoyed it.

"Sorry, but he's working for the other side this time. We're on a break while he investigates, which honestly gives me even more incentive to find out quickly what happened to Cam. Do we have any thoughts about who might want to see him dead?"

George thought about it, and then said, "We can't discount Hannah herself. She's bound to still have keys to the building, so that gives her access."

I recounted seeing them arguing in front of Donut Hearts, and Grace nodded. "Don't forget, Evelyn used to work for Hannah, too, and if Cam tried to get in the way of her beating your mother for mayor, she might just be crazy enough to kill him."

"It's hard to imagine she'd go that far to get a job I doubt she really wants," George said.

He clearly hadn't seen the side of her that I had earlier. "It's not about the job. It's about punishing my mother for stealing her husband, no matter how crazy that might sound," I said. "She has to go on our list. Anyone else?"

Grace nodded. "William Benson is a suspect."

"William?" I asked, surprised by the mention of his name. William ran an arcade on the other side of town, a place the kids — and many adults — loved. In fact, many of the kids in April Springs called him Uncle William, including me. "Why should his name be on our list?"

"I was going to the Boxcar to meet Peter two days ago, and I was waiting outside when I heard an argument. Cam and William were around back, and from what I heard, they were ready to come to blows. It seems William wanted to put in a go-cart course, and Cam personally stopped the permit process. It sounded as though Cam was shaking William down for a little something under the table to let the permit go through, and William wasn't having any of it."

"You didn't tell me about that," I said. Normally, Grace and I shared things like that.

"I meant to. As a matter of fact, I had my phone out to call you, but Peter showed up just then and it slipped my mind."

"I'll talk to him tomorrow," George said. "William and I go way back. Do you two want to tackle the women?"

I thought about facing Evelyn Martin, and honestly, I wasn't too keen on the idea, but

I'd had to ask tough questions to people in the past who'd liked me even less. "We'll do it." I turned to Grace. "Can you take a few days off?"

"I already did," she admitted. "Peter and I were going away, and I put in for my vacation two weeks ago. I can't change it now, so I'm sorry, but you're stuck with me."

"Does that mean you'll be volunteering at the donut shop every morning, too?" I asked with a smile.

"Sure, if you change your hours. Why don't I take advantage of my time and sleep in? Then, when you're ready to close shop for the day, I'll be ready to help you investigate."

"That sounds like a plan to me. So, we all meet up tomorrow evening, right back here."

"That sounds good," George said as his phone rang. "Excuse me." After a hurried conversation, he hung up. "That was a friend of mine on the inside. Cam was spotted an hour before you found the body, so we've got a timeline to work from. He was murdered between ten thirty and eleven thirty in the morning."

"Can you trust your source?" I asked.

"With my life," he answered. "We need to make tomorrow's meeting before dinner. I can't come back here and eat again so soon."

"Why? Didn't you like what you had tonight?" I asked.

He looked flustered and was clearly searching for the right thing to say when I added, "George, you're always welcome here. I was just kidding."

"I love your mother's cooking," he said. "I just can't make a habit of it." He stood, and I saw a trace of the limp he'd been doing his best to overcome. I for one would be glad when it was completely gone, since it was a reminder of a time I'd put him in harm's way with one of my investigations. It had nearly made me stop digging into other people's troubles, but I couldn't do that, especially not now. Momma had asked for my help, and I wasn't about to turn her down.

"See you ladies tomorrow," he said as he climbed off the porch.

I looked around for his car, but I couldn't find it. "Where are your wheels, George?"

"I'm out walking for physical therapy," he admitted. "Treadmills bore me these days."

"I'd be glad to give you a ride home," I said.

"No, thanks. I need the exercise." He waved as he walked around the corner, and

I felt Grace's hand touch my shoulder.

"You need to stop beating yourself up about that, Suzanne. It wasn't your fault."

"He was there because of me," I said.

"George is a grown man. You couldn't have stopped him even if you'd tried."

I turned back to her. "That's the thing, though, isn't it? I didn't try, not one little bit, and now he's got a limp because of me."

"Which is getting better every day," Grace said.

Momma came outside with a serving tray and four bowls. "I've brought out the apple crisp," she said, and then noticed George's absence. "Oh, dear, I assumed he'd still be here."

"I'll eat his," I said with a grin.

"Not without a fight. I'll flip you for it," Grace added.

"There's no need to argue over the extra portion. There's plenty left."

"Yeah, but it's more fun acting as though it's the last one," I said with a smile.

Baked Fruit Delight Donuts

We've been trying to eat a little healthier lately, so I've been playing with more baked, and less fried, donuts. You can achieve some surprisingly good results, and once I got my stand-alone baked-donut maker, I found that making donuts couldn't be easier. These donuts in particular produce a fruit-filled explosion in your mouth with every bite.

Ingredients

Wet
- 1 egg, beaten slightly
- 1/2 cup whole milk (2% can be substituted.)
- 1/2 cup granulated white sugar
- 1 tablespoon butter, melted (I use unsalted; salted can be used, but cut the added salt by half.)
- 1 teaspoon vanilla extract

Dry
- 1 cup all purpose flour (I prefer unbleached, but bleached is fine, and so is bread flour.)
- 1 teaspoon baking powder
- 1 teaspoon baking soda
- 1/2 teaspoon salt

- 1/2 cup dried fruit (any combination of fruit bits like raisins, cranberry [Craisins], apple, apricot, plum, peach, cherry)

Directions

Combine the dry ingredients (flour, baking powder, baking soda, and salt) in a bowl and sift together. In another bowl, combine the wet ingredients (beaten egg, milk, butter, sugar, and vanilla extract). Slowly add the wet mix to the dry mix, stirring until it's incorporated. Don't overmix.

The donuts can be baked in the oven at 350 degrees for 10–15 minutes in cupcake trays or small donut molds, or for 6–7 minutes in a countertop donut baker.

Once the donuts are finished, remove them to a cooling rack. These are best served as is, but they can be embellished with any topping of your choice. Sometimes I make an apricot glaze by reducing apricot jam on the stovetop by half, and then use that to lightly cover the tops.

Makes 5–9 donuts, depending on baking method

CHAPTER 6

To my surprise, the next morning Emma was in front of the donut shop, waiting for me though she wasn't due in for another half hour. I hated that she'd been standing out in the cold. She must have been freezing.

"What's going on?" I asked as I unlocked the door and let her in. "You're here early, aren't you?"

As she rubbed her hands together, she said, "Don't worry, I'm not on the clock. I found out some stuff from Dad that I just couldn't wait to tell you."

As we both hung up our coats, I said, "I don't want to get you into trouble with him. Are you sure he's okay that you're sharing?"

Emma laughed. "It was his idea. He's hoping that if you and your gang crack the case, you'll give him a heads-up so he can write it up for the newspaper."

"As much as I appreciate the spirit of cooperation he's proposing, I'm not sure I can do that," I said. Getting Ray Blake's take on things could be helpful, but if he printed anything that disparaged Jake or even the police chief, I would hate to feel responsible for it.

"How about this: What if you just did whatever you were most comfortable with doing?" she said.

I decided that I could live with that. "What have you got, then?"

She clearly couldn't wait to tell me. "Dad was able to uncover two pretty big bombshells. You know what a ladies' man Cam always thought he was?"

I'd had a few friends who'd made the mistake of dating him, though he'd never been crazy enough to ask me out. If he had, I would have turned him down, even before Jake came into my life. Cam wasn't my type, more flash than substance, trying to impress women with his wad of money more than his personality. "He was delusional," I admitted.

"Well, it turns out that some women weren't quite as discerning as you. He dated the vet in town, didn't he?"

"Sherry broke up with him," I said. "She told me that she was glad to be rid of him."

"Well, clearly not everyone he ever dated

121

felt that way. It turns out that he dumped a woman named Kelly Davis four days ago, and it was a bad breakup. From what Dad heard, she threatened to kill him for dumping her, in front of witnesses, too."

"I didn't even realize they were dating. Has Jake heard any of this?"

"I don't know about that, but Dad's going to tell Chief Martin the second the newspaper hits the stands today. He won't give up a scoop, but he's going to make sure he doesn't help a murderer get away if she killed him, either. Is Jake in town?"

"I'm not sure," I said.

Emma looked puzzled. "That doesn't sound good. You two didn't have a fight, did you?"

"We're not seeing each other at the moment," I said, and before I could finish, Emma looked as though she wanted to cry.

"That's terrible! You two are perfect for each other, Suzanne. You have to make this right while you still can."

"Easy, let me finish. As long as Jake's here working on the case, we aren't going out, but we're still solid. There's no reason to worry about us," I said.

"Are you sure? That doesn't sound all that solid to me."

I took her hands in mine. "Emma, it's

what we have to do, and we both understand it." It was time to get her off my love life. "Who else did your dad come up with?"

Emma took a deep breath, and then let it out. "William Benson made his list, too."

I knew about William as a suspect, but I didn't want to say anything just yet. I wanted to know if Ray was working off of the same information we were. "William's always had a pleasant word for me and a nice smile whenever he comes by the donut shop. What did your dad find out about his relationship with Cam?"

"They had a problem about money," Emma said.

It sounded as though we had the same information. "Cam expected to be paid off for the go-cart permit, right?"

"How did you know?" Emma asked, clearly disappointed that I knew about the scheme.

"Don't worry, it's good to hear it confirmed from a different source."

Emma shook her head. "Do you really think that William might have killed him? I have a hard time believing that."

"Don't worry, we'll talk to him," I said.

My assistant looked expectantly at me. " 'We,' as in 'the two of us'?"

I had to nip this right now. "Emma, you

know the rules."

She was clearly deflated by the reminder that I'd promised her parents not to involve her in any of my criminal investigations. "Okay, fine."

"Anything else?" I asked.

"Do you know about Harvey Hunt?"

"The contractor?" I asked. I'd heard about him around town, but to my knowledge, he'd never stepped one foot into the donut shop. Plenty of his men had, though, and if they were any indication of their boss's disposition, he wouldn't be an easy man to deal with.

"That's the one. Dad found out that Harvey owed Cam a tidy sum of cash, and the mayor was pressing him hard for it."

"What was the money for?"

"Dad has two theories, but he's not sure which one is true. One is that Harvey still owed the mayor for a payoff for getting the bid on the city hall renovation three months ago."

Sadly, I had no trouble believing that. "What's his other theory?"

She grinned. "I shouldn't smile, but I find it ironic that despite his crooked business practices, Harvey's construction company was in financial trouble."

"Why should that make you happy?"

"Dad thinks that Harvey had to borrow money from Cam to pay off some creditors, cash that Harvey had originally paid our mayor for bids that he'd gotten in the past. Either way, it was a tidy sum of money."

"How did your father find out about the loan in the first place?"

"It was supposedly from a call-in tip from an anonymous source. At least, that's what Dad said."

I could see that she was holding something back. "But you're not sure you believe him, do you?"

Emma shrugged. "My father is the poster child for not telling anyone everything he knows, including my mom. I've got a feeling that he's got an inside source at the construction company. He gets this particular smile when he knows he's onto something solid, and when Dad told me about this, he was grinning like the Cheshire cat."

"I can't wait to hear what else you've got for me."

"That's it, but I'll keep paying attention to what's going on, and if there are any new developments, I'll let you know."

"Thanks," I said as I stood. "I appreciate that."

"Just trying to help where I can, boss," she said with a smile.

"Then maybe we can start making do-nuts," I said with a grin of my own.

Just before six a.m., I picked up my phone and called Grace's answering machine. I knew she left her ringer on silent mode on her home telephone, so I didn't have to worry about waking her up. I left her a brief message about Kelly and then told her that I'd see her after work. It was time to open. I left the kitchen to turn on the lights out front and unlock the door. Sometimes I had early risers waiting for me, and other times I didn't, but I'd noticed that since we'd pushed our hours back some, we had more customers the first thing.

To my delight, Jake was standing outside, and better yet, he was alone.

"Hey there," I said, wanting to hug him, but afraid someone might see. My boyfriend was a stickler for how things looked, and I was going to respect that.

"Hi, Suzanne. You look great." His smile nearly melted me.

I glanced down at my jeans, an old T-shirt, and my apron. "You've been out to sea too long, sailor. I'm a wreck, and I know it."

He shook his head and grinned. "I don't think so. Can we chat for a second?"

"What happened to keeping a low profile?" I asked.

Jake looked around. "I made sure no one else was around when I waited for you to open. Nobody's here yet, but if Emma could watch the front, we could talk in the kitchen, if you're interested."

"You bet I am." I smiled as I called out, "Emma."

"What's up, boss?" she asked as she came out drying her hands on a dish towel. The second she saw Jake, she started grinning. "Hey there, stranger. It's good to see you."

"Hey yourself," Jake said.

I took Jake's hand and told Emma to watch the front. She gave me a mock salute, and I led my boyfriend back into the kitchen, away from prying eyes. The second the door was closed, I kissed him and then gave him a huge hug.

"I missed you so much," I said, the words spilling out of me. "I can't believe we have to hide like a couple of teenagers."

"I can't, either," Jake admitted. "I'm sorry, Suzanne. I shouldn't even be here right now. I know what I said earlier, but I can't just ignore you. You mean too much to me."

"I'm glad," I said as I finally released him. "I can't believe you're staying in town and I can't even see you."

"Well, if we can pull off a few more of

these early-morning visits, I'm game."

"I've got an even better idea," I said. "Instead of waiting out front, why don't you come in the back way around fifteen till six. I can have Emma stock the cases, and we can have a few minutes alone every morning away. What do you say?"

"If anyone sees us, it's going to kill my ability to investigate this case," Jake said reluctantly.

"I understand," I said, and then hugged him again. "You're right, of course."

As I pulled away, he asked, "What was that for?"

"I'm putting a few hugs in the bank before you have to go," I said.

"I can only stay a few minutes," he answered. "I'm going to have to sneak out the back as it is."

"Give me a second and I'll get you some breakfast," I said.

"I don't want to waste my time with you by eating," he answered.

"Boy, you really must be in love," I replied with a grin. "You have to want coffee, though."

"That would be good," he admitted.

"Hang on then, I'll be right back." I ducked up front and found Emma waiting on an older couple, with three more folks behind them.

"Sorry to do this to you," I said as I poured Jake a cup of coffee and bagged a few donuts for him. I knew how much Emma didn't care for working the front, and I tried to spare her every time I could.

"Take your time," Emma said. "It's all good out here."

"Yes, by all means," a well-dressed man in the back of the line said sarcastically. "Take your time. We have all morning."

I smiled at him and then told Emma, "Give them each one free donut, courtesy of Donut Hearts." I turned to the man and asked with a grin, "Better?"

He nodded, and after a moment, added a fleeting smile.

Jake was waiting for me when I rejoined him.

"Thanks," he said, and then put the donuts and coffee down on the prep table.

He kissed me again, and then said, "I hate to do it, but I've got to go."

"You need to hear something first." It didn't take much of an internal debate to decide that I was going to tell him what Emma had told me earlier. He was the official police investigator on the case, and he deserved to have all of the information that I'd acquired. "There are two more suspects that need to go on your list."

"And you're just handing them over to me?" he asked. "What's the catch?"

"I'm going to keep digging myself," I admitted.

He shrugged. "What have I got to lose? You'll do that whether I get the names or not."

"True, but at least this way I won't feel so guilty about it."

He laughed and said, "Fine. What have you got?"

I told him about Kelly Davis, Harvey Hunt, and William Benson, and as he jotted their names down in his notebook, he asked, "Care to tell me who your sources are?"

"Sorry, it's confidential," I replied. "What's mentioned in the land of donuts stays in the land of donuts."

"Suzanne," he said, drawing my name out.

"I mean it. I can give you the scoop, but I'm not at liberty to tell you where I heard it. Take it or leave it."

"I'll take it," he said. "Thanks, for breakfast, *and* the information."

"Just act surprised when you hear those names from another source," I answered.

"I can do that. Now, will you let me out the back way so I don't have to deal with any of your customers?"

"I'd be glad to. Just pay the toll first and you're free."

"What's the toll?" he asked.

"One kiss, however long you'd like it be," I answered with a smile.

After he more than paid for his passage, I opened the back door, peeked outside to make sure no one was out there, and then said, "Scram. The coast is clear."

Jake left and I bolted the door again. I was thrilled that he'd come by. I didn't need to have a man in my life, but it could make my life more interesting when there was one I cared about. Now maybe I'd be able to enjoy the rest of my day and keep digging into Cam's murder. I didn't care which one of us found the killer first. I just wanted my family's name cleared, and my boyfriend back.

When I walked back up front to take over, Emma said softly, "You let him out the back way, right?"

"He's gone," I confirmed. There were a few customers in line, new ones since I'd been in the dining room last.

"We're here for our free donuts," one of the guys said.

"What are you talking about?"

"I just got a text on my phone that you were giving food away," he admitted.

131

"Sorry, you had to be here in line at the time to qualify, but come back tomorrow. You never know," I said, pretty certain that I wouldn't be giving any food away then.

"Aw man, that stinks."

There weren't many people there, so I said impulsively, "Okay, my offer of one free donut stands."

Instead of thanking me, he pulled out his telephone instantly and started typing, so I added, "But you have to be here right now to get it, and if you call, text, tweet, or tell anyone else what I'm doing in any way, you have to pay double from now on."

He dropped his phone back into his pocket and shrugged. "I give up. No harm, no foul."

It cost me three more donuts, so it wasn't all that bad. I knew how fast people, especially young ones, communicated with their phones, but I was an old-fashioned kind of gal myself. I might be a dying breed, but I didn't feel the need to communicate with everyone I knew around the clock and tell them whatever I was doing, no matter how mundane. I honestly didn't know how people had time to even think these days, the interruptions seemed to come so fast and furious.

■ ■ ■ ■

I couldn't wait to close the donut shop at eleven, but it wasn't because I was tired of offering my treats to the world. A dozen folks who'd come into Donut Hearts had been more interested in my take on the mayor's murder than they were about what I had to sell, and I wasn't about to say anything that might get my mother in any deeper with her fellow townsfolk. The worst of the lot were the pair who'd just left, congratulating Momma and hinting that she'd done the town a favor by getting rid of Cam, something I would never have imagined before then. A man was dead, and all they could focus on was their unhappiness with the way he'd done his job.

I felt sorry for the late mayor, never believing that particular emotion would be possible for me to experience.

Emma came out as I was running the report.

"We had a good day, didn't we?" she asked.

"In some ways, I suppose we did," I said, still in a touchy mood from my last bloodthirsty customers. I'd been so frustrated by the last exchange that I couldn't even focus on writing out the deposit slip for the day's receipts.

"Okay, maybe we didn't do as well as I thought," she said. There were a scant dozen donuts left from our day, so I understood her confusion about my reaction. Then again, she hadn't stood out front with me dealing with the questions, comments, and innuendos I had all morning. "I'm sorry," I said. "I had a tough time with some of our customers today, but that doesn't give me any right to take it out on you."

"Hey, you're the one on the front lines. I like being in the kitchen. By the time we're ready to close, I like to have the dishes done and the floor swept. When I leave here, the donut shop stays right here. As the owner, though, I'm sure you have a lot of it on your shoulders even when you're not working."

I tapped the pen on the counter. "You know, mostly I love everyone who comes in here, and I've made more friends than I ever could have imagined running the shop, but there's one day in a hundred when I wish I worked for someone else in a nine-to-five job I can leave at the end of my day."

"It's got its perks," she said with a grin. Emma pointed to the deposit and asked, "Want me to do that?"

"I think I can handle it. Go on, you can

take off."

"Thanks, I think I will."

There was something about her light attitude that made me wonder about something. "There's not a new man in your life, is there?"

"No, not yet, but you never know, do you? Why do you ask?"

"You seem happier than usual," I admitted.

"Suzanne, I know better than anyone how often my good moods are tied into the new men in my life, but I'm just happy to be alive right now. Have you ever had one of those days when everything just feels right?"

I nodded. "I'm sure I have, but they're hard to come up with at the moment."

Emma touched my arm gently. "The mayor's murder has you on edge. It's perfectly understandable. Don't worry, I know that between you and Jake, one of you will find the killer and clear your mother's name."

"Thanks for the vote of confidence," I said. "Have a nice afternoon."

"Right back at you," she said as I let her out of the donut shop.

I finally managed to make out the deposit slip without messing up and tucked it into my bank bag, along with the cash and

135

receipts for the day.

I was about to head out when there was a tap at the door. Grace was there, dressed in jeans but still managing to look elegant somehow. I waved the bag in the air, shut off the lights, and at the last second grabbed the remaining box of donuts before I headed out.

"For me?" she asked with a grin when she saw the box.

"Sure, why not?" I said.

She looked tempted but shook her head. "I'd better not."

"Don't tell me you're back on another health kick."

Grace frowned a little, and then said, "Honestly? I'm trying to drop a few pounds."

I studied my friend, trying to see where she could afford to lose an ounce. "Why in the world would you want to do that?"

"Peter told me before he left how nice it would be if I could fit into a dress he just bought me. I don't know if he realized it, but it was a size too small, and I can't take it back and exchange it, since he bought it in Atlanta."

That was going too far, and I wasn't about to let this guy get away with so egregious a foul. "Seriously? He thinks you're overweight? What does he say about me?"

Grace shook her head. "It's not like that, Suzanne. I'm sure he didn't mean anything by it."

I wasn't about to argue the point with her. Maybe it was just the fact that I was having a rotten day, but I didn't want to add any problems with Grace to it. It was her life, anyway, and maybe I should start keeping what I thought to myself. Maybe it was an innocent error, but then again, maybe it wasn't. Either way, it wasn't my battle, so I decided to drop it. "Are you ready to do some crime fighting?" I asked.

"I'm all yours. I have to admit, I loved sleeping in this morning." She must have realized how that sounded, knowing when I had to get up every day. "Sorry, I shouldn't be rubbing it in."

"Are you kidding? With my new hours, I'm getting all kinds of sleep."

Grace laughed. "Oh yes, I'm sure of it. Two thirty in the morning is a lazy girl's wake-up time."

"It is, compared to one thirty," I said. "Do you mind if we drop by the bank before we talk to our first suspect today?"

"I figured we were heading there anyway," Grace said.

"Because of the bank deposit?" I asked.

137

"No, I found out before I came over here that Kelly Davis just got transferred to our bank branch in town."

"Where was she before?" I asked as Grace and I got into my Jeep.

"She was at the Union Square branch, but she wanted to be closer to Cam, and by the time the transfer finally came through, she couldn't say no, so she had to come here despite their split."

It was my turn to be impressed. "Grace, how'd you happen to find all of that out? I just left you that message this morning."

"I have a friend who works in Union Square, and I knew Kelly lived there, so I gave her a call after I checked my machine."

"Did you find anything else out?" I asked as I drove to the bank.

"Apparently Kelly was telling anyone who would listen that Cam was The One. She already bought her wedding dress, if you can believe that."

That was news. "Did Cam know that?"

Grace grinned. "That's why he dumped her, from what Annie said. He came over to her house early to pick her up for a date, and she was trying it on. Can you imagine how that must have looked?"

"That must have been a shock for both of

them," I said as I pulled into the bank parking lot.

"You'd better believe it." She put a hand on my arm and turned to me before I could get out of the Jeep. "Before we go inside, there's something you should know. Annie said that Kelly has the meanest temper she's ever seen, and that's saying something. We need to tread lightly here if we're going to learn anything."

"I'll do my best to watch my step, but I can't make any promises. We need to get an alibi for her and then figure out if she could have done it."

"Lead on. Just don't say you weren't warned."

We walked into the bank, and though one teller was free, it wasn't Kelly. When Jackson waved me over to his window, I smiled but shook my head. He looked puzzled by my behavior, and maybe even a little bit hurt, but I couldn't explain it at the moment. I decided I'd give him the box of donuts in my Jeep to make up for my slight, but it was important to speak with Kelly.

When she was finally available, I slid my bank bag across the cage to her.

"I'm so sorry for your loss," I said as she pulled out the contents and began to count.

"Pardon me?" she asked. Kelly was a

pretty blonde, but in kind of a trashy way. Her outfit was just on the edge of office acceptability, with a skirt that was too tight, a hem that was too high, and a blouse that barely managed to contain her pretty ample cleavage. I felt sorry for the two top buttons in particular, and was going to be careful if they popped. It would be a bad way to lose an eye.

"I'm the one who found Cam's body," I said. "I'm kind of surprised you came into work today after what happened yesterday."

She frowned at me for a moment before she spoke. "I have to work. I'm out of vacation and sick time, so if I don't show up, I get fired."

Funny, but her eyes weren't even red. If she'd been crying, you couldn't prove it by me. "Still, you must be shattered by your loss."

"It's a nightmare," she agreed.

I saw her stiffen suddenly as she glanced over my shoulder, and when I turned, I saw Officer Grant come in.

"Something wrong?" I asked.

Kelly ignored me, and then made it a point not to look like she noticed the police officer, who walked to Jackson's window, made a quick withdrawal, and then walked back out.

"No, everything is fine." She had lost count, so she had to start over on my bills.

I couldn't leave it alone, no matter how much she clearly hoped that I would. "Since you two broke up, you'll never be able to make things right again. That must be awful."

"We had a spat. We never broke up," she said, an edge in her voice now. It appeared that I was finally getting to her. "Cam and I had them all of the time."

This conflicted with what I'd heard about them before. "Are you saying that you were still together when he died?"

She nodded. "Of course we were." Kelly seemed to realize how that must have sounded, because she quickly added, "Well, not at that moment, but as a couple, yes. We were just on a break, but we both knew that we'd end up together."

"Where were you when he died?" I asked. It was the entire point of interviewing her, and I hoped to get an answer.

"Tell me exactly when he was murdered, and maybe I'll let you know," Kelly said, all pretense of courtesy now gone from her voice.

I was ready with my answer, since I already knew the approximate time that Cam had been murdered. "Tuesday from ten thirty to eleven thirty in the morning."

Kelly looked surprised to hear the news. "On second thought, there's really no reason I should tell you anything." She'd stopped counting altogether now, and her voice was loud enough to attract attention from some of the other folks at the bank.

The manager, a man who came in for donuts now and then but made no effort to get to know me, came over and asked, "Is there a problem here?"

"No, sir," Kelly said quickly.

He looked at me, and I shook my head. "We're all good."

He clearly didn't believe it, but he went back to his office, though I noticed that he kept an eye on us.

Kelly was all business now. She balanced the deposit against my cash and receipts, then handed me the slip along with my bag. "Have a nice day."

She'd put just a little too much emphasis on the "nice," but I had no choice but to leave. As I stepped away, I saw the manager approach her, and then I heard him tell her to take her lunch break. That was perfect.

If she hadn't brought her lunch, which I somehow doubted she'd ever done in her life, then I could ambush her in the parking lot before she could get away.

CHAPTER 7

We got to my Jeep, I reached in back, and then handed Grace the donuts. "Would you take these in to Jackson for me and tell him that I'm sorry for the way I behaved?"

She took the donuts from me and asked, "I'm happy to do it, but why don't you?"

I smiled firmly. "I'm going to brace Kelly when she comes out."

"That sounds like more fun to me," Grace said as she tried to shove the box of donuts back in my hands. "Why don't you make your peace offering and I'll deal with Kelly."

I shook my head, hoping that Kelly would delay a little before she came out. "If she thinks we're ganging up on her, she might not talk. Please?"

It was clear that Grace wasn't all that thrilled to miss the confrontation, but she nodded anyway. "Fine, but I'll be right back."

Kelly brushed past Grace as she hurried

out of the bank, but I wasn't going to let her get away. "I'm not finished talking to you yet," I said as I approached her.

She had the keys to a black Trans Am out and was unlocking her door even as I approached. "I don't have anything to say to you."

"It won't take a second." I was beside her now, and much harder to ignore.

I was shocked when Kelly spun around and grabbed my arm. I tried to pull it away, but the girl was strong. Her voice was nearly a hiss as she said, "You almost got me fired in there. Leave me alone, or you'll regret it."

There was no doubt in my mind that it was a direct threat, and the strength she used to hold my arm made me realize she was fully capable of killing a man. I couldn't let that stop me, though.

Trying to keep the panic out of my voice, I said, "What I heard is true, wasn't it? You've got quite a temper."

She acted as though she hadn't realized that she was still gripping my arm. She released it, and I saw her handprint still there on my flesh. "I'm sorry. I shouldn't have done that. I'm just at a loss right now, and I'm not myself."

It was a nice apology, but I wasn't sure I

144

should believe a single word of it. "Then you'll answer my questions?"

"I'm not *that* sorry," she said as she got into her car.

As Kelly drove away, Grace came rushing out. She joined me as I watched the car speed away.

"What did I miss?" she asked breathlessly.

"Kelly just grabbed my arm and threatened me. Tell Annie she's right: that girl has a real temper."

"Enough to kill Cam?" Grace asked.

"With plenty left over," I said.

Grace looked pleased. "So that's a good thing, right? Kelly stays on our list."

"As far as I'm concerned, she can move right up to the top," I said, rubbing my arm, trying to get some of the pain out of it.

"Who do we tackle next?" Grace asked as we got into my Jeep.

I started my car and said, "It's either Hannah or Evelyn, and to be honest with you, I'm not up to interrogating the police chief's ex-wife just yet. Arguing with Kelly was a bit much to take. Why don't we start with Hannah?"

"That sounds good to me," she said.

As I drove to Hannah's house, I asked, "What did Jackson say about the donuts?"

Grace smiled. "He told me he was taught

early and often that when someone offers you a gift, you say thank you and take it. Honestly, I think he loved them."

"Good. It might pay off having a friend working so close to Kelly."

Grace looked at me with a frown. "Is that why I gave him those donuts? Were they really just a bribe?"

"Of course not," I said. "But I need some inside information, so why shouldn't I ask Jackson about her? There's nothing nefarious about that."

"As long as it wasn't part of your plan all along," Grace said.

I had to laugh. "Trust me, I'm nowhere near that devious. You should know that about me better than most."

"I do," she acknowledged. "How are we going to tackle Hannah?"

"I think the truth might be our best chance," I admitted. "Unless you have a better idea yourself."

"No, I think the truth will work just fine."

We drove to Hannah's place, a retreat that she'd built just outside town. The lawn in front of the place was a lush and lovely meadow during the summer, but even in February it was delightful. The small pond was still free of ice, though the water had to be frigid, and the bird-feeding station she'd set up on its bank was unbelievable. As I looked up at the house, I could see that Hannah James's place was a log cabin, but there was nothing small about it. Timbers rose to two stories, and the logs were stained dark brown. The green metal roof caught a hint of sunlight, and the broad porch looked really inviting.

That's where we found Hannah, painting at an easel. She had a fireplace on the porch, and a few logs were cheerfully burning.

"Good afternoon," I said as Grace and I walked up onto the porch. "Mind if we take a peek at your work?"

"It's still rough," she said, biting her lip. "I'd really rather you didn't."

"I understand completely," Grace said. "You're entitled to be private about your works of art in progress."

I took in the scene and added, "You've certainly got lots to paint here."

Hannah, a thin woman in her sixties who was built like a willow, nodded. "I wanted to see a picture every time I woke up. I've made all four seasons a delight."

"It's great that you've got all of this," I said.

As Hannah cleaned her brushes, she said, "When my father died, he left a hole in my heart and more money than I knew what to do with. I closed my business, moved out here to his place, and fell in love with it all over again. It's amazing the way he designed the layout to offer lovely views wherever I look."

"You must miss him terribly," I said.

"I do," she said. "What brings you ladies out here on such a beautiful day? I know it's not to admire my vistas. Most folks think it's too chilly to spend much time outdoors in February."

"Actually, we're looking into Cam Hamilton's murder," I said simply.

Hannah shook her head, looked as though she wanted to cry, and then said, "I'm sorry. I can't help you. I didn't have anything to do with that."

"It happened in your shop," Grace said gently.

"My former shop," she corrected her, and then turned to me. "If I'm not mistaken, your mother owns it these days."

"Yes," I admitted. "She had a reason to dislike Cam, but I've heard that you did yourself."

Hannah shook her head. "I don't know what you're talking about."

There was nothing I could do but tell her what I'd seen. "I saw you two in front of Donut Hearts not a week ago," I admitted.

"You looked as though you were ready to kill him." It was a poor choice of words, something I instantly regretted. "Maybe that's a little strong, but you were both extremely upset."

Hannah frowned, and then put the brush she'd been holding down. "I suppose it will come out sooner or later." She pointed to the adjacent land. "Cam bought that property a month ago, and he planned to bulldoze every tree on the lot."

I looked at the majestic trees there: oaks, maple, hickory, and pine. "Why on earth would he do that?"

"He wanted to put a condominium complex there," she said, spitting the words out as though they burned her as she spoke them.

"No wonder you were angry with him," Grace said.

"I was upset, but not enough to kill him," she said.

"What's going to happen now?" I questioned her, honestly curious about what the mayor's death would mean to the project.

"Next door?" she asked, as though she hadn't given it a bit of thought. "I suppose someone will inherit the land, but if there are no heirs, it might go to public auction by the bank."

"Would you buy it?" I asked, wondering if the land acquisition might have been her motive all along.

She nodded. "Why not? I offered Cam good money for it, and I'll do the same with the bank if they take it over."

"But either way, there won't be any condos going in," I said.

Hannah pointed a finger at me as though it were a laser. "I already told you, Suzanne: I didn't kill him."

"But surely you still have a key to your old shop," I said. "You could have gotten in there without a problem."

Hannah looked clearly surprised by my statement. "Are you saying that your mother never changed the locks? Are you serious?"

"She hadn't gotten around to it, since the building wasn't being occupied," I said, feeling the need to defend my mother's failure to do such a simple task.

"Well, if you ask me, that was just plain careless of her," Hannah said.

"Who else might have a key?" Grace asked clearly, trying to cool the tone of the conversation.

"Anyone who ever worked for me probably had a key," Hannah admitted. "I've never been fond of mornings, so I allowed anyone who could stand it to come in early, and that required them to have a key."

"Does that include Evelyn Martin?" I asked.

Hannah's eyes narrowed. "Do you think she might have murdered Cam?" She paused to think about that, and then nodded. "Yes, I can see that."

"Anyone else?" I asked, wondering what names might pop up that we hadn't uncovered yet in our investigation.

Hannah shrugged. "I've been thinking about it, making a list in my mind. A rather handsome young state police investigator came by earlier, and I'm compiling it for him."

So, Jake hadn't wasted any time following up his leads. "Could we get a copy of it as well?" I asked.

"I don't see why you'd need it," Hannah said. "Honestly, I can't believe your mother approves of you trying to solve crime while we have perfectly capable police officers handling things."

"She asked me to do this," I said, probably saying more than I should have.

"She must be really desperate, then," Hannah said. "Not that I blame her."

I was losing my patience. "Where were you on Tuesday morning between ten thirty and eleven thirty?" I asked.

Hannah laughed at the question. "I had to tell the police, but I won't indulge you. You should be careful, Suzanne. I'd hate to see you get hurt."

"Is that a threat?" I asked. "I seem to be getting a lot of them lately."

"No, of course not," Hannah said, clearly uncomfortable with the implication. "I just think the game you are playing is dangerous."

"Trust me, it's not a game," I said.

Grace touched my arm, and when I looked at her, she shook her head slightly. It was time to go before I damaged my relationship with Hannah beyond the point where I could ask her any more questions later. "Listen, I'm sorry if I was rude a little earlier. I love my mother more than anything else in this world, and I hate the idea of her living under everyone's suspicion that she might be a cold-blooded killer. Do you forgive me?"

They were powerful words, and I meant them. I'd been harsher with Hannah than she'd deserved, and I wanted to make amends for it. The fact that she'd bit right back didn't have anything to do with me. My only hope of getting anyone to cooperate with me was to try to keep from alienating them, something I hadn't managed too well so far. It had to be because Momma was in trouble. There was no objectivity in me at the moment, and if I wanted to keep detecting, I was going to have to learn to take a softer approach with the folks I questioned.

"Of course I do," Hannah said softly. "It's perfectly understandable, and while we're asking for apologies, I'd like to ask you for one as well. I'm a little sensitive when it comes to Cam Hamilton's murder. He was killed in my old shop, we have land that abuts that he was going to defile, and enough folks in April Springs know about it all to put me under the gun as well. To tell you the truth, I want you to find the killer myself."

"Then would you give us your alibi?" Grace asked. "It might really help." I was startled by the question, but knew that there couldn't have been a better time to ask than right then, as long as she was the one posing the question.

"I was being stubborn not telling you before. I'm afraid it isn't anything that can be verified. I was here, walking my land. I was alone, I'm sorry to say, another habit of mine, and then I started on this painting."

"You didn't see or talk to anyone the entire time?" I asked, knowing that it would be impossible to prove one way or the other without a collaborating witness.

"No one," she said. "I'm sorrier than you could imagine. Good luck, ladies, and I mean it."

After we drove off, Grace said, "I was worried we were going to blow it, but that apology came at just the right time."

"It was sincere," I said. "I was too tough on her." I looked over at her for a second and added, "As a matter of fact, I was kind of wondering why you didn't stop me."

She smiled at me. "I thought we were trying out a new investigative technique, bad cop/bad cop."

"You could always be the good cop for a change," I suggested.

Grace laughed long and loud at the suggestion. "Have you met me, Suzanne? Is there any way you can see me as the good cop?"

"You've got a point," I said.

Grace sighed heavily and remarked, "I'm afraid we're no better off than we were before, though, are we?"

"I don't see it that way," I said. "We have a motive for Hannah we didn't have before, and we already knew that she had the means and the opportunity."

Grace took a moment to process that and

then said, "I don't know, I can't see her as a killer."

I shook my head. "If we've learned anything over the years, it should be that killers come in all shapes and sizes."

"I know," she said. "I guess that just leaves one more name on our list we need to speak with today."

With a growing sense of dread, I nodded. "It's time we talk to Evelyn Martin."

"I suppose we could always talk to her later," Grace suggested.

I shook my head. "I don't think so. We want to resolve this as quickly as we can."

Grace took a deep breath and said, "Suzanne, remember a long time ago when you asked me to tell you if you were being too pushy with people?"

"Sure," I answered.

Grace nodded. "You're there. You can't treat Evelyn the way you just did Hannah. Hannah's good-natured enough to forgive you, but we both know the chief of police's ex-wife isn't nearly as even-tempered."

"I'm sorry," I said. "I admitted that I was wrong, but you have to give me some credit. I did apologize."

"And you'll do better with Evelyn, right?" she asked lightly.

"I promise," I said. I knew I could get

edgy at times, and a little snarky attitude could slip out when I was frustrated, but Grace was right. It was no way to deal with people.

We parked in front of the Martin household, but before I could ring the doorbell, Grace asked, "Are we good?"

"Better than good. We are golden," I said. "Thanks for keeping me grounded."

"Hey, that's what friends are for."

Evelyn opened the door wearing an unattractive muumuu, looked at us both, and then said, "I'm not interested in donuts, or donut makers."

"Can we just have a second?" I asked, using my best smile.

"You're here about Cam's murder, aren't you?" Evelyn asked.

"What makes you say that?" I countered.

She laughed. "Come on. Do you actually think it's a secret that you two snoop into anything that happens in April Springs? Well, you might as well give up, because you aren't getting anything out of me."

"Why did you hate Cam so much?" I asked softly.

She just laughed. "You haven't disappointed me, I'll say that. I've been waiting for you to come around all day, Suzanne."

"So you could help us?" I asked in my nicest voice.

"No, to do this," she said, and then she slammed the door in our faces.

I turned to Grace and smiled. "How did I do?"

"Outstanding," she said, answering with a grin of her own.

I had to laugh. "That went well, didn't it? Should I ring the bell again?"

Grace shook her head. "I think we learned enough, don't you? Evelyn may have killed Cam, so I understand why she wouldn't talk to us; but then again, she may just not be all that fond of either one of us, especially since your mother is dating her ex-husband."

"It's got to be the dating thing," I said as we got back into my Jeep.

"Why not the other?" Grace asked.

"How could anyone not like us?"

She laughed. "It's a mysterious and baffling event, isn't it?"

I let out a breath I hadn't realized I'd been holding. "I don't know why, but Evelyn's reaction suddenly made me feel better."

"Me, too," Grace said. "Any idea why?"

"I think it could be because she didn't hold back about how she felt about us, and let the consequences be what they may. A little open honesty, even if it is all wrapped

157

up in hostility, isn't all that bad a thing."

"It does limit us to how we can question her," Grace said.

"We'll figure out a way around it," I said. "What should we do now? We have a little time before dinner. You're eating with us again, aren't you?"

Grace shook her head. "Two nights in a row? I'd better not. I don't want to wear out my welcome."

I had to laugh at that. "Are you kidding? I think Momma would prefer your company to mine most days."

She was about to answer when my phone rang. Oddly enough, it was my mother.

"Hey there, we were just talking about you," I said.

"You and Jake?"

"No, I'm with Grace."

"Oh," she said, sounding a little disappointed by my admission. "Are you two going to have dinner together tonight?"

"I thought we might," I said.

"That's nice. Don't wait up for me, then. I'll be late."

"Late? Where are you going?"

Momma sounded pleased as she said, "Phillip is taking me to Union Square for dinner. I told you yesterday."

If she had, it had completely slipped my

mind. "Have fun."

"If I come in late, I'll see you tomorrow."

I hung up and turned to Grace. "So much for my invitation. Momma's got a date, so she's not cooking. If you'll brave it, I can whip something up for us at home."

"I've got a better idea," Grace said. "Why don't we go to the Boxcar instead?"

"Are you saying that you don't like my cooking?" I asked with a grin.

Grace tried to hide her smile as she said, "You made donuts all morning. Tell me you want to go into the kitchen to make dinner for us tonight."

"You sold me," I said. "Besides, I like hanging out at Trish's."

I glanced at my watch and saw that it was almost five. "Is it too early for you to eat now, or should we try to come up with someone else to talk to?"

"I vote we eat now," Grace said. "I know how your schedule is. You must be starving."

"I could eat," I admitted.

Trish met us at the door when we walked into the Boxcar, but instead of her usual smile, she was frowning.

"What's wrong?" I asked.

She pointed to the back. "I don't want to do it, but if those two don't lower their voices, I'm going to have to throw George and his friend out of my diner."

OLD FASHIONED
VANILLA DONUT DROPS

These are light and tasty, a sure winner. We really like the simple lines of the vanilla flavoring, but other extracts can be used, such as orange and even peppermint.

Ingredients

Wet
- 1 egg, beaten slightly
- 1/2 cup granulated white sugar
- 1/2 cup whole milk (2% can be substituted.)
- 1 tablespoon butter, melted (I use unsalted; salted can be used, but cut the added salt by half.)
- 1 teaspoon vanilla extract

Dry
- 1 cup all purpose flour (I prefer unbleached, but bleached is fine, and so is bread flour.)
- 1 teaspoon baking powder
- 1/2 teaspoon nutmeg
- 1/4 teaspoon salt
- Enough canola oil to fry donuts

Directions

Heat canola oil to 365 degrees.

Combine the dry ingredients (flour, baking powder, nutmeg, and salt) in a bowl and sift together. In another bowl, combine the wet ingredients (beaten egg, sugar, milk, butter, and vanilla extract). Slowly add the wet mix to the dry mix, stirring until it's incorporated. Don't overmix.

Drop teaspoon-size balls of batter into the oil, turning as they brown.

Remove and drain on a paper towel, then enjoy. You can add as a topping powdered sugar, frosting, or icing, or make an array of dipping stations that feature lots of different tastes. The beauty of these drops is that they highlight just about any topping you choose.

Makes 5–9 drop donuts, depending on baking method.

CHAPTER 8

We started to walk back to George when the man he'd been speaking to got up abruptly and stormed out, nearly knocking me down in the process. His back had been turned to us, so I hadn't recognized him at first, but when I saw his face, I was surprised to see that it was William Benson, owner of our local arcade, and someone everyone in town generally thought of as a nice guy.

As he walked past Trish, she said, "William, you haven't paid yet."

He tossed a ten-dollar bill at her, shaking his head in anger as he left.

"Hey, that's a nice tip," Trish said with a smile. She nodded back toward George. "You two sitting with him?"

"We are," I admitted. "Could we have our usual?"

Trish nodded. "The most recent one? Let's see, lately you've both been having two cheeseburgers, two fries, and two

Pepsis," she said. "Or would you rather have iced tea instead?"

"Soda sounds great today," I said. I was a true daughter of the South, with sweet iced tea running through my veins, but sometimes I felt like a soda. I'd drunk Coke for a long time, but Momma and our chief of police had recently taken a trip to New Bern, a town that happened to be in North Carolina, and also the place where Pepsi had been invented. She'd come back with a few trinkets for me, along with a new penchant for Pepsi. I'd tried it, liked it more than I remembered, and now I was hooked. It wouldn't take the place of sweet iced tea, but it made for a nice change of pace now and then.

"Got it," she said.

George hadn't even noticed us come in, something out of character for the former cop. He stood abruptly when he realized that we were approaching him. "Ladies," he said. "Would you mind if I join you?"

"Actually, we were thinking of sitting with you," I said. "After all, you were here first."

George frowned as he considered this. "Let's find another table, shall we? This one still has an unpleasant feeling to me."

As we found another table and sat down, I asked, "What was that argument about?

I'm guessing William wasn't all that pleased with your line of questioning."

"That's putting it mildly," George said. "I thought he was going to take a swing at me for a second there."

"How did you manage to inspire that kind of anger? I didn't think the man had it in him," I said.

George took the salt shaker and slid it across the table in front of him from hand to hand. It made a scratching sound as it moved, and George's focus seemed to be on only it as he spoke. After a few moments he said, "I asked him about the payoff Cam demanded for a permit, and by the way he denied that it ever happened, it was pretty clear that he was lying about it. I pushed him on it and he got angry, more than I would have imagined."

"I hate to be the one to say it, but didn't he kind of have a right to be upset that you were asking him such delicate questions?" Grace asked.

The salt shaker paused, and George looked at her as he spoke. "Sure, I don't blame him for that, but he hesitated too long when I brought the issue up, almost as though he were trying to figure out how to react before he got upset. There was something calculating about the way he did it that makes me wonder about the man."

"It's hard to imagine that Uncle William could kill Cam."

"I believe that anybody can kill, if the motivation is strong enough," George said.

"Yeah, but you were a cop a long time," Grace said.

George looked at her quizzically, not sure how to react to that statement. "What does that mean?"

"Take it easy," I said. "Grace is just saying that it's perfectly understandable if you assume the worst in most folks."

"I don't, though," George said, clearly unhappy with the idea. "I know I dealt with a lot of criminals over the years, but I met a lot of good people on the job, too. I'm telling you, there's something darker than a permit payoff going on here."

"So we all keep digging," I said, trying to lighten the mood. "Here's our food," I added as I saw Trish approaching.

"Here you go," she said as she slid our plates in front of us. For George, she had a piece of homemade apple pie.

"I didn't order this," George protested.

"What can I say? You look like you could use a treat about now. Am I wrong? I can always take it back."

George put a hand on the plate and

166

smiled. "Thanks, Trish. Just add it to my bill."

She scowled at him. "I'll do no such thing, George. It's a gift." She started to leave, and then, as if it were a last second thought, she added, "Oh, one more thing. If you ever have another argument like that in my diner again, you're going to have to find somewhere else to eat. Understand?"

"Yes, ma'am," he answered solemnly.

"Wow, that was masterful," I said after Trish was gone.

"What's that?" George asked.

"Trish nearly killed you with kindness by bringing you a free slice of pie, then in the sweetest way imaginable she threatened to throw you out if you step out of line again, and you weren't even that upset about it."

"Well," he said after he took a bite of pie. "She *was* nice about it, and she was right. It wasn't fair of me to brace William here, where I knew he'd be bound to react to my questioning. And lastly, she brought me free pie."

I tried to hide my smile, and the best way I could think to do it was by taking a bite of my burger. I knew George ate a great many of his meals there with Trish, so her threat was no small matter. What amazed me was how diplomatically she'd handled it. The next time I had to throw someone out of Donut Hearts, it was going to be with a few glazed donuts thrown into the mix. If it worked for Trish, it might just work for me.

As we ate, I asked George, "Did you have a chance to talk to Harvey Hunt yet?"

He shook his head. "No, he was in Charlotte on business all day, but I've got an appointment with him first thing in the morning. How about you two? Have you had any luck with the ladies you're supposed to talk to?"

I wasn't all that pleased with the progress we'd made, but I owed it to George to tell him what had happened so far. "Well, we got a few answers, raised some new questions, and had a door slammed in our faces, so all in all, I wouldn't call it a roaring success."

George grinned at us. "I don't know, it sounds like a fun day to me. Tell me what happened."

After we'd recounted our experiences to him, he smiled. "I probably should have taken Evelyn from the start. I'll handle her myself."

I couldn't believe George was offering. "Seriously? I'm not sure you know what you're getting yourself into. That woman is in no mood to discuss Cam's murder with anyone."

"I think she might talk to me," George said, a little too smugly for my taste. What did he know that I was missing? I had to ask.

"Really? What is it? Do you think she won't be able to resist your manly charms?" I smiled as I said it. I'd never known a man in my life who didn't think he had a way with the opposite sex, whether it was true or not. Maybe that wasn't fair. Since my failed marriage to the Great Impostor, maybe my vision had been a little tainted as well. I was teaching Jake to open his heart again after his family's sudden end, and he was showing me that not all men were lying dogs. It was more than a fair trade-off, in my opinion.

"No, it's nothing like that," George said. "Evelyn's dad and I were good friends before he died, and she's always treated me like an honorary uncle as well. Believe it or not, when Evelyn was younger, she used to be quite lovely. When she and Phillip first married, I honestly thought that it would last forever."

"What happened?" I asked, not able to keep from being so nosy. It was hard to imagine our chief of police and his wife ever having a good life together, but then again, all I'd ever seen from them was a dysfunctional pairing that never should have happened.

"Well, no one likes to talk about it, but everything was fine until their baby died," George said sadly.

"What? I didn't know about that," I said.

He looked surprised by my reaction. "Why should you? It was just before you yourself were born. Evelyn carried that baby full term, but something went tragically wrong with the delivery. I helped pack up the nursery after it happened, and her dad and I even repainted the room from pink to tan. Something happened to her that day, to them, really, and they never were able to bounce back from it. Evelyn got more and more distant, and by the time they finally divorced, I'm sure it was a relief to everyone involved, no matter how Evelyn is acting now."

I suddenly had a lot more sympathy for Evelyn than I could have imagined. I'd never been pregnant when I was married to Max, but I had thought many times how nice it would have been if we'd had a child together. At least then there would be something positive, some purpose that could have come from our union. I couldn't imagine losing a child like that. I suddenly realized that if their daughter had lived, she and I would have known each other pretty well. After all, in a small town we would have been thrown together with school, church, and half a dozen other ways.

Grace broke my train of thought when she asked George, "Have you stayed close to her since then?"

George shrugged. "After what happened, she wasn't close to anyone anymore, and it nearly broke her father's heart when she turned her back on the world; but since the divorce, Evelyn and I have shared a few meals together. If I ask her about Cam, I'm pretty sure that she'll tell me."

I put down my burger and touched George's hand lightly. "You don't need to do this. I hate the thought of you jeopardizing your relationship like that, especially when it's on such shaky ground."

George shook his head after he finished the last bite of pie. "Suzanne, I don't want to think that she's capable of murder, but if she is, she needs to pay for what she's done."

"And if she's innocent?" I asked, not believing I was even saying the words.

"Then I'll find a way to make things right between us again." George stood and then said, "Don't worry, I'll leave the tip with Trish. See you two later. Happy hunting."

171

"Good night," Grace and I said in perfect unison.

George hesitated up front, then had a small and private conversation with Trish, and she finished it with a hug. I was certain George had apologized for the earlier commotion, and knowing Trish, I was equally sure she'd accepted it.

After he was gone, I looked at Grace. "What do you make of all of that? Did you have the slightest clue about what happened between the chief and Evelyn?"

"I'm surprised by the news, but now that I've heard it, it makes sense to me. It seems Evelyn had a reason to be bitter with the world."

"But it still doesn't explain why she might have hated Cam enough to kill him," I said.

Grace shrugged as she looked out the window. "We'll let George talk to her tomorrow and see if he comes up with more than we could."

"It would be hard for him to learn less, wouldn't it?" I said with a slight smile.

"Hey, don't be too hard on us. We came up with a few nuggets today."

I nodded and pushed my plate away. "I hope Jake had better luck than we did, though."

Grace said, "He can follow his leads, and

we can follow ours. George is going to talk to Evelyn and Harvey tomorrow. What's our game plan?"

I didn't even have to think about my answer to that. "Well, I'm making donuts, and after that we'll just have to see what happens."

"Wow, at least we have a plan," Grace said as she pulled more than enough money to cover both our tabs.

"Hey, you don't have to treat me to dinner," I protested.

"It's my pleasure. I just got a big bonus," she added with a grin. "My district exceeded every sales goal we had since I took over, and management decided to show their appreciation with a nice fat check."

I laughed. "I should have gotten dessert, then."

"It's not too late," Grace answered with a smile.

"No, I'd better not. I'm stuffed, and if I eat too much more, I'll never get to sleep tonight. Thanks for dinner, though. Man, it must be nice being you."

"It can be," she said, happily.

After Grace paid Trish, we walked outside together into the chilly night air. The stars were out in all of their brilliance, and I marveled that they seemed brighter somehow in the winter months, as if trying to make up for the cold we were enduring.

"Well, if it's not the two crime busters," James Settle said as he started toward the Boxcar Grill. "I hear you two are digging into the mayor's murder."

The blacksmith had come to town looking for old railroad tracks for his craft, and had ended up staying, opening up a forge and art studio on the outskirts of town.

"Where did you get that idea?" I asked, curious to know how folks had found out so quickly.

"You're kidding, right? It's all over town," James said. He was a brawny man, a look that fit his profession perfectly. "What I want to know is, are you having any luck?"

"Why are you interested?" Grace asked.

"It's no secret that I wasn't any fonder of our mayor than anyone else. We had a few run-ins, too." He looked at me and grinned. "Oops, I just put myself on your suspect list, didn't I? I can't imagine how long that must be. You could probably use the town records for that. I'm curious. Was there anyone around here who actually liked the man?"

"I'm sure he had his supporters," I said. Why was I defending Cam Hamilton all of a sudden? Was it because I meant it, or was it just that James Settle was still an outsider, though he was now an April Springs resident as well? We tended to keep things close to the vest in our part of the country, and it was a lot like family. It was okay to squabble within, but to the outside world we always tried to present a united front.

James seemed to consider that, and then he said, "I'm not so sure that's the truth, but if I were you, I'd take a look at his last girlfriend or his best friend."

"Why would you do that?" I asked, honestly curious about his reasoning.

The blacksmith ran a hand through his hair. "Think about it. Someone got Cam into that abandoned shop, and I'm guessing it was someone he trusted pretty well. Why else meet someone there? It had to be someone close to him. Have you thought about it from that angle?"

"We've already spoken with his ex-girlfriend," I admitted.

"Then there you go. What about a guy friend? Just about everyone I know has one."

"Who's yours?" Grace asked.

Settle shrugged. "I haven't been in town long enough to make one yet here, but give me some time; I will. Now, if you ladies will excuse me, my dinner is calling my name."

After he had gone inside the Boxcar, I

asked Grace, "Is it just me, or does what he just said make sense?"

"I have to admit, he's got a point," Grace said.

A thought suddenly occurred to me. "There's something else we need to consider."

"What's that?"

I didn't like where it was heading, but it was a possibility I had to consider. "What if James is just trying to send us up a blind alley? It's perfect, if he did it on purpose. First, he tells us that he had a reason to want to see the mayor dead, and before we could even process that, he gave us not one but two possible suspects we should be looking at instead of him."

Grace shook her head. "Do you really think he's that clever?"

"I don't know. I haven't known him that long, or that well," I said. "I say we put his name on our list and we also try to find out who Cam's closest friend was."

"It can't hurt," Grace said.

She glanced at her watch, so I asked her, "Am I keeping you from something? I thought Peter was out of town."

"He is," Grace said. "I'm expecting him to call, though."

"I can take you home if you'd like," I

volunteered.

"No, it's not for another hour."

Wow, she really was watching the clock. He wasn't even in town and he was finding a way to run her life. "What do you want to do in the meantime, then?"

"Do we really have time to talk to anyone else?" she asked. "We're getting pretty close to your bedtime, aren't we?"

I stifled a yawn as I said, "I'm fine."

"Suzanne, if I tried to keep your hours, it would kill me in a month. Are you telling me getting a little extra sleep would be a bad thing?"

"I could always use sleep, but I want to solve this case," I protested.

"So do I, but we've got a big day tomorrow. Why don't you let me ask around a little on my own? I'll make a few telephone calls and see if I can find anyone who Cam was particularly close to. Tomorrow we can brace them together if I have any luck tonight."

"You're not going to go after someone who might be the killer by yourself, are you?" I'd sent George out once on his own, and he almost hadn't come back, so there was no way I was going to let Grace risk her life for an investigation.

"I won't even whisper the guy's name. No

one will know what I'm up to," she said.

I thought about it and realized that she probably was right. I was beat, there was no doubt about it. I'd had a little too much excitement lately, and not enough rest. Besides, with Momma out on a date, I'd have the cottage to myself. Having Jake over was my first choice, but since that wasn't exactly an option at the moment, I'd take some time sleeping as my second choice. "Okay, you've convinced me. Just be careful."

"I will." She paused, and then added, "You know I'm not trying to get rid of you, don't you?"

"I know. You're right. I'd offer to drive you to your car, but it's right there." Her company car was still parked in front of the donut shop.

"I think I can make it on my own," she said.

"I'll make sure you get there," I said with a grin, and I watched her as she walked to her vehicle, started it, and drove home. I followed, and as we got to her house, I honked once and continued the rest of the short distance back to my place.

I wasn't all that excited about being home, though, once I got there.

My ex-husband, Max, was sitting on the hood of his car, clearly waiting for me.

CHAPTER 9

"What do you want, Max?" I asked as I got out of my Jeep. I'd gotten over my anger with him, well, most of it, but that didn't mean he was my best friend.

Max tried his most charming smile out on me, but I was immune to it through years of aversion therapy. "Hey, is that any way to treat your husband?"

I had to laugh at that description. "Max, I can't tell you how happy it makes me to put 'ex-' in front of that. What's going on? Are you having trouble with your latest production?" Max was a sometime actor and an always wannabe director. Since no one in their right mind would give him a job doing that, he often volunteered at the senior center to stage their productions. The twist was that the theatrical group always insisted on playing role that were quite a bit younger than they were in actuality.

Max grinned. "No, it's going fine." In a

more somber voice, he said, "I heard you were digging into Cam Hamilton's murder."

First James Settle, and now Max. Did everyone in April Springs know what we were up to? "Are you even surprised? My mother is one of the main suspects. Of course I'm going to do everything in my power to solve it."

"I thought your new boyfriend was on the case," he said cagily.

"He is, but he doesn't mind if I dig around the edges. I know it must sound crazy to you, but he actually values my opinion."

Max shook his head sadly, a movement that looked rehearsed to me, though someone less cynical than me might have bought. "That's not fair, Suzanne. I always did, too."

What was going on here? Why was Max suddenly so in need of my approval? "Do you really want to discuss how you compare to Jake in my mind?" I didn't say it with any hurtfulness intended, but from the way he flinched, it was clear that was how he took it. To soften the sharp edges of my comment, I added, "Max, I know it's not late by most people's standards, but I am really beat. I'm sorry if I'm being a little crabby. Was there something you wanted?"

He took it in, seemed to accept my apol-

ogy for what it was worth, and then nodded. "Actually, I have a crime-buster tip for
you."

"I'm listening," I said. There was no doubt
in my mind that Max probably had some
excellent sources in the community.

Max got that look on his face that said he
knew he had something I wanted, but to be
fair, he didn't try to hold it from me. "I saw
our fair mayor in a parked car downtown
near the big clock three nights ago around
midnight, and he was with someone."

"It wouldn't surprise me at all to hear that
Cam had a date," I said.

"That's the thing. He wasn't with a
woman; it was a man, and there was no love
lost between them, from what I heard."

"What were you doing out that late yourself?" I asked.

"I was jogging," he explained. "I've got to
keep myself in shape. You never know when
Hollywood's going to call again for my next
gig."

I'd had enough of this. "Who was it,
Max?" My ex could drag a story out when
he wanted to, and clearly that's what he
wanted at the moment, but I wasn't playing
any more games with him tonight.

"That's the kicker. It was none other than
our very own chief of police," Max said.

I knew that the two men had a relationship that was strictly business, but I was still surprised that Max would report something like that to me. "Do you honestly think that our chief of police had something to do with our mayor's murder? That sounds like something you saw on Court TV."

"I'm not trying to spin anything," he said. "I'm just telling you what I saw and heard. I thought you might appreciate the tip."

"I do," I said, shivering a little as I accidently repeated those fateful two words I'd spoken to him years ago in front of all of our family and friends. "Did either one of them happen to see you?" I asked.

Max frowned. "Not a chance. The second I knew what was going on, I dodged behind the building, but I know what I saw." Max got off the hood of his car and then opened the front door.

As he started to get in, I said, "Thanks for coming by and telling me that."

"You're most welcome," Max said, and then he got into his car and drove away.

I wasn't sure how confidential Max thought our conversation was, but the second his taillights were out of sight, I got out my cell phone and called Jake. This sounded like something he needed to know.

■ ■ ■ ■

"This is Inspector Bishop. Leave a message, and your number."

What a charmer my man was. I told him to call me, either within the hour or at the shop tomorrow morning. I'd just barely hung up when my phone rang.

It was Jake. "Speak of the devil and he appears," I said, with a grin.

"Not sure I like the reference, but at this point I'll take it. How did my name come up in one of your conversations?" he asked.

"I just left you a message on your cell phone," I admitted.

"Should I hang up and check it?" he asked, and I could almost hear his smile in his voice. Jake sounded tired, but I knew that wasn't all that odd when he was on a case.

"Let me tell you myself. Max was just here."

The joy in his voice suddenly vanished. "At your house? At this time of night? I need to talk to that man until he understands that it's over between the two of you."

I wanted to laugh at the very thought of that ever happening, but I didn't want Jake to think that for one second I was laughing at him. "He wasn't trying to woo me, Jake. He came by to give me some information about Cam's murder."

"Suzanne, if you think that's the only reason he came by to see you tonight, you're nuts."

"Trust me, he knows that I love you," I said. "Do you want to hear his tip?"

Jake paused a moment, and then said, "Sure, go ahead. I'm not above taking charity from even him at this point."

I conveyed what Max had told me, and Jake whistled. "That's not good."

"Why?" I asked.

"I interviewed Chief Martin this afternoon, and he never said a word about it. He should have come clean with me from the start if that conversation was innocent."

I couldn't believe I was about to defend our chief of police, a man I continued to butt heads with, but for Momma's sake I asked, "Why would he voluntarily give you a reason to suspect him, Jake? Maybe it just wasn't all that important."

"Sorry, but that won't fly. That's just not how we think," Jake said.

"The two of us?"

"Lawmen," Jake said simply. "He should have told me, and he knows it. The only question is, why did he feel as though he

185

had to hide it from me?"

I suddenly felt bad about passing on the information. "What are you going to do?"

"First thing tomorrow morning, Chief Martin and I going to have a little talk."

"Leave Max's name out of it if you can," I said.

"Why should I do that?" Jake asked, clearly unhappy by my request.

Why *had* I asked that? I didn't owe Max a thing after catching him with Darlene, but I still didn't want to throw him to the wolves. "He told me in confidence, but he had to know I'd tell you. Give him a break, Jake. The war is over. You won."

For just a second, the smile was back in his voice. "I got the girl, huh?"

"Don't get cocky, mister. You still have to work hard to keep her." My grin had to be obvious to him as well.

"You never have to worry about that, Suzanne. I won't ever take you for granted," he said, the playfulness now completely gone.

"Right back at you," I said as I pulled my jacket closer. It was time to go inside where it was warm. As I walked up the porch stairs, I said, "Anyway, I just thought you should know."

"Thanks, Suzanne. Have a good night."

"I hope you do, too." Then I had a sudden thought. "Is there any chance I'll see you tomorrow morning again when I open?"

"You never know. We can only hope," he said, and then hung up.

I went inside, feeling glad that I'd told him what Max had said, but somehow hoping that it wouldn't come back to bite me later.

I got ready for bed, climbed in, happy that tonight, I was finally going to get enough sleep so I wouldn't be groggy throughout the next day.

And of course, I couldn't fall asleep to save my life.

My mind was whirling with too many suspects, too many reasons folks around town wanted Cam Hamilton dead. How in the world did the man keep getting elected mayor with the enemy list he had? It didn't make any sense, until I remembered something Momma had told me long ago when she'd been fussing about our congressman, a man entrenched in his job who was good at only one thing: getting reelected every two years.

"Suzanne, folks may complain and groan about government, but when it comes to voting out their representatives, it usually takes an act of epic proportions to unseat the scoundrels. Everyone says they want change, and then they turn around and elect the same folks year in and year out."

That wouldn't be happening this year, though.

Cam Hamilton would not be running for reelection ever again.

I finally managed to fall asleep, though it happened later than if I'd just stuck to my normal routine, so I was a little edgy the next morning on the dark drive to the donut shop. It was Emma's day off today, so I'd be working alone, which suited me just fine. One day a week I had Donut Hearts to myself from three until six: three hours of silence other than the sound of my mixer and the oldies station blaring out tunes on the radio.

I started every morning I worked alone smiling, but truth be told, by the time I opened my doors at six to the public, I was ready for some company. I'd have to work an extra hour cleaning the kitchen after I closed at eleven, but for now I could stay up front and sell the fruits of my labor.

After unlocking the door and serving a few early risers, I kept looking for Jake. He hadn't exactly promised he'd come by, but

I was hoping for it nonetheless. When my cell phone rang, I picked up it quickly.

It was indeed my boyfriend. I asked in my most cheerful voice, "Hey, mister, care for a donut on the house?"

"I wish I could," he said, "but the chief and I are about to have a chat, so I wanted to call you first. My phone's going to be off all morning, and I didn't want you to worry about me if you tried to call."

"Well, aren't you sweet," I said.

"I do what I can," he replied.

I was about to ask him what he was going to say to the police chief when Jake said, "Gotta go. Love ya."

It wasn't exactly flowers and a box of chocolates, but he'd thought of me, and that was what counted. I made sure that he'd get credit for it.

But I hoped one of us solved this case soon. I missed my boyfriend, and while it might not have been as valid a reason as some, it was good enough for me, even if my mother hadn't been involved up to her eyebrows.

"Good morning, Suzanne," Momma said as she came into Donut Hearts a little later in the morning. She wasn't exactly a regular at my shop, but it was nice to see her from

189

time to time. Though her makeup was expertly applied as always, I could tell that she'd been crying, and recently.

"Hi, Momma. How are you?"

"I'm fine. Why shouldn't I be?" she asked.

If she was going to play it that way, I had no choice but to follow her lead. "May I get you something this morning?"

She studied the display cases, and then said, "Just coffee, please." As she looked around the shop, she added, "Where is Emma this morning?"

"It's her day off," I explained as I fetched her a large coffee.

Momma didn't approve of our arrangement, and she wasn't all that shy about sharing her opinion with me. "Suzanne, this is too much work for one person. Why don't you consider shutting down instead of working by yourself? Surely one day a week won't kill you."

She hadn't lowered her voice, and there were a few customers in the shop at the moment, but if they were listening to us, they weren't doing it openly. Still, I had a feeling the conversation we were having would be repeated more than a few times over the next few hours, so I had to make it good. "Business is booming," I said loudly. "That's one of the reasons I stay open seven days a week. I'd hate the thought of disappointing my loyal clientele by not being here for them."

Momma shrugged. "It's your decision, of course. You're just not getting any younger, and the hours you work can't be helping with the aging process."

I put a hand to my face inadvertently. I wasn't in the mood to have any of these conversations at the moment, so I switched her coffee from the mug to a cup to go without even asking. "Here you go," I said as I slid it to her.

As she reached for her purse, I added, "Don't worry about it. It's on the house."

"That hardly seems fair," Momma said as she pulled out a dollar bill. "I'll pay my own way, Suzanne. I always have and I always will."

I didn't have the heart to tell her that a buck wouldn't cover the blend I'd just poured her. Better to take a slight loss than listen to a lecture on how high my prices were at the donut shop.

As Momma started to leave, she hesitated at the counter and said in a soft voice, "I hope that exchange will appease anyone listening that things are fine in our world. Suzanne, we need to talk somewhere in private."

"Do you mean you didn't just drop by for my coffee?" I asked, matching the low volume of her words.

"Of course not," she replied.

"I'm sorry, but I can't leave the front, since I'm all alone. If we talk low enough, no one will hear us."

Momma considered it, and then nodded. "Are you making any progress in the case?"

"We've added some suspects," I replied.

"Is that good news?" Momma asked impatiently.

"We're all working as hard as we can," I said, "but these things take time. Jake's doing some digging of his own, too. Don't worry, we'll get to the bottom of this. If my gang can't solve the murder, I'm certain that Jake will be able to do it."

"Yes, Phillip called me just a few minutes ago. I'm well aware of your young man's current line of inquiry, Suzanne."

It was clear from her tone of voice that Momma wasn't pleased with Jake's investigation when it turned to her boyfriend, but it had to be done, no matter how unpleasant any of us found it, and I was sure she knew it, at least on some level. "He's got to do this by the book, now more than ever. Every suspect has to be considered, no matter who they might be."

192

"I fully realize that," she said. After a momentary pause, she asked, "Is there anything I can do to assist you and your team in your investigation?"

I had to look twice to be certain that she was serious. "Thanks, but I think we're good."

She wouldn't accept that, though. "You'd tell me if I could help, wouldn't you?"

I knew Momma had resources I couldn't match, so perhaps I was being a little hasty when I rejected her offer out of hand. Then again, I wasn't at all sure how it would look if she started digging into Cam's murder herself. Folks expected that kind of behavior from me, but for my mother, it might make them leap to conclusions that weren't in any of our best interests.

"If I can think of something that doesn't directly involve you, I'll ask, trust me," I said, expecting her to protest.

Instead, she nodded her head wearily, and I found myself worrying about her. "What are you going to do with yourself today, Momma?" I asked.

With the resolve and backbone I knew my mother possessed, she said proudly, "I'm going to put on a brave face and parade myself around town as though I were running for homecoming queen. I want folks to see that I have nothing to be ashamed of, and that I'm not afraid to be seen out and about. I won't campaign, we've already discussed that, but I will do my best to give everyone the impression that the weight of this murder isn't crushing me like a car sitting on my chest." For just a moment I'd seen the real vulnerability in her eyes, and it was something I hated finding there. I had to do everything in my power to solve this case, and sooner rather than later.

It was nearing eleven, and I was ready to close for the day. It seemed to take forever when I was working alone, and I realized again how much I loved having Emma there with me during the morning. Honestly, if I hadn't cut my hours so recently from noon to eleven, I might have locked the doors early, but I couldn't see doing that now.

In the end, I was glad I didn't.

Two of my favorite customers, Terri Milner and Sandy White, came rushing in as I was wiping down the tables.

"Are we too late?" Terri asked breathlessly. "Please tell us we aren't too late."

Sandy added, "We will die without éclairs."

"You're in luck," I said with a grin. "I happen to have two left."

"Excellent," they said as I went back behind the counter and plated them. "Would you like a pair of coffees, too?"

"Oh, yes," Terri said. "If I were a drinking woman, I'd have you put a shot of something extra in it."

"Did you two have a rough day?" I asked as I poured two coffees to go with their éclairs.

"We took a field trip," Sandy said.

"To the Bowling Row," Terri added.

"And the kids all bowled," Sandy said.

Terri paused and then said, "I have to give them credit. Most of them went toward the pins."

"But not all of them," Sandy added.

"Was anyone hurt?" I asked as I took their money and handed over the change.

"Mostly just feelings and pride," Terri answered.

"But it was so loud, my ears are still ringing," Sandy complained.

"The pins couldn't come close to matching the voices of our little angels," Tina said. "Some genius decided to give them cupcakes before they even started to bowl. Imagine twenty-six kids crashing around, every last one of them on a sugar high."

She must have thought I'd take offense to that, because she quickly added, "Not that there's anything wrong with that."

"Hey, I'm a firm believer in moderation," I said. "I'm just glad it wasn't donuts. I get enough heat as it is for what I serve."

As they took up their favorite spot by the window, I saw Terri tap Sandy's arm. "Do you hear that?"

She clearly tried to hear what her friend was talking about, but she finally shook her head. "I give up. What is it?"

"The sound of silence," Terri said.

"Don't get too used to it," Sandy said. "It's a half day at school today, remember? We have to pick them up as soon as we finish here."

"What maniac decided to take our kids bowling in the morning and then send them home with us in the afternoon?" I knew how much these women loved their kids, and what they'd sacrificed for them, so I didn't take anything they said to heart.

"If you two don't mind, I'm going to start cleaning up," I said when I noticed that it was three past eleven.

Terri looked at Sandi, clearly mortified. "We forgot again."

"She closes at eleven now," Sandy said.

They both stood and I said, "I'm not trying to run you off. If you want to stay while I work, you're more than welcome to.

196

Honestly, I wouldn't mind the company."

"We'd love to," Terri said, "but we really do have to get going. Thanks so much for the offer, though."

They both took final bites and last sips, and then left.

As I flipped the OPEN sign to CLOSED and locked the door, I had to laugh. Terri and Sandy had been some of my very first customers when I'd first opened the shop, and I always loved having them visit, even when they had their kids in tow.

Well, maybe not *always* then. Thomas liked to show off for the twins, while Mary and Jerri did nothing to discourage him.

Boys, I decided, no matter what their ages, never seemed to change.

EASY, DELICIOUS DONUTS
ANYONE CAN MAKE!

We were desperate for donuts one day, and I didn't feel like going to much trouble, so I raided my pantry to see what I could use. I found a packet of Martha White chocolate chip muffin mix and decided to play with it. I split the mix in half and used whole milk with one half and 2% chocolate with the other and made fresh donuts. The whole-milk ones were really good, but the chocolate milk batch was fantastic! This one is now a hit with my family, and we're branching out to try other mixes in the Martha White line as well.

Ingredients

- 1 packet Martha White chocolate chip muffin mix (7.4 oz), split in half
- 1/4 cup whole milk (2% can be substituted.)
- 1/4 cup chocolate milk, whole (2% can be substituted.)

Directions

Combine half the mix with whole milk, and the other half with chocolate milk.

And that's it!

The donuts can be baked in the oven at 350

degrees for 10–15 minutes in cupcake trays or small donut molds, or in a dedicated donut baker for 6–7 minutes.

Once the donuts are finished, remove them to a cooling rack. These are best served as is, but they can be embellished with any topping of your choice. Sometimes I make an apricot glaze by reducing apricot jam on the stovetop by half, and then use that to lightly cover the tops.

Makes 5–9 donuts, depending on baking method

CHAPTER 10

I didn't get out of Donut Hearts until almost noon. It just hadn't been my day. The cash register report was over by an odd seven dollars and thirty-nine cents, something I couldn't attribute to a simple mistake in making change. Maybe I'd entered a number or two into the register wrong when I'd rung up a sale, or even worse, I'd either charged someone too much for their donuts or cheated them on their change. Either way, I felt like a heel, and I never did manage to figure it out. On the rare days when that happened, I noted the discrepancy in the log, and then did my best to forget it. Added to that, Emma had moved a few things around since the last time she'd been off, and I couldn't for the life of me figure out her new system.

At least the donut count was close to being spot-on. I had just six donuts left from a day of selling, and for some odd reason, the times I kept my waste under a dozen were counted as good days for this donut maker. There had been times in the past, beyond my control, when I'd ended up with dozens upon dozens left at the end of the day, and I always felt bad when that happened. I didn't even need a box today. Instead, I just put the unclaimed donuts in a bag and headed out on my way.

I didn't get very far, though.

George was waiting for me ten paces from my front door, and judging by the expression on his face, he wasn't very happy.

"Like some donuts?" I asked, trying my best to cheer him up a little.

"You don't have any coffee left, do you?" he asked, sort of growling out the question. "I could really use some right now."

"No, but come on back inside. I can make some in a jiff."

"I won't have you doing that on my account," he said. "Do you have a minute?"

I glanced at my watch. "I'm meeting Grace at one, so I've got nearly sixty of them. What's got you so upset?"

"Who said I was mad?" he asked.

I touched his shoulder lightly. "First of all, I said 'upset,' not 'mad.' And second of all, I know you well enough to be able to tell that you're not happy about something. Come on, you can talk to me."

"I just spoke with Evelyn," George admitted, "and it didn't go all that well."

I found a nearby bench that was unoccupied and steered him toward it. "Let's go over there and you can tell me all about it."

He followed me, and after a bit of coaxing, George took the bag and demolished the donuts I'd had left. I wanted to supply him with coffee, too, since that was our agreement for his help in my investigations, but he'd said no with enough force to make me realize that he'd meant it.

"Talk to me," I said after he finished the last one.

"She threw me out after a few minutes," he said, his voice falling flat as he told me. "We were just starting to connect again after her father's death, and now it's all ruined."

I felt like crying. I'd cost George his health in the past, endangered his life even — but this was somehow worse. "I am so sorry. I had no business letting you to speak with her."

"What are you talking about?" George asked. He clearly wasn't happy with my comment. "It's not your fault, Suzanne. You can't keep blaming yourself for every bad thing that happens in my life."

"Maybe not," I said, "but I'm the one who sicced you on her."

"I volunteered, remember?"

"Well, I still feel responsible."

"Don't," he said as he took the empty bag and began to wad it up into a tight ball. "It was pretty clear that Evelyn was gunning for me the second I walked in the door. It appears that she believes Jake is going after her ex-husband, and she's mad enough to spit fire about it. There's something that woman is hiding, I can feel it in my bones, but I don't have a clue what it might be." He shook his head, and I could see the pain in his eyes as he added, "There's a secret there. She wanted to tell me, I could see it in her eyes, but I must have pushed her too hard, and she ended up shutting down on me."

I remembered Jake telling me earlier that morning that he'd be talking with Chief Martin about the murder, but how had Evelyn found out about it so soon?

"I didn't think it was public knowledge that Jake was talking to Chief Martin," I said. "How did she know? A lot of folks seem to know about what happened already."

George shrugged. "Jake probably wanted to keep things friendly, so they spoke at the

Boxcar, and Evelyn must have overheard them there."

I fully understood why Jake hadn't brought the chief to my donut shop, but I hadn't realized that they'd been that close by. "Was it honestly that bad?"

George nodded somberly. "According to Evelyn, Jake ended up accusing the chief of murder, point-blank."

"I can't imagine he'd do that without a lot of provocation," I said.

"Trust me, I know the professional side of him better than you do. It's so out of character for the way Jake investigates that I didn't believe it for one second. I knew that Evelyn was blowing it up out of proportion, but I when I tried to assure her of that, she threw me out. There's no way she's going to tell any of us anything now. Sorry if I killed that line of inquiry."

I patted George's shoulder again. "We can do without her information, but if it's important to you, you need to go back there and make things right between the two of you, even if means throwing Jake, Momma, and even me under the bus to do it."

He looked shocked by the suggestion. "Suzanne, I'd never do that. You shouldn't even suggest it. It's not my style."

I had to get through to him that his

relationship with Evelyn was more important than our investigation. I could see the
pain he was in looking into his eyes, and it
was more than I could take. "I know that.
All I'm saying is that I know how bad it
made you feel losing that relationship in the
first place. If you can, you owe it to yourself,
and her father, to try to save it."

George shook his head. "In my heart, I
know that you're most likely right, but I
can't do it, not right now. I've got an appointment in ten minutes with Harvey
Hunt, and I need to keep it."

I had a sudden inspiration. "Don't worry
about it. I'll talk to him myself," I said.

"Without Grace?"

It seemed that George wasn't all that
certain that I could handle the meeting on
my own, but it wasn't time to have that
particular debate. "Fine. I'll call Grace, and
if she can make it, that's great, but if not,
I've got it covered. Where are you two supposed to meet?"

"By the bench closest to the town clock,"
he admitted reluctantly. "I don't feel right
you doing this, though. Talking to Evelyn
can wait."

"What would her father want you to do?"
I asked. It was probably a low blow, but
sometimes George needed a little push in

the right direction.

"I don't even have to think about it. He'd want me to go see if I could fix things with her right now," George said. "Okay, you convinced me." As he stood, I saw that there was just the slightest hint of hesitation in his movements, and I was glad that his physical therapy had worked so well. As George began to walk away, he turned back and said, "Watch your step with him, and don't turn your back. Not for a second."

His words chilled me a little, though the sun felt warm on my face. "Is there something you're not telling me?" I asked. "Do you think he's dangerous, even in public in broad daylight?"

"Better safe than sorry, that's all I'm saying," George said.

As soon as he walked away, I dialed Grace's number, but either she was on another call or she didn't have her phone with her.

It seemed that I was going to have to tackle Harvey Hunt on my own.

I got to the clock fifteen minutes before I was supposed to meet Harvey Hunt, but I could see that a man was already waiting there, sitting on a nearby bench and looking up and down Springs Drive. He had gray hair at the temples, and cold brown eyes that shook me as we made eye contact.

"You're Harvey Hunt, right?" I asked as I approached him.

He nodded and said, "Sorry, I can't talk right now. I'm meeting someone."

"George sent me instead," I said. "He was called away on an emergency. I'm Suzanne Hart," I added as I stuck my hand out.

He made no move to take it, though. "I know who you are. You run the donut shop. What kind of emergency did George have?"

"It was personal," I answered as I sat down on the bench beside him.

Harvey clearly didn't like that idea at all. He stood and said, "Talking to me sounded pretty important to him yesterday. How bad is it?"

"Well, it's not life or death," I conceded, "but he hated missing you. It would be great if you'd talk to me instead."

Harvey studied me a moment, and then shook his head. "I don't think so. I don't deal with lackeys. Tell him to come see me himself if it's that urgent."

I wasn't all that fond of being called a lackey, but I decided to let that slide. Before Harvey could leave, I had to figure out a way to stop him. "You can tell me what happened with you and the mayor, or you can tell the police. George was just trying to protect you, and I thought I was doing you a favor by coming here so I could hear your side of it."

He didn't storm off, so at least that was something. At least I managed to get his attention. "Protect me from what?"

"More than you're willing to risk losing," I said, hoping that it was true.

He sat back down and said, "You have one minute."

"What happens to the money you owed Cam Hamilton now that he's dead?" I asked. There was clearly no room to play cat and mouse with him, and if I was going to uncover anything, it was going to have to be from blunt and direct questions.

Instead of getting upset, Harvey studied me for at least ten seconds. "What makes you think I ever owed him money?"

I grinned at him as I said, "That's a nice response, but unfortunately, you took too long answering to be very convincing."

Harvey shook his head in disgust. "Does the whole town have to know my business?"

"It's the price you pay for living here," I said. "I'm still waiting for your answer."

"Fine, I'll tell you," he said, clearly disgusted. "I don't see what it could hurt now. I paid Cam off the morning he was murdered at nine."

"Really?" I asked. "I don't suppose you can prove it."

"The mayor wasn't about to give me a receipt for my money," Harvey said. "If I'd waited a few hours, I wouldn't be in the jam I'm in right now. The guy I got the money from to pay him off is a lot less understanding than Cam was, that's for sure."

I was intrigued by the brutal honesty of his response. "Then why did you borrow the money in the first place?"

Harvey just shrugged. "Cam was hounding me for the money, and he was starting to make things a little uncomfortable for me around here, so I wanted to get him off my back once and for all."

Harvey was telling a good story, but I didn't know how much of it I could actually believe. "How can I be sure anything you've told me is true?"

He stood, and it was clear he had no intention of sitting back down again. "Lady, quite frankly, I don't care what you believe. Tell George the next time he sends one of his flunkies around, we're going to have some real trouble."

I had to get one last question in before he stormed off. "I'm curious. Why did you agree to meet him in the first place?"

"I owed him a favor, but as far as I'm concerned, we're square now. You tell him that, would you? I'm finished here."

As Harvey walked away, I wondered if there was any part of what he'd said that was the truth. I liked to think of myself as a good judge of whether someone was lying to me or not after my years of training with my ex-husband, Max, but Harvey had just taken it to a whole new level. I'd have to mention my conversation with him to Jake the next time we spoke. If Cam had a large sum of money on him when he was killed, it could be a motive for murder that we hadn't even considered yet. Was it possible that our mayor had been mugged for the money he was carrying on him? If he'd been found in an alley, I might have believed it, but showing up inside Hannah's old storefront was too much to explain.

Unless the person who'd robbed him had had a key.

It was another twist in a case that was already complicated enough.

I was still sitting on the bench, thinking about what had just happened when Grace showed up.

"Sorry I'm late," she said. "I just got your message."

"Why didn't you pick up when I called?" I asked.

"I was on the phone with Peter," she explained. "He had a few minutes and I didn't want to miss the chance to talk to him. What did Harvey have to say?"

My first reaction had been to scold her for not taking my call, but then again, could I say that I wouldn't have done the same if it had been Jake on the phone with me? I didn't get much time with my boyfriend, and his job didn't exactly allow him to check in anytime he wanted, so when I got a call from him, I tended to give it top priority. If Grace decided to do the same thing, who was I to judge her? It was time to get off her back about being a low priority.

"He claims he paid Cam off close to when the mayor was murdered."

Grace frowned. "That's pretty convenient, isn't it? I don't suppose there were any witnesses to it."

I grinned. "I asked him if he could prove it, and he said that Cam didn't give him a receipt. Trust me, he wasn't too happy talking to me at all."

Grace frowned as she looked at me. "Then we can't prove it, one way or another. It's a real mess, isn't it?"

"Aren't they all?" I asked as I stood. "Do

you still have some free time this afternoon?"

"I'm all yours," Grace said. "What did you have in mind?"

"I think it's time we have another chat with Kelly Davis."

"Because the last one went so well?" Grace asked with a smile.

"Hey, somebody's got to talk to us eventually. If Kelly won't, then we'll have to tackle Hannah again."

"I never dreamed so many people would be so unhappy to see us," Grace said while we walked toward my Jeep.

"Funny, I've been amazed that it hasn't happened more often before now."

Unfortunately, Kelly wasn't at the bank when we went inside. Grace pretended to study a brochure at the table they had set up so I could do a little more digging on my own. There were times when it was good having two of us interview people, but sometimes folks were more likely to talk to me if I was alone.

I found my donut-loving friend Jackson, the teller, and got in line to ask him where Kelly might be as soon as it was my turn at the window.

At least he didn't have any problem talking to me. "She called in this morning and took a personal day," he said when I asked him. "Why are you looking for her? She had some pretty rough things to say about you the last time you were here, Suzanne. I'm not sure I'd go out of my way looking for her if I were you."

"It was all just a simple misunderstanding," I said, trying to come up with an excuse on the spot. "That's why I wanted to speak with her. I feel bad the way we left things."

Jackson seemed to think about that, then lowered his voice and said, "If I had to guess, I'd say she's looking at antiques in Hudson Creek. I overheard her talking to someone yesterday about going there."

"Thanks, Jackson," I said.

"Just try to straighten things out with her," he said. "She's a decent friend, but trust me, you don't want that woman as an enemy."

"Why is that?" I asked. If Kelly had a history of bad behavior in her past, it would be good to know about it before I tackled her again.

He was about to tell me when his manager approached. The last thing I wanted to do was get Jackson in trouble, so I said, "Thanks for clearing that up. I'll be back

213

later with my deposit."

"You're very welcome," he said, and winked at me, something I was certain his boss couldn't see.

I nodded to Grace, who walked out of the bank with me.

Once we were out in the parking lot, I asked, "Do you feel like doing a little antiquing?"

"I'm always up for that, you know me, but I thought we were on a case," Grace said.

"This is a part of it. Jackson told me that Kelly is probably in Hudson Creek shopping. It's what she does when she wants to get away from April Springs."

"Then I say we go shopping. Maybe we can drop in on Bill while we're there," Grace suggested.

"It would be nice to go into Yesterday's Treasures without an agenda," I said, remembering the last time Grace and I had gone there.

"You mean having a reason that doesn't directly involve my friend," Grace said.

"That's right. The strip's not that big, so we shouldn't have any trouble finding Kelly on Antiques Row."

"It sounds great," Grace said, and then offered, "Why don't we take my car? You know I love your Jeep for short trips, but there's no reason we shouldn't drive in style if we're going all that way."

"I'm not even going to argue with you about it," I said. "Get in and I'll take you back to your car."

We switched vehicles, and I settled into the passenger side while Grace drove to Hudson Creek. It was good spending time with my best friend, even if it was investigating a murder case. As we drove, we chatted about a thousand things. I wasn't sure if it was on purpose or not, but the men we were seeing and the murder case we were investigating were two topics we strictly avoided.

I almost hated it when we crossed the town limits of Hudson Creek, but I reminded myself this wasn't a joy ride, or an afternoon we were killing.

It was time to keep digging into Cam Hamilton's murder, and at the moment, Kelly Davis was in our sights.

As we walked into Yesterday's Treasures, Bill, tall and lean as ever, met us near the door. "If it's not two of my favorite ladies in the world," he said with a smile. It faded slightly when he saw that we were empty-handed. "What? No donuts today?"

"Sorry, we had a good run at the shop and there weren't many left," I told him. "Next

215

time, though, for sure. How have you been, Bill?"

He waved a hand around his shop, empty of shoppers, but full of neatly displayed items and signs that carefully stated what was in each section. "Business is just booming," he said, smiling. "Can't you tell?"

"I'm sorry," I said. "Is it that bad?"

"Actually, we're finally slowing down a little. It's nice to get a breather every now and then. Folks are finally starting to find us, and things are really looking up."

"That's wonderful," I said. "Have you by any chance had a customer today named Kelly Davis?"

"I'm not sure. What does she look like?" he asked.

Without thinking, I blurted out, "She's a pretty blonde, young, and she likes to dress kind of trashy."

"Suzanne," Grace said, "that's a little harsh, isn't it?"

"It might be," Bill said, "but it's dead on the spot. Actually, she was here about twenty minutes ago."

So, we'd just missed her. "Any ideas where she might have gone to next?"

"Are you two digging into another murder?" We'd involved Bill in one of our investigations before, so he had a right to

216

question us.

"What makes you ask that?" I asked as innocently as I could.

He laughed. "Come on, I know you aren't here to shop. That would be out of character when the two of you are together."

"One of these days we'll come back just to check out your inventory," Grace said.

"With donuts," I added.

"That's fine, but if you expect a discount when you come, I'd better see a load of donuts in your arms."

"You've got a deal," I said.

As we walked out onto the street, Grace and I looked up and down in search of Kelly. If she was still on Antiques Row, she was in one of more than a dozen shops that specialized in antiques of one kind or another.

The question now was: which one?

CHAPTER 11

"Kelly Davis! What a coincidence running into you here," I said when we finally found her browsing through a shop that specialized in antique uniforms, buttons, and ribbons. I'd wanted to skip that one, since it didn't look promising at all, but Grace had insisted. I didn't know if she had some kind of weird sixth sense about it, but she was right.

"Suzanne," she said tepidly. "I see you brought along reinforcements this time."

I smiled my brightest smile. "Grace and I are out shopping, just like you."

She didn't look as though she was buying it, not for one second. "Here? Excuse me if I have a hard time believing that."

"Grace's uncle loves this stuff," I said as aloofly as I could manage. "I might ask the same thing of you."

"My dad is nuts for antique uniforms, and his birthday is tomorrow." She looked around and then said, "I was looking for a nice present for him, but I'm afraid this place is way out of my price range."

An older man with mutton chop sideburns said, "Make me an offer, then. I'm not afraid to dicker with you; I told you that before."

"Maybe later," Kelly said as she headed for the door, leaving us behind.

I picked up an item at random and without even looking at the price, I said, "I'm sorry, but you're out of our league, too."

As we were leaving, the man repeated, "Don't just leave. Make me an offer. Any offer."

When we were all out on the sidewalk, I had a rash idea. "Kelly, I'm glad we ran into you. I want to apologize. I didn't mean to jump all over you yesterday. Could Grace and I buy you a late lunch? There's a place called the Popover Diner down the street that's supposed to be very good." I wasn't sure about that, but it was the only card I had to play at the moment.

"I suppose I could eat," Kelly said.

"Then it's settled," I said as I started down the road. Kelly moved out a little in front of us, and Grace winked at me and smiled as she caught my eye.

I just shrugged. I'd gotten lucky so far,

219

but I couldn't count on that to get us through the interview. We had to ask some tough questions. I just hoped Grace and I would find a way to word them so we didn't cause another scene. We'd already discovered that Kelly's temper lived up to its billing.

The Popover was no Boxcar Grill; that was certain. Trish's place was fun and light and welcoming, but the Popover hadn't been that way since the fifties, judging from the décor of the place. That was most likely the last time the red vinyl covering the booth benches might have been new. The linoleum floor had chunks missing, showing the battleship-gray concrete underneath it, and the curtains had all faded so much it was nearly impossible to decipher what their original colors might have been.

"Isn't this nice?" I asked, trying to put the best face on it I could.

"It's really quaint," Grace chimed in, trying to support me.

From the expression on Kelly's face, it was clear she wasn't buying it, though. "What a dump. Do you think the food is even safe to eat here?" It was obvious that she didn't care what the people there thought about her.

"I know that it's not the Ritz," I said, a

massive understatement. "Why don't we think of it as an adventure?"

"I just hope I survive it," she said.

As we sat down, a brunette waitress barely out of her teens with LULU stitched on her apron approached us. "Sweet Pea?"

I had to have misunderstood her. I knew that some waitstaff in the South liked to use "Honey," and "Darlin'," but I wasn't certain I'd ever been called "Sweet Pea" before.

"Ya'll want three?" she asked, as though we were all hard of hearing.

Then I got it. "Three sweet teas sound great. What's the special today?"

Lulu smiled. "We serve a mean veggie plate," she said, then added, "This place doesn't look like much, but the food is good and the service is friendly." She said the last bit with a wink, and I felt myself warming to her. I turned to Kelly and Grace and asked, "Shall we place ourselves in Lulu's capable hands?"

There were two nods, one enthusiastic and one quite a bit more reluctant, and Lulu left to get us our food.

"Any bets on how much of what we get is fried?" Kelly asked.

"No takers there," I said. I wanted to talk to her about Cam, but I wasn't sure exactly how to bring it up. I was still trying to think of an angle that wouldn't enrage her when Grace beat me to the punch.

"I understand that you and Cam were meant for each other," she said. If I'd said it, there was no way I would have been able to utter those words without laughing, but Grace had delivered the line with exactly the right amount of class.

"It's true," Kelly said softly. "He was my soul mate, and now he's gone."

I couldn't believe it. Somehow, with one line, Grace had gotten through Kelly's defenses. That was just one more reason I was such a big fan of my best friend. When it came down to it, she was excellent at getting to the heart of what motivated people.

I said, "We really do hate what happened to him. That's why we're digging into his murder. Is there any way you could help us? It could mean the difference between success and utter failure." Even as I said it, I hoped that I hadn't spread it on too thick.

Kelly studied me for a moment as I did my best to mimic Grace's appearance of sincerity. A friend of mine had once told me that once she'd learned how to fake being sincere, the rest was easy. She'd been joking, at least I hoped she had, but it was important to get Kelly's trust if we were going to get anything out of her.

Kelly frowned at the tablecloth and said, "You're just trying to save your mother."

"I'm not denying that," I replied, "but in a way, that sort of puts us on the same side. We both want Cam's real killer brought to justice."

Kelly looked up from the tablecloth and stared straight into my eyes. "Unless your mom is the one who killed him."

This was going downhill fast. Maybe I should have let Grace handle the interview after all. Everything I said seemed to be skewed in a way that made Kelly angry.

I looked at Grace, and she knew without a word what to do next.

"How about me, then? I'm not biased," she said. "I honestly just want to find out who killed Cam."

"No matter who did it?" Kelly asked, not taking her eyes off of me for a second.

"No matter who," Grace said, and I trusted that she was telling the truth, so there was no reason that Kelly shouldn't. I had to believe that Grace didn't suspect my mother, but there were no outward signs that was true, and if she had killed the mayor, Grace wouldn't flinch in trying her best to bring her to justice. I honestly couldn't say if I felt the same way. After all, she *was* my mother.

"Okay, how can I help?" Kelly asked as Lulu came back to our table. As our waitress passed out the food, she said, "You get a better deal if we do this family style, so I took the liberty to save you a few bucks. There should be plenty enough for everybody." Lulu passed out three empty plates and then gave us stocked platters overflowing with sweet potatoes, sautéed broccoli and zucchini, cooked carrots, and corn. The only fried thing we got was okra, something I really loved.

Lulu left the table for a second, came back long enough to top off our drinks, and then gave us some space. She was getting a generous tip, no doubt about it, no matter what the quality of the food. I would take a pleasant server and average food over excellent cuisine and a rude waiter any day.

We dished food onto our plates, and I noticed that Kelly took some fried okra, too. I kept the observation to myself, though. It was time for me to fade back and let Grace take the lead in the questioning.

I was beginning to wonder if she was going to say anything, but after ten minutes Grace finally asked, "Since you knew Cam better than anyone else, can you think of anyone who might have wanted to kill him?"

I was having second thoughts about bracing her so quickly, though. It was risky asking her in the middle of our meal, but I realized that Grace was right. If we waited until we were finished, we might never get the chance.

Kelly speared a piece of okra, ate it, and then said, "It's a lot tougher being mayor than most folks realize. There were a handful of folks who resented the way Cam did his job, and he's been threatened more than once over things he's done for the good of the town."

"Do you have anyone in particular in mind?" I asked. I knew that I'd promised to keep my mouth shut, but I'd failed epically.

"Do you mean besides your mother?" Kelly asked.

Grace shot me a warning glance, but I didn't need it. Any more questions were going to have to come from her, and as tough as it was, I was going to do my best to keep my mouth shut from here on out.

"Of course she does." Grace took a sip of tea, and then said, "We heard that Uncle William was unhappy with him."

Kelly nodded vigorously. "He wanted to triple the size of his arcade. Can you imagine what an eyesore that would have been? Cam had to look out for the good of April Springs, and when he said no, William flipped out. I heard him threaten Cam my-self."

"You were actually there when it happened?" Grace asked.

Kelly looked uncomfortable with the question, and finally admitted, "Not face-to-face, but I was in the other room."

"We need more than that," Grace said, the sympathy clear in her voice. "If we confront William, we need details that will show him that we're telling the truth."

Kelly scowled and said, "I'd been visiting Cam in his office, and I was in his private restroom, when William came storming in. I'm guessing that he didn't even know that I was there."

"Then how can you be certain that you heard it right?" Grace asked.

"The door was ajar, and besides, William was pretty intent on threatening Cam with physical violence. He was yelling loud enough so that I would have been able to hear him even if the door had been shut."

I'd known William a long time, and I couldn't imagine the circumstances where he'd threaten anyone, especially by yelling. Now was not the time to share that opinion, though, and I knew it.

"Is there anyone else that comes to mind?" Grace asked. "It's important."

After a few moments to think, Kelly said, "You should try Hannah James."

"Is that about the land Cam bought beside her?" I asked. I knew I should have been quiet, but I couldn't resist butting in after all. I was going to have to learn some serious self-restraint. I just wasn't sure how.

"How did you know about that?" she asked me, her food on her plate now forgotten.

"Hannah told us herself," I said.

Kelly looked smug as she asked, "Did she happen to mention she said she'd shoot Cam before she'd let him spoil that land?"

"You heard that, too?" Grace asked. I had to wonder how many of the mayor's conversations Kelly had been privy to. Had anyone been aware of her presence in his office besides the two of them?

"No," she conceded reluctantly. "Cam told me later, but I know that it was true. He bought that land to build a house for us to share together after we got married." Kelly started crying then, a soft sob that seemed to fill the air around us. "I'm sorry, but I just can't talk about this."

With that, she got up and rushed out the door.

I started to stand, but Grace said, "Leave

227

her alone, Suzanne. She's done talking to us."

"We're just giving up?" I couldn't believe Grace didn't want to go after her, too. "What about the condos Hannah told us about? Kelly was lying."

"Please, those were crocodile tears," Grace said as she waved a hand in the air. "She was looking for a way to get away from us, and the second she found one, she bolted. Kelly wasn't about to say another word to us."

I settled back down into my seat as Lulu approached our table and asked, "Is there anything wrong?"

I smiled at her. "No, everything is fine. Our friend is just a little emotional lately."

Lulu nodded. "I've got a friend just like that. She treats a greeting card commercial on television like it's some kind of Greek tragedy." She looked at our plates and then asked, "Can I bring you some dessert?"

"No, we're good. Just the check, please," I said.

"How was it all?" she asked.

"Excellent. You were right to recommend it."

She looked pleased by my acknowledgment. "I'm glad you liked it."

As she slid the check across the table to

me, she added, "Come back anytime."

"The next time we're in town, we will," I said. "Thanks for making us feel so welcome here today."

I studied the check, figured out a nice tip, took the cash out of my wallet, and headed to the register. Lulu was there waiting on us.

"I thought we already said our good-byes," I said with a smile.

"Otis is in the back, so you get me again at the cash register."

I handed her the money and the check, and she started to give me the change, when I said, "Keep it. The rest of it is for you."

"Thanks so much," she said as she slid the tip into her apron pocket. "I hope you have a nice afternoon, and that your friend feels better soon."

"We do, too," I said.

Once we were outside, I looked in my wallet and counted my money. After a second, I turned and asked Grace, "Did I just give her a twenty or a fifty?"

"I didn't see," Grace asked.

I checked my wallet again, and sure enough, I saw that I'd grabbed the wrong bill. Lulu's tip was quite a bit more substantial than I'd planned, but I couldn't exactly go back in and tell her I'd made a mistake.

I didn't have to. Grace and I were still standing there when Lulu rushed out. "That tip was too generous," she said as she offered me a twenty back. "Don't think I didn't appreciate it, though. It was nice to meet you. You managed to brighten up a pretty dreary day."

I felt like a heel taking it, and in the end I just couldn't bring myself to do it. "No, that's not fair. It's for you," I decided rashly. After all, the mistake had been mine, not hers.

"Sorry, but I can't do it," she said, smiling, still holding the twenty out to me.

I finally took the bill back and said, "Thanks, I appreciate your honesty. Lulu, if you're ever in April Springs by eleven in the morning, come by my donut shop and I'll fix you up with whatever you want, on the house."

"You own Donut Hearts?" she asked.

"I do. Have you ever been there? I'm sorry if I don't remember you, but we get a lot of customers there."

Lulu grinned. "I came once on my day off, but I don't blame you for forgetting me. The place was jammed with customers, and I saw a sign about a dollar deal you were having. Do you do that often?"

I remembered Emma's mistake placing an

ad once, and the crowd that had descended on my shop like a plague of locusts. "Just the one time," I said. "It just about killed us, but we managed to live through it."

"I can't imagine doing it even once," she said. "Well, I'd better get back in there. Otis will dock my pay if I'm out here too long."

"Thanks again," I said, waving the bill in the air.

"Hey, we working gals have to stick together."

"That was nice," Grace said after Lulu was gone.

"It was more than that. I know how hard it must have been for her to do that."

"She's our kind of people," Grace said. "So, what's next for us?"

I looked at my watch and realized that by the time we got back to April Springs, it would be time to eat dinner. "Momma and I are having leftovers tonight, but you're welcome to join us."

"Thanks, but Peter's supposed to call, and I don't want to miss it," she said.

I wasn't about to argue with that. As we drove back toward April Springs, I said, "Cam surely had more than his share of enemies, didn't he?"

"And that's just the ones we know about so far," she said.

"My goodness, do you think we'll keep finding them?" The thought troubled me, not just because of the mayor, but because of the additional suspects we'd have to eliminate until we found the real killer.

"It wouldn't surprise me one bit. Where's our list stand at the moment?"

"Well, besides jilted Kelly," I said, "There's rebuffed William from the arcade; poor Harvey, who says he paid Cam off but can't prove it; next-door neighbor and mortal enemy Hannah; and the chief's not-so-lovely ex, Evelyn." I hesitated a moment, then added, "Say what you will, but I refuse to put Momma's name on the list."

"I never would have asked you to," Grace said. "You know I didn't mean what I said to Kelly, right? There's no circumstance imaginable that I can see your mother killing Cam Hamilton."

I shook my head. "I know she didn't do it myself, but that might not be how it seems to the police. Jake firmly believes that anyone, and he means anyone, can be backed into a corner where committing murder looks like the only option you have."

Grace shivered a little as I said it. "I hate to think that's true. What a way to live your life."

"It doesn't exactly make human nature

look good, does it?"

"Regardless," Grace said, "your mother stays off the list until we have a photograph of her standing over the body with the murder weapon in her hands."

"Thanks for that," I said. "There's no worries, though. We still have enough suspects to keep us busy."

As Grace drove on, I said a little later, "I wonder if there's someone we're still missing."

"What do you mean?" she asked me.

"Well, Kelly said it herself, and you backed it up. There were a great many folks who weren't pleased with Cam, and from the sound of it, they all had their reasons. Could we be harassing these poor people and not even have the real killer on our suspect list?"

"We can't focus on that, Suzanne," Grace said. "We have enough to do with the suspects we've been able to uncover so far. It doesn't do us any good thinking that none of them are guilty. If we clear these, then we can start poking under more rocks."

"I'm just saying, we need to keep in mind that there may be more out there lurking in the shadows."

It was a somber thought, and by the time we got back to my Jeep, I was still having trouble coming to grips with the ramifications of this case. Grace had sped all the way home, and I had to wonder if that call was coming sooner than I'd realized. I barely had time to get out of her car before she raced off toward home.

UPSIDE-DOWN DONUTS

It's been so long since I first created this recipe, I honestly don't remember why I called them upside-down. I imagine in years to come when my family makes them after I'm gone, they'll wonder about it, but there aren't any answers, and I smile a little when I think about the puzzled looks I might be creating someday with one of my recipes. It's a good, solid mix, though, and the orange extract gives it a particular kick.

Ingredients

Wet
- 1 egg, beaten slightly
- 3/4 cup granulated white sugar
- 1/4 cup whole milk (2% can be substituted.)
- 1/4 cup buttermilk
- 1 tablespoon butter, melted (I use unsalted; salted can be used, but cut the added salt by half.)
- 1/2 teaspoon vanilla extract
- 4 drops orange extract

Dry
- 1 cup all-purpose flour (I prefer unbleached, but bleached is fine, and so is bread flour.)

- 1 teaspoon baking soda
- 1/2 teaspoon baking powder
- 1/4 teaspoon salt

Directions

Combine the dry ingredients (flour, baking soda, baking powder, and salt) in a bowl and sift together. In another bowl, combine the wet ingredients (beaten egg, milk, buttermilk, butter, sugar, vanilla extract, and orange extract). Slowly add the wet mix to the dry mix, stirring until it's incorporated. Don't overmix.

The donuts can be baked in the oven at 350 degrees for 10–15 minutes in cupcake trays or small donut molds, or in a donut baker for 6–7 minutes.

Once the donuts are finished, remove them to a cooling rack and top as desired.

Makes 5–9 donuts, depending on baking method

CHAPTER 12

"Suzanne, what's wrong?" Momma asked as I walked in the front door of the cottage we shared together.

I must have been brooding about Peter without realizing that it showed on my face. "What? Nothing at all. Why do you ask?"

"You just came in with a scowl on your face that was troubling. Did you have a bad day working on your own?"

"No," I said, trying my best to lighten up. "Not really. There were a few frustrations, but that's to be expected, isn't it? We're making some progress on the case, but I can't talk about it." I wasn't sure that was exactly the truth, but hopefully it would get her to drop the subject.

She wouldn't, though, and Momma took my hands in hers and looked deep into my eyes. "There's something more to it than the case, so don't bother trying to hide it from me. Talk to me."

I realized that even with my Momma's problems, she was always there for me, and there was no one else I could vent to about what was on my mind, not even Jake. Especially not Jake. Our conversations these days were too rare to muddy with my problems with Grace's boyfriend.

"I suppose what it all boils down to is that I'm not a big fan of Grace's boyfriend, Peter," I said.

Momma frowned a little. "To be honest with you, I've never liked him myself, but I believe we are in the minority around town. He can be very charming, when he wants to be."

"Exactly," I said. "A little too charming, if you ask me."

"Could it be possible that he reminds us both too much of Max?" Momma asked.

"It would explain a lot about the way I feel about the guy, wouldn't it? Wow, I want to tell Grace to dump him as fast as she can and run the other way, but I know it's not my place to say a word to her about it."

"Did something in particular happen today to make you feel that way?"

I considered it, and then realized that saying anything aloud would just sound petty, but she'd asked, and I felt I owed Momma an answer. "No. It's just that Grace rushed home to take his phone call and dumped me out of her car so fast, I nearly fell on the pavement. I kind of wonder why she wouldn't just talk to him in front of me. I'm not going to embarrass her."

Momma shook her head. "Suzanne, that's not it at all. You know how you like privacy when you speak with Jake."

"Am I that bad?" I asked, looking for an honest answer, which I was fairly certain my mother would give me. "To be honest with you, it's not that attractive when I'm looking at things from the other side. Perspective means a lot, doesn't it?"

She patted my hand. "Don't worry. You and Jake are cute together."

I wasn't sure how I felt about that description, but I wasn't going to argue with her about it. "Thanks. I feel better."

"Are you certain it wouldn't help to talk about your investigation?"

"I suppose it wouldn't be too bad," I said. "We keep finding suspects, but unfortunately, we aren't doing much to eliminate them. Momma, how did Cam ever get elected in the first place? Everywhere we turn, we find enemies of his."

"Cam was a great deal savvier than most folks gave him credit for at first," Momma said. "I spoke with a few of the town's lead-ing citizens about getting their support in the election before Cam was killed, but every last one of them turned me down."

"I can't believe that," I said. My mother was not only very popular around town, she was also an influential businesswoman.

"Believe it," she said. "Cam had dirt on just about everyone who matters, and he was clearly not afraid to use whatever he had to keep everyone in line."

"Was he actually blackmailing them?" I asked. After what I'd been learning about Cam's life, it wouldn't have surprised me.

"Not for money, but I believe he used his knowledge to push those who might have been reluctant to support him into his camp. I'm honestly not at all certain I would have beaten him out for the job if he'd lived. He would have been a tougher opponent than I ever anticipated."

And then something hit me, something I'd been ignoring all along. "Momma, maybe we're going at this the wrong way. Who profited most when the mayor was murdered?"

"I thought that's what you've been exploring," she said, clearly a little confused by my question.

"No, I mean in business. He won the bid for the new sewer plant, but who did he beat out for it? That might just be a motive we've been missing so far."

"I don't know, but I can find out. Let me make some phone calls," she said as she reached for her phone.

"Can I get dinner while you're calling?"

"It's in the oven, reheating. I'm not sure I'll be finished in time, though." She glanced at her watch. "This might take a while. Would you like to eat first, or wait until after I'm through with my calls?"

"Make the calls first," I said, remembering my big lunch. "This is important."

She nodded. "Fine. What are you going to do in the meantime?"

I thought about it and said, "It's a nice evening. I think I'll take a walk in the park. Maybe it will clear my head some."

"Be careful, and take a heavy jacket," Momma said, almost by rote.

I smiled but did as she asked, and walked outside to stroll around the park that was right outside our door. Walking helped me think, and I needed that more than anything else at the moment, time to process everything I'd learned in the course of the murder investigation.

I wasn't going to get it, though.

As I neared the Patriot's Tree, a scene of death and vengeance several times over the years, a man stepped out of the shadows, nearly scaring me to death in the process.

"What are you doing here?" I asked laughing as I collapsed in Jake's arms. "You scared the wits out of me."

After a long-overdue kiss, Jake pulled away. "Sorry about that. I should have warned you I was coming, but to be honest with you, I couldn't stand not being able to see you."

"Not that I'm complaining, but how did you know I'd be out here?" He smelled wonderful, and I had to keep touching his chest to make sure that my boyfriend was really there with me, and not just in my imagination.

"I didn't. I was about to call you when I saw you come out of the house. I'm just lucky, I guess."

"You could have rung my doorbell," I pointed out.

"I would have been tempted, but I'm not sure it would have been a good idea." He kissed me again, and then wrapped me up in his arms. "I miss you."

"I miss you, too. It sounds silly, since we're both in the same town, doesn't it?"

"Not silly at all," he said. "If we can't be together, does it really matter how much space is between us?"

"That's about the most romantic thing anyone's ever said to me," I said.

"Hey, I have my moments."

I kissed him again, and then asked, "Are you making any progress on the case?"

"You know I can't really talk about an active and open investigation, Suzanne, even with you," he said.

"Not directly, anyway," I answered with a grin. "Do you know Morse code? You could tap out some hints for me."

"Do you know it yourself?" he asked, clearly curious.

"Oh, yes. Grace and I learned it so we could chat in school during class time. It drove most of our teachers crazy hearing rhythmic taps all of the time."

He shook his head, but I could see his smile. "Why am I not surprised? You must have been handfuls back then."

"Some folks think we're pretty tough to handle now," I replied.

"I don't doubt it." Jake took a breath, then asked, "Why don't you tell me what you've been up to? I know you haven't been in town all day."

"How could you possibly know that? Are you stalking me, Jake?" I asked playfully.

"No, but I saw you and Grace drive into

town earlier. I was tempted to pull you over and give her a ticket for speeding."

"She was rushing home to talk to her boyfriend," I explained.

"Then I might have had to let her off," he said. "Seriously, I'm not above taking a little help on this one. What have you found out?"

I didn't even play games; I told Jake everything we'd all learned, and all of my suspicions. He whistled softly as I finished. "Wow, you *have* been busy."

"Don't forget, I had some help from my friends, too," I said.

He tilted his head to one side. "No doubt. You've turned up a few good leads there, I have to give you credit for that."

"Which ones in particular?" I asked, trying to get a little information out of him.

"Let's just say there a few angles I haven't had a chance to hit yet. I'm particularly interested in hearing about Harvey Hunt and the money he claimed to have paid Cam before he was murdered."

"I've been dying to ask you. Did you find any cash on the mayor?" I asked.

"No, but I'm going to take a closer look at his bank accounts and then poke around his house to see if I can uncover something." Jake took a deep breath, then said, "Suzanne, there's something I can tell you that

244

might be related to all of this, but you have to promise not to tell anyone where you heard it."

"I promise," I said, meaning every syllable of it.

Jake nodded. "Harvey Hunt is the bidder who came in second on the sewage plant bid, and the project defaults to him now."

I couldn't believe it. "So it looks like he had two motives to want to see Cam dead, didn't he?"

"That's what it sounds like to me." Jake glanced at his watch and said, "Sorry I can't stay longer, but I've got a meeting in ten minutes."

"With Harvey?" I asked.

Jake just laughed. "You know that I can't say," he said as he nodded his head up and down and grinned. "I love you, Suzanne."

"I love you, too, and I never get tired of hearing you say it."

After Jake was gone, I headed back to the cottage, feeling a little of the load of the world lift off my shoulders with every step I took. It was good having Jake in my life, and if Peter made Grace feel one thousandth as good, I wished her the very best.

Momma was in the kitchen when I got back. "I tried every contact I had, but with those sealed bids, I couldn't find out who Cam was bidding against," she said, removing some meat loaf, mashed potatoes, and green beans from the oven.

"It was Harvey Hunt," I said. "He gets the contract by default now."

Momma looked at me and must have seen my smile. "Jake told you."

"How could you possibly know that? Did you see him?" I asked as I looked out the window toward the darkened park.

"I didn't have to," she answered with a smile of her own. "You always get that goofy grin on your face whenever he's around."

"Guilty," I said.

As Momma plated up our food, she asked, "So, did Harvey just go to the top of your suspect list?"

"More important, he's there on Jake's. Congratulations. You've been unseated."

"It's a number one spot I'll gladly give up any day," she said.

"Don't worry," I answered. "We'll figure this out."

"I just hope someone does it quickly," Momma said. She was about to add something else when her frown disappeared. "Now, are you ready to eat?"

"More than ever," I said.

The world was suddenly brighter, and I

had renewed faith that the killer would be unmasked soon.

I just hoped that it was true.

As I drove through town the next morning in the dark, I found my spirits lifting a little, knowing that Emma would be back at work today. Every time she was gone, I found myself missing her presence working beside me.

I was still smiling as I walked up to the door of my shop, but the smile faded in an instant.

My store's front window, so carefully painted with the Donut Hearts logo, was shattered and lay in a thousand pieces on the floor inside. As I glanced in, I could see from the light of a nearby streetlight that there was a brick resting on one of my couches with a note wrapped around it. I knew I should wait for the police before I looked at it, but there was a part of me that wanted to see what I'd done to stimulate that kind of atrocious action. I had to know.

I had decided that the cops could bark at the moon and started to put my key into the front-door lock when a patrol car came driving up, its lights flashing, though the siren was silent.

Officer Grant, a customer and a man who

was slowly becoming my friend, got out holding a long, heavy flashlight on me. "What's going on here, Suzanne?"

I pointed to the broken window. "Somebody's clearly not happy with me. How did you know this happened? I just found it myself."

"We got a tip," he said. "Is the door locked?"

I tried it and found that it was.

"Unlock it, and then stay here," he said.

I did as I was told, and as he walked inside, Officer Grant drew his weapon, along with the flashlight he was carrying.

I must have held my breath as he investigated, but to my relief, he finally came back out front, flipping lights on as he approached.

"Nobody's here," he said. "You can come on in."

As I did, I went to the brick, but he stopped me. "The chief is going to want to see that first."

"Too bad. I'll show it to him when he gets here," I said as I reached for it.

Grant asked softly, "Please? It will make my life easier if you don't touch it first."

I couldn't do it, not with that plea. "How long will it take him to get here?"

Officer Grant looked outside, and then

nodded. "Unless I miss my guess, that's him on his way right now."

The chief joined us, dressed in slacks and a polo shirt instead of his usual uniform. He barely glanced at me, then carefully picked up the brick with gloved hands.

"You can't seriously get prints from that, can you?" I asked.

"The gloves are for the note," he explained. "We might be able to trace the brick a different way."

Instead of untying the knot, Chief Martin cut the hemp rope with a pocketknife and then slid the coil into a paper bag. "Might be important," he said. He carefully removed the note, then held the brick out to Officer Grant, who was waiting with a bag of his own for it.

Finally, after taking forever, the chief opened the note, looked at it, and then started to put it into a clear bag of its own.

"No way you're not showing that to me," I said with enough force to let him know I meant it.

He appeared to think about it, then shrugged and opened it toward me.

BUTT OUT.

That was all it said, but it was enough, backed up with the violence of the shattered window. "Any chance you'll take this advice?" the chief asked me.

"What do you think?"

Officer Grant snorted once to cover up his smile. After a second, he excused himself and went out to his patrol car.

When he was gone, the chief asked, "You need someone to fix this for you?"

For a split second I thought about calling my favorite handyman, Tim, but he wasn't around anymore, a victim of murder himself not that long ago. "Don't worry. I'll find someone to do it."

The chief surprised me by saying, "I've got time. I'd be glad to take care of this myself."

"Aren't you on duty?" I asked. Was he feeling genuinely nice toward me, or was this just a ploy to get closer to my mother? Not that he needed my help.

"No, I'm strictly a day-shift kind of guy. I've got some plywood in my basement, and while it might not be much, it'll hold until someone can get here and replace the glass."

"Thanks, that would be wonderful," I said, honestly meaning it. Even if the gesture was more for my mother's sake than mine, the chief had been making a real effort to get along with me lately, and I wasn't about to rebuff him. Besides, I didn't have all that many options without a handyman I could count on.

"I'll be right back," he said.

I grabbed a broom and started sweeping up, and was almost finished when Officer Grant came back in. At least it wasn't summertime. Since it was February, I hoped that the bugs that got into the shop would be minimal.

Grant handed me his clipboard and said, "Just sign this and you can give it to your insurance company to get reimbursed for your window."

"I'll probably just pay for the glass myself, since my premiums will probably go up if I report this."

"Either way, you're covered," he said.

I signed the form, and then got a copy so far back that it was barely legible.

"Want me to stick around until you get this fixed?" he asked. "I don't mind lingering a little if it would make you feel any safer."

I doubted the chief would have wanted him there, and besides, I was in my own shop, and no one was going to scare me enough so that I felt I needed protection there. It was my safe haven from the evils of the world, and I wasn't about to let one brick-throwing fool spoil it for me.

"I'm okay, but thanks for offering," I said.

"Suit yourself," Officer Grant said as he headed for his patrol car.

The chief was as good as his word, and he was back quickly with everything he needed to temporarily patch my window. He had just mounted the plywood over my empty window frame when Emma came in.

"What happened here?" she asked as she shivered a little.

"I'll tell you in a minute after I turn the heat up. Flip the fryer on, will you? And you might want to get out some of the ingredients for our cake donuts."

"Will do," she said, and quickly disappeared into the back. With any luck, our donuts would be ready, right on time. The donuts must go on, or the show, or whatever. I wasn't about to disappoint my customers, and in the process, let the person trying to scare me out of my shop feel like they managed it.

"Can I pay you for the plywood?" I asked the chief as the last screw went into the frame and he stood back looking at it, satisfied with his work.

"No, it was just taking up space, anyway. This should hold for now."

"Thanks, Chief," I said, and to both our surprise I leaned forward and kissed him on the cheek.

He made an excuse and was gone in a heartbeat before either one of us could say another word.

As I walked into the kitchen, Emma asked incredulously, "Did I just see you kiss the chief of police on the cheek?"

"Why weren't you working instead of snooping?" I asked with a laugh.

"Are you kidding me? I didn't want to miss the show."

As I started my prep for the cake donuts, I said, "Someone tried to warn me off from my investigation with a brick through our front window, and the chief was nice enough to lend a hand to patch it until I can get the glass replaced."

Emma looked at me carefully and asked, "You're not backing off, though, are you?"

I didn't even have to think about it. "No way. This just means I'm getting closer to catching the killer if he has to resort to this kind of stunt."

Emma nodded. "But you don't have any idea who it might be yet, do you?"

I grinned at her. "Honestly? Not really. I seem to have plenty of suspects, but there aren't really any front-runners so far."

Emma bit her lower lip, then said, "Maybe something Dad learned could help. Did you know that William Benson had more reason to want to see Cam out of the picture than what happened with his permit?"

"No," I replied as I finished mixing the batter for my basic cake donut. "Why else would he want to see the mayor dead?"

Emma nearly crowed as she reported, "It turns out that William was interested in Kelly himself."

"Romantically?" I found it hard to believe that sweet old Uncle William could be interested in a younger woman like Kelly. I knew some men were attracted to flashy, trashy women, but I didn't think William would be one of them.

"Oh, yes. He had a major crush on her, from what Dad heard. William wanted to get rid of his competition, and Cam knew it. That was the real reason why he denied William a permit to expand. It was a way to show him that Cam had all of the power, and from what Dad learned, it just about drove William crazy."

"It's another good motive for one of my suspects," I said. "I don't mean to be greedy, but was there anything else?"

I started feeding the batter into my dropper, but I wasn't ready to put any in the oil yet. It required swinging the dropper back and forth in order to drive the batter to the bottom, and it wasn't safe for anyone else to be around when I did. As long as Emma could feed me more information, I would just have to hold off on donut making.

"I've got something else, and it's a real whopper. It turns out that Evelyn was near Hannah's just before Cam's body was discovered."

I almost dropped the tool in my hand. It would have been a major mess to clean up with the raw batter, but at that moment I didn't care. "What? How could he possibly know that?"

"It's a little harder to prove," Emma admitted. "Actually, Dad got the tip from one of his readers."

"Really?" I asked. How many crackpots read the *Sentinel*? Probably most of them, I figured.

"Hey, it might be true," Emma said.

"Then again, it might not be," I countered.

"Don't worry. Dad won't print it unless he's got a confirmation he can count on. Still, it's good information to have, don't you think?"

I'd been meaning to tell Emma that I'd passed everything I'd learned from her on to Jake, and now was as good a time as any to do it. "You know I'm telling Jake everything we talk about, right?" I asked.

"Of course," she said as she edged away to the door. "I'd be surprised if you didn't. Go ahead and make those donuts, and then we can talk more."

She ducked out, and I dropped perfect little donut rounds into the hot oil. After giving them two and a half minutes, I flipped them with my long wooden skewers, waited until they were finished on the other side, and then drained them. One last drop got the last of the dough into the oil, and I called out to Emma, "You can come back in now. It's safe."

Emma came in and took the dropper from me, rinsing it in the sink for my next batch. While she did that, I watched the donuts, pulling them out when they were finished. It was more of an art to doing it properly. Timers and gauges could malfunction, but I could tell by the aroma and the shading of the donuts when they were ready.

Emma drenched all but four in icing, and as she did, I prepped a new batch. We were a nearly perfectly functioning machine in the kitchen, something that was quite clear after spending the day before there on my own.

"Was there anything else he was able to uncover?" I asked.

Emma looked really uncomfortable as she

said, "That's all for now, but there is something else I need to talk to you about."

I didn't like her tone of voice. It sounded much more serious than I was ready for. "What's going on, Emma? No one's dying, are they?"

"It can wait until after our cake donuts are finished and we start on the yeast ones," she said, carefully avoiding my question.

I laughed. "Emma, there is no way I can wait an hour to hear what you've got to say. I'll start imagining all kinds of scenarios, and they'll get worse by the minute. Tell me now so we can both breathe a little easier."

She nodded, then took a deep breath before she said, "I don't know quite how to say this, but I'm leaving Donut Hearts at the end of the month."

That time I did drop the tool filled with batter, splattering the mixture all over the floor.

CHAPTER 13

As Emma and I cleaned the mess up together, I asked, "Is it something I said? I didn't do anything, did I? Do you want a raise? I can't afford to bump you up much, but I'll give you what I can." I knew that I was blabbering, but I couldn't help myself.

"It's not that, Suzanne," she said. "I finally saved enough for two years of college away from home, and I've got to go while I still can. I've done all I can at the community college. It's just time, that's all."

"Speaking of time, what school starts new classes this time of year?"

"I'm going to State Tech, and they're offering a brand-new independent quarterly program for new students that I'm opting into so I don't have to wait to transfer. I'll switch over to the standard calendar in the fall, but this is a way for me to get started right now."

"Do you know what you want to study?"

"Well," she said with a grin. "I've had so much fun working for you that I'm going to get my degree in Restaurant Management."

"I'm happy you're finally going to get to live your dream," I said as I hugged her. I knew she'd wanted to go away since she'd first come to work for me, and I'd been dreading the day when she'd be able to. I just hadn't realized that she'd been that close. "That's wonderful," I said, hoping my voice didn't sound as flat as I felt. "You've worked really hard for this."

"Don't worry, I'm not abandoning *you*," Emma said. "We'll always be friends. At least, I hope so. I'll come back home every summer, and if there's room for me here, I'll work for you then."

"Of course there will be a spot for you," I said, not even having to think about it. I couldn't imagine running Donut Hearts without Emma, and if she wanted to come back, I would never stop her, no matter what its impact on the bottom line.

"Don't make any promises too quickly," she said. "I know you have to replace me. This place is tough enough to run by yourself one day a week. It's not possible to do it all seven."

She had a point. I'd have to find someone who would put up with my killer hours for not a lot of pay. It had been a miracle when Emma had fallen into my lap, but that miracle was about to end.

"I have to find someone to take your place," I said, just now realizing it. I'm not a weepy kind of gal normally, but it took everything I had not to start crying.

Emma hugged me. "Don't worry. You'll be fine. I've got a few folks already lined up who might be interested, if you'd like some names and numbers."

"That would be great," I said.

"It's going to be okay, boss," she said, trying to show a brave smile.

"I hope you're right."

After Emma washed the donut dropper, she handed it back to me. "Can you make another batch of apple donuts?"

"Trust me, that's the least of my worries," I said.

As Emma ducked behind the door, I watched her go.

Whether I liked it or not, my world was about to undergo a drastic change. In less than three weeks, Emma would be gone, and I'd be on my own again until I could find a replacement for her.

"Suzanne? What happened to your window?"

I'd answered the question two dozen times already, so I gave my stock answer without even looking up. "Someone decided to redecorate for me. I'm having it fixed soon, hopefully this morning."

"This is a bad time, isn't it? Is there any chance that you're ready for us?"

Ready for what? I wondered as I looked up to see exactly who was talking. I was still in a funk over Emma's news, though it was nearly ten. We'd both tried our best to ignore the fact that she'd just given me her notice, but there was a very real uneasiness in the air between us.

I was surprised to see that it was Jennifer, the head of the book club that met at Donut Hearts once a month.

"Is that really today?" I asked. How had I managed to lose track of the time so thoroughly?

"If this isn't going to work for you, we could come back tomorrow," she said. "I'm sure the other ladies will be fine with it."

I couldn't let all of these outside events influence the way I behaved. Maybe having the book club meeting would give my life a little normalcy. "No, I'm ready. Let me get Emma to cover the front, and we can get started."

Jennifer paused, and then asked softly, "Is

everything all right? I'm guessing something bad happened to your front window, and we all heard about what happened to the mayor. You must be beside yourself, what with your mother directly involved in it all."

"That's not it. We're fine," I said. The words nearly stuck in my throat as I explained, "Emma just gave me her notice."

Jennifer looked appropriately stricken. She knew how much I depended on my assistant. "Don't worry. I'm sure that you'll find someone else."

"I hope so," I said. There was no way I was going to let my gloom infect the club meeting. "Do me a favor. Don't say anything to Hazel and Elizabeth, okay? I don't want to bring the entire group down."

"I promise," she said. "Take your time. We'll be over there when you're ready."

I called Emma up front. "Can you take over for half an hour? The book club is here."

"Is it that time of the month already?" she asked, drying her hands on a dish towel.

"I know. It caught me by surprise, too," I said.

"Go on. I've got this covered."

I grabbed four coffees, added matching cinnamon swirl cake donuts, and headed to the couch and chairs where my group was waiting for me. The three women, as always, were dressed elegantly, and I felt a little out of place in my blue jeans and T-shirt.

"I've been dreaming about this for a month," Hazel said as she swooped down on one of the donuts before I could even put the tray down.

"We serve them every day of the week, you know," I said, smiling at Hazel despite my dour mood. "You're welcome to come by any time, even if we don't have a book club meeting scheduled."

Elizabeth laughed. "That's not it. She's on a diet, and she's just allowing herself one big treat a month, so you're it for her this month."

"Is one donut enough, then?" I asked. "You can have mine, too, if you'd like. I certainly don't need it."

Hazel looked tempted, but then finally shook her head. "Thanks for the offer, but I've got to stick to my diet this time."

"Is there anything in particular going on in your life?" I asked.

Elizabeth grinned as she explained, "She's renewing her vows with her husband. In two months. In Hawaii."

"Wow, that sounds wonderful," I said.

"The renewal, or the trip?" Hazel asked.

"Both," I said. "Congratulations. How

many years have you been married?"

"Thirty, if you can believe that," she said.

"You must have been a child bride."

Elizabeth started laughing, and I looked at her quizzically. "Did I say something wrong? I didn't mean to."

"No, I'm sorry, it's not that. It's just that I was at her original wedding, and that's exactly what she was."

"I was twenty-one years old," Hazel said with an air of authority. "That's hardly a child. I was a grown woman ready to start a new life with the man I loved."

Jennifer added, "I didn't think I was all that young when I was in my twenties myself, but it's difficult not to look at it that way now. It's funny, but the older I get, the later middle age becomes for me. I see people listed in the obituaries who have lived into their sixties and seventies, and the first thing I think of is how tragic it is that they all died so young."

We all nodded at that, sharing the experience of starting to grow older. Jennifer clapped her hands together twice, and then said, "Now, on to our topic. Today we're discussing men who write mysteries under female pseudonyms. In particular, we've got Lee Parsons on tap with his latest, *Half-Baked Murder Pie,* written under the name

Melissa Brighton. Any thoughts, ladies?"

"I love all of his books, but I don't know why he can't just write everything under his own name," I said. "He must have half a dozen names floating around out there, and most of them are women. It's pretty confusing keeping up with them all."

"Can you all honestly even tell that a man wrote these books?" Hazel asked. "Because I can't. That man can really get inside my mind. It's as though he knows how I think."

"I wrote him an e-mail after I read *Half-Baked,*" Elizabeth said quietly.

"Did he answer?" I asked. I always wondered about the authors I loved, and if they enjoyed getting mail from readers, or if it was just a part of business for them.

"He did. I asked him why he used so many names, and he told me if it were up to him, everything he wrote would be under his own name, including his grocery list. Unfortunately, he said his publishers wouldn't let him, so he does what he has to in order to stay in print."

"That must be sad, not being able to claim his own work," Jennifer said. "I honestly don't care what name he's using at the time, though: I love his books."

I smiled. "I do, too. He used to do crafting mysteries as Amanda Bartilloni. It took me a while to get it, but I was watching a sitcom rerunning on television one day and one of the characters mentioned that another character must be a female impersonator, because he'd chosen the name Amanda: a man, duh. Lee must have seen it, too. I just love his sense of humor."

Jennifer tapped the book in her hands. "How about his culinary mysteries? Did you all enjoy *Half Baked*?"

"I thought it was his best one yet," I said. "I don't know if it's because I'm a donut maker by trade, but the guy honestly knows how to bake. I love the way he weaves the recipes throughout the plot, and you can tell he's done his fair share of time in the kitchen as well as sitting at his computer."

"I'm not so sure I agree. The murder weapon was a little too fairy-tale-like for my taste," Hazel said.

"You didn't like the poisoned apple in the apple pie?" Jennifer asked.

"I thought it was cute," Elizabeth replied.

"That's because you two are pen pals. Don't worry, I like his books, too. Has anyone heard what the next book in the series is going to be called?"

"*Overcooked,* I read somewhere," I said.

"Great title," Jennifer said. "Now, what did you all think of his use of metaphor when he first picked the apples for the pie in the old, forgotten orchard on a dark, overcast day?"

"It was just creepy enough for me," Elizabeth said. "I like my murder mysteries nice and clean."

"Except for the whole dead-body thing," Hazel said with a smile.

"Except for that, of course. If I could, I'd move right into any of the towns Lee's built in his imagination over the years. They're what home should be like."

We chatted for another half hour about the book, and then it was time to break up. As I gathered the dirty dishes together, I asked Jennifer, "Any idea about what next month's book is going to be, or should I wait for your e-mail?"

"I've got it right here," Jennifer said as she reached into her massive purse. She pulled out a paperback with a signpost on the front. "It's called *Coventry's End,* and it's a real corker."

"I'll see you all next month, then," I said.

Jennifer held back and offered me a twenty. "It's my turn to treat."

"I thought this month was on me," I said, refusing her money. I took too much enjoyment from being in the book club to ever charge my group for their refreshments, but they'd insisted, and in the end, I gave in.

"We took a vote this morning outside. You provide the location, so the three of us will be taking turns paying for the refreshments. You're out of the rotation." Before I could protest, she said, "Suzanne, you might as well take it. If you don't, we decided we'd start ordering things we weren't going to eat just to make up for it. You really don't want us throwing away your delightful treats, do you?"

"No, I'd hate it, to be honest with you. Thanks," I said as I took the bill and headed for the cash register to make change.

"No change is necessary," Jennifer said.

"I insist," I said, and handed her the remainder.

She took it with a smile, and then dropped it into our tip jar. I knew it was useless to protest, so I just did my best to smile and thank her for the tip.

"See you next month," Jennifer said. "And don't worry, things will start to look up soon, I'm certain of it."

After the ladies were gone, Emma asked me, "What was that all about?"

"They heard we were looking into Cam's murder," I said, not wanting to lie to Emma, but not exactly eager to share with her that I'd told Jennifer she was leaving.

268

Emma accepted it at face value, then disappeared back into the kitchen. As I watched her go, I suddenly realized that what she was doing was exactly right. It was a big world out there, and she didn't want to spend her years working in the back of my donut shop. I decided then and there that I was going to stop feeling sorry for myself and be happy that one of my dearest friends was doing something she'd always wanted to do.

No self-indulgence would be allowed. And then I looked at the display case and saw the apple fritters there, dark brown with sparkling glaze on them, and I decided that a little self-indulgence might not be so bad.

As I took my first bite, I knew that it was worth every calorie.

It was nearing eleven, and I decided that there was no way the glazier was going to show up to fix my window today. The police chief had done a solid job blocking out the opening, but I'd hoped for a little more than plywood for a view. Momma came into the shop, frowning at my front window.

"That hasn't been taken care of yet?"

"I was hoping someone would be here before I closed," I admitted.

She took out her cell phone and started

dialing. "We'll just see about that."

The last thing I wanted was to give my mother something else to worry about. "Momma, it's okay. You don't have to go to any trouble on my account."

"It's no trouble, young lady, but even if it were, you're my daughter. A little trouble comes with the territory," she added with a twinkle in her eye. "I still wield a great deal of influence in this town. Don't worry, you'll have your glass soon."

I knew better than to try to stop her. After a brief conversation, she hung up, and I was glad to see a full-blown smile on her face. "They'll be here in fifteen minutes." As she glanced at her watch, Momma added, "That's a little after you close. Do you mind waiting around?"

"For new glass? No, ma'am, I'd be happy to," I said. "Thank you."

"No need, Suzanne. If you don't mind, I'm going to stay until I'm sure they live up to their word."

"Be my guest. Would you like some coffee or a donut while you wait?"

"Coffee would be great, and maybe one of those donut holes as well."

The glazier did better than he promised, and two minutes before we were set to close, he walked in. After studying the

270

plywood in place of the glass, he asked, "Who did this?"

"The chief of police," I answered, and Momma looked at me quizzically, the surprise clear on her face. "Phillip fixed this for you?" she asked.

"He was off duty and he volunteered," I admitted. "You don't mind, do you?"

"Mind? Of course not. I'll have to thank him for it."

"I already did, but I'm sure he'd like it better coming from you," I said with a slight smile.

Emma came out to dispel any reply Momma might have made, something I was grateful for. "The back's clean, so I'm ready to take care of the racks up here," she said. "Hello, Mrs. Hart," she added when she saw my mother. "I didn't know you were here."

"Hello, Emma." Momma looked closely at her, and then asked, "Have you been crying, child?"

"Crying? No, of course not," Emma said. "Why would I have any reason to cry?" She grabbed the racks and hurried back to the kitchen without even boxing the remaining donuts first.

"What's wrong with her?" Momma asked as the glazier began removing the plywood.

"She's leaving," I said.

"You fired her?" Momma asked, incredulous.

"I would never do that. She turned in her notice; she's finally going off to college." As the plywood came down, I suddenly realized just how dark it had been in the shop. I needed that window, and was happy that Momma had pulled some strings to make it happen sooner rather than later.

"Good for her," Momma answered. She was a firm believer in education, as was I. Momma patted my shoulder and said, "I'm sure you'll find a suitable replacement."

"I wish I were as certain," I said.

"Suzanne, I know how special Emma is to you, but you have to let her go. You might as well make her remaining days here as pleasant as possible. You want her to always remember Donut Hearts with fond memories, and what you do for the rest of her time here is crucial for that."

As usual, my mother made a good point. "I'd pretty much come to that conclusion myself earlier," I said.

"I'm not at all surprised," she answered. "You always were savvy when it came to dealing with people." Momma's cell phone rang, and she stepped outside to take it, though she knew she was welcome to take it there. I wondered what she might be hiding, but I knew better than to ask her to stay.

Once she was outside, the glazier turned to me and asked me, "I'm just curious, but what do you do with the donuts you don't sell at the end of the day?"

"We usually donate them somewhere," I said.

He looked disappointed, so I added quickly, "But the soup kitchen is overflowing with them at the moment, so I'm sure they'd appreciate a break. Would you like some?"

"I'd be happy to pay full price for them," he quickly said. "I just got pulled away from my lunch to do this job, and I'm going to be jammed for time the rest of the day, so the chances aren't good for me eating anything."

I suddenly felt bad about Momma throwing her weight around just so I could have my window back. "Tell you what. I'll throw in half a dozen donuts and a large mug of coffee as my gratitude for your prompt service. How does that sound?"

"Like my wife's going to kill me."

"She doesn't let you have donuts?" I asked.

"Not six at a time she doesn't," he grinned.

I went into the kitchen and found Emma finishing up the last rack. "I'll take off now, if you don't mind."

"That's fine. I'll see you tomorrow," I said as I got a plate and put the donuts on it.

She started for the door, and then paused. "Suzanne, this was the hardest decision I ever had to make in my life. You know that, don't you?"

I put the plate down and hugged her. "Emma, you deserve a chance to live your dreams. I'm proud of you."

After a minute she pulled away. "Then we're good?"

"As gold," I said.

She clearly felt better as she walked out of the kitchen, and truth be told, so did I. I hated for there to be any tension between us. Our time together ought to end the way we'd spent it, with friendship and laughter.

I got back out to the kitchen and handed the glazier the donuts, stopping to pour his coffee along the way.

"Thanks," he said. "Can I get these to go? I'll be back in an hour with a helper."

"You don't have the glass with you?" I asked, disappointed.

"No, I have to go back to the store and cut it. Don't worry, you'll be set before one." I meant to ask him to reinstall the plywood before he left, but I was so surprised by his sudden departure that I didn't think of it until he was already gone.

I looked outside for Momma after the glazier left, but she must have already left, too. Was that mysterious phone call related to Cam's murder, or did it involve something else entirely? Either way, I'd have to wait until later to find out.

I ran my cash register report, balanced the till, made out the deposit slip, and still had forty minutes left to wait. I couldn't just leave Donut Hearts open and vulnerable like that.

Soon enough, though, that's exactly what I wished I'd done when an unfriendly face popped into my open window.

OLDIE GOLDIES

This is an old-time drop-donut recipe for frying in oil. I like canola oil, but peanut oil can be used as well. The taste of this recipe is a little too subtle for most palettes, but the folks who love them swear by them. Truth be told, I don't make them that often, but when I do, for some odd reason it's usually raining outside and a little cold. Not the greatest donuts in the world, but certainly not the worst ones I've ever made, either.

Ingredients

Wet
- 1 egg, beaten slightly
- 1/2 cup granulated white sugar
- 1/2 cup sour cream
- 1/2 cup buttermilk

Dry
- 1 1/4 to 2 cups all-purpose flour (I prefer unbleached, but bleached is fine, and so is bread flour); enough to stiffen the dough
- 1 teaspoon baking soda
- 1/2 teaspoon cinnamon
- 1/2 teaspoon nutmeg
- A dash of salt
- Enough canola oil to fry donuts

Directions

Heat canola oil to 360 degrees while you mix the batter.

Combine the dry ingredients (1 cup flour to start, baking soda, cinnamon, nutmeg, and salt) in a bowl and sift together. In another bowl, combine the wet ingredients (beaten egg, sugar, sour cream, and buttermilk). Slowly add the wet mix to the dry mix, stirring until it's incorporated. Don't overmix.

Take a teaspoon worth of batter and rake it into the fryer with another spoon. If the dough doesn't rise soon, gently nudge it with a chopstick, being careful not to splatter oil. After two minutes, check, and then flip, frying for another minute on the other side. These times may vary given too many factors to count, so keep a close eye on them. Drain and top with powdered sugar if desired.

Makes about a dozen small donuts

CHAPTER 14

"What happened, Suzanne? Doing a little remodeling?"

"Hello, Max. What's going on?" He had flowers in his hand, and my ex was wearing his best suit. Oh, no. Was this idiot actually trying to win me over again? "Please tell me that those aren't for me."

My ex-husband looked at me as though I'd just lost my mind. "Sorry, but no."

I laughed out loud, maybe a little too long. "Trust me, I'm relieved, not disappointed. Who are they for?"

"Emily," he said.

"You're not, Max. She's through with you. She told me so herself." Emily Hargraves ran a newsstand in town called Two Cows and a Moose, a place I loved to visit. It was named after three childhood stuffed animals which Emily liked to dress up for special holidays in costumes she made herself. At first I thought it was a bad idea, but Emily claimed that it brought in unbelievable business, and I didn't doubt it. Cow, Spots, and Moose presided over the place from a shelf above the cash register, and they must have more than pulled their own weight bringing customers into her shop.

"I refuse to accept that she's truly finished with me," he said.

"You're setting yourself up for failure, Max, you know that, don't you?"

He shook his head with a determination I hadn't seen all that often. "I have love on my side. There's no way I can fail."

After he was gone, I immediately called Emily. "You might want to lock your door, pull the blinds, and turn off all of your lights."

"I'm game, but would you mind telling me why? What happened?"

"I just saw Max walking toward your newsstand. He was wearing his best suit, and he had roses."

"For me?" she asked incredulously. "That's ridiculous."

"That's what I told him," I said. "Anyway, I just thought you might like a heads-up. You should sic Spots on him."

Emily laughed. "Max wouldn't stand a chance if I did that. He's ferocious when it comes to defending me. Don't worry, I can handle him myself."

After we hung up, I realized that she was right. Though Emily had fallen under my ex-husband's spell once, I had a feeling that it wasn't going to happen again.

Soon enough, the glazier and his assistant were back, and the window was quickly put in place. "Sorry I can't do anything about the lettering," he said as he handed me his bill.

"I'll take care of it myself," I assured him, looking at the large number at the bottom of the invoice. I'd have to sell a lot of donuts to replace that glass, but it was still better than turning it over to my insurance company.

It just gave me one more reason to track the killer down and make him pay for what he'd done.

I called Grace as soon as I was free, but her phone was busy, and she didn't use her call waiting to see what I wanted. I wasn't sure if she was dealing with another crisis at work or if she was talking to Peter, but I didn't want to keep investigating without her. It was nice out, so I left the Jeep at the donut shop and walked over to her place.

Her car was in the driveway, but she didn't

answer the door after three rings. Whatever it was must have been important. I sat on one of the chairs on her front porch, trying to decide if I should wait, or go on and talk to Evelyn on my own. The police chief's ex-wife was on the outs with everyone I knew, so I decided that it wouldn't hurt to push her again myself. Since there was no way I could know how long Grace was going to be, I decided to tackle Evelyn alone.

I was on the sidewalk, heading back to the shop, when Grace's door flew open.

"Sorry about that," she said as she beckoned me to join her.

"I was worried about you," I said, and then I noticed that her eyes were red, and it was pretty clear that she'd been crying. "Grace, what happened? Is everything all right?"

"I'm fine," she said as she dabbed at her nose with a tissue. "It's all good."

"Why don't I believe you?"

She looked at me a second, took in a deep breath, and then blew it out. "It's nothing. Peter and I had a little spat, that's all. It happens to every couple now and then, right?"

"I suppose so," I said.

She studied me for a moment, and then asked, "You and Jake fight, don't you?"

I thought about my relationship with Jake, and I knew that the question was more complicated to answer than it might seem to Grace. I wasn't exactly sure what Jake and I did when we disagreed could be called fighting, certainly not compared to my stormy relationship with Max during our marriage. "Every couple have to find their own way," I said.

"That's not much of an answer, is it?"

"I know, but everyone's different. Listen, if you want to skip sleuthing with me today, that's not a problem at all. I don't mind a little digging on my own."

She shook her head. "The last thing I need right now is time alone. I'll be okay. Just give me a minute to get ready. Do you want to come inside?"

"No, thanks. I've been cooped up in the shop all morning. I think I'll stay out on the porch, if it's okay with you."

"That's fine. See you in a jiff."

As Grace went inside, I had to wonder what Peter had said to upset her so much. Grace wasn't usually so emotional, at least not outwardly. I knew that couples disagreed, but I hated seeing Grace torn up like that. As tough as it was minding my own business, Grace knew that I was there for her if she wanted to talk. Until she said something to me, though, I was going to do my best to stay out of her love life. After all, I'd asked her to stay out of mine.

She came out a few minutes later, all signs that she'd been crying now gone. Grace was in the cosmetics business, after all, and she was a whiz at using their products to mask and conceal her pain.

Unfortunately, I knew that, like beauty, it was only skin-deep.

"Where are we off to?" she asked, her voice laced with more cheerfulness than I knew she felt.

"It's time to go after Evelyn with our guns blazing," I said. "Since no one seems to be able to get through to her, I think it's time for a direct confrontation."

"That might be dangerous, given the woman's attitude toward you," Grace said as we got into her car.

"Maybe, but I don't have any better ideas, do you?"

She shook her head as she drove to Evelyn's. "So, it's going to be bad cop/bad cop again today."

"I don't see how else we can handle it."

We got to Evelyn's place and parked out in the street. As we walked up the path, I looked over to the right when something caught my eye. There was a line of old brick pavers there, laid out in a grid that must have acted as a patio of some sort at one time, but that wasn't the first thing I noticed.

The bricks looked suspiciously like the one that had been thrown through my window; worse yet, one was missing from the grid, as clear as a cheerleader missing her front tooth.

"Look over there," I told Grace as I put a hand on her arm.

She glanced over and said, "Not a great place to entertain, is it?"

That's when I remembered that Grace hadn't seen the brick that had been thrown through my window. As soon as I brought her up to date, she said, "Surely Evelyn isn't stupid enough to use one of her own bricks to threaten you."

"What if she's trying to be cagey? Would anyone, even the police, think she was that dumb? I'm guessing it might just be a ploy to keep the suspicion away from her."

Grace frowned. "Do you see Evelyn acting that subtly? I have a hard time believing she thought it out, if she was the one who broke your front window."

"I don't know one way or the other, but I'm going to ask her the second I see her." Then I had a sudden thought. "Hang on a second."

I walked over and pried up another brick, brushed the dirt off of it, and then looked at Grace. "Let's go."

"You're not going to retaliate, are you?"

"Not in the way you're thinking," I said.

I walked up, with Grace on my heels, and rang the doorbell. I was counting on Evelyn not noticing us outside before. If she had been watching me when I took the brick, my bluff wasn't going to work.

She answered the door with an angry expression. "What do you two want?"

I didn't have to feign anger as I said, "I just wanted to bring your brick back to you. You left it inside my donut shop this morning."

I watched her face, but she looked honestly surprised by my accusation. "I don't know what you're talking about."

"You tossed this through my window and told me to butt out. Did you honestly think I wasn't going to know that you're the one who did it?"

Evelyn's bewilderment just seemed to increase. "Suzanne Hart, have you lost your mind? I never did any such thing."

I pointed to the patio. "Funny, but it's a perfect match to the ones you have left."

"Anyone could have taken a brick from

there. They aren't exactly under lock and key, are they?"

"Then you're denying it?" I asked, trying to make my voice sound as disbelieving as I could.

"Of course I am. Why would I do such a thing?"

"To warn me to stop what I'm doing," I said. "Trust me, it's not going to work."

"Stop doing what, exactly? Making donuts?"

"We're not fools," Grace said, chiming in. "You know we're investigating Cam's murder, and you must be afraid that we're getting too close to the truth if you feel as though you have to threaten Suzanne's donut shop like that."

Evelyn held her hands up as though she were trying to slow us down. "Hang on a second. I thought this happened at your cottage."

I couldn't believe it, but I found myself beginning to think that she hadn't done it after all. "It was at my donut shop, and you know it."

"I know no such thing. I didn't do it," Evelyn said.

"Then help us figure out who did," I answered. "The only thing you have to lose is being a suspect in Cam's murder."

286

"I don't care what people think," she said flatly.

"Not even when you're suddenly a candidate for his old job? Or are you going to drop out now that Cam is gone? Have you decided to let my mother have the job without a fight?"

"Don't believe that for one second. When the truth finally comes out, I'm going to crush her," Evelyn said.

I shook my head. "I don't think so. The only way you're even going to have a chance is to prove that you didn't kill Cam."

"How do you prove a negative?" she asked.

"An alibi would be a nice start," I said.

"Sorry I don't have a convenient witness around, but remember, my husband left me, and we never had children, so I live alone. I was here the whole time."

"Don't lie to me. That's not what I heard," I said, deciding it was time to use the information I'd gotten from Emma.

She looked at me angrily. "Suzanne, you need to back off. I don't know what you're talking about."

I looked at her steadily as I said, "There's an eye-witness who places you near Hannah's just before the mayor was murdered."

"That's a lie," she said harshly. "Who is this supposed witness?"

"I'm not at liberty to reveal that yet," I said, since I didn't have a clue who might have tipped off the newspaper about Evelyn's proximity to the scene of the crime.

"Well, when you are, bring him to me, and I'll call whoever it is a liar to his face."

"What makes you think it was a man?" Grace asked.

Evelyn looked at my friend as though she wanted to swat an annoying fly. "It was a generic term. Bring her, then. I don't care who said it. I was never there."

"Never?" I asked.

"Not since I worked my last day for Hannah."

"Then you have to stay on the list," I said.

We started to leave, and to my surprise, Evelyn called us back. "Listen, I want this thing resolved myself. I want to beat your mother fair and square, and I might be on the suspect list, but from what I've heard, she's at the top of it. Do you think the folks around here will vote for her any more than they will for me, given the circumstances?"

"That's why I want this settled before the election, too," I said.

"If you come up with anything useful for me, I'm always here," she said.

"We'll keep that in mind," I said as we got into Grace's car and drove off.

We got around the block and Grace pulled over. "Do you believe her?"

"About which part? I have to give her credit. She seemed genuinely surprised that one of her bricks was used to break my window."

"I agree," Grace said. "But just because she might not have sent that warning doesn't mean she didn't kill Cam."

"Do you really think they might not be related?" I asked.

"It's a possibility. If our snooping has caught someone else's attention, there's a chance they're afraid of what we might find, and it doesn't even have to be related to the mayor's murder."

"That's depressing," I said.

"Why is that?"

"Because I hate the idea that someone *else* in town has a secret that big to hide."

"Most everyone I know has a secret or two," Grace said with a little more gravity than I liked in her voice.

"Maybe so, but I hope they all aren't worth killing to protect."

"It would wreck our small-town lives, wouldn't it?" Grace said.

"I don't even want to think about it," I said. My phone rang, and I found myself hoping that it was Jake.

289

No luck, though.

George said, "Hello," when I picked it up.

"Hey, George. What's going on?"

"Where are you right now?" he asked.

"We just left Evelyn's place," I said.

"What? I thought we agreed that you'd leave her to me." It was clear that George wasn't happy about our actions, but I couldn't let that stop me.

"When you think about it, it's better this way," I said. "If Grace and I question her, you can try to reconnect on your own. I thought you'd be pleased."

"Grace was with you, too? Did you two gang up on her?"

"George, you should take a deep breath and then think about what you're saying. I know you're emotional about this, but you can't take it out on me."

He did as I asked, and after a long pause, George said, "Sorry about that. Forgive an old man for his outburst?"

"Not necessary," I said. "There's a lot of emotion running through this thing."

"Where you able to find out anything?"

I explained, "Well, she claims she didn't throw a brick through my window, and I believe her."

"Hang on a second. Someone vandalized Donut Hearts?"

"I found it first thing this morning when I got there," I replied. "If you didn't know that it happened, how did you guess that it was at the shop?"

"I just assumed it. Why, was it at your house?"

"No, it was at the donut shop, but Evelyn thought it was at the cottage."

I heard George take a deep breath and then let it out again. "Is that significant?"

"I'm not sure. I just think it's interesting," I said.

"What else have you been up to?"

I didn't really have an answer for that. "That's it. How about you?"

"I just had a long talk with William, and I'm not all that happy about some of the things he said."

"Why don't we meet somewhere and talk about it?" I asked.

"Tell Grace to look in her rearview mirror," George said.

I heard a car door open behind us, and Grace and I both looked back to see George approaching on foot.

"Did you even see him pull up?" I asked.

"No, I was too busy trying to listen in on your conversation," Grace admitted.

"Some sleuths we are."

"Hey, we do what we can," Grace said as

the backseat door opened and George climbed inside.

"Hello, ladies."

"Hi, George," we said in unison.

"So, tell us what William said," I added.

George smiled. "To start with, he has a huge crush on Kelly Davis, did you know that?"

"Yes, but it's good to hear it confirmed," I said.

George looked a little deflated. "Who told you?"

"I just found out early this morning," I said.

"I didn't ask when," George reminded me.

I knew he'd keep pressing me if I didn't answer. "No one is supposed to know this, but Ray Blake found out last night, and Emma told me this morning."

"So the newspaperman got one right," George said. "You should have seen the look on William's face when I brought Kelly's name up. Uncle William wasn't around at that moment, I can tell you that."

"Could he have been motivated enough to kill Cam for her attention?" Grace asked.

"I hate to say it," George said. "But the passions run deeper in that man than I ever would have suspected."

"So we have a double motive for him," I

said. "Shouldn't we be focusing more on him?"

"That's why I called in the first place," George said. "I just softened him up. Now it's time for you two to follow up with him before he has a chance to catch his breath."

"We can do that," Grace said with a grin.

"Then I'll leave you to it," George answered.

"What are you going to do next?" I asked as George started to get out of the car.

"I thought I'd have a talk with Harvey myself. Anybody mind?"

"You're welcome to him," I said, remembering my brief conversation with the man.

"How about if we meet up later this evening?" Grace suggested. "We can have dinner at my place and compare notes."

"My schedule's pretty flexible at the moment," George said. "Should I bring a pizza?"

"Are you saying something about my cooking?" Grace asked him.

"No, I was just trying to be nice." He looked a little worried by Grace's reaction, and I knew George didn't want to hurt their friendship.

"I'm just teasing. You were," Grace said. "Actually, pizza sounds great."

"See you later, then," George answered as

he got quickly out of the car.

"You don't even like to cook," I said to Grace after he was gone.

"No, and I'm the first one to admit that it's not my area of expertise, but I wasn't sure I liked George saying something about it."

"So then it's a win-win."

"That's the kind of situation I like," she said.

As Grace started the car, I asked, "How do you feel about going to the arcade and having a chat with dear old Uncle William?"

"I haven't been there in years, but I'm game if you are," she said.

"All puns aside, we have to forget about the sweet man we know and understand that he might just be a murderer. Don't turn your back on him for one second, Grace."

"I don't plan to," she said, "and I expect you to do the same."

As we drove to the arcade, I kept wondering if either of William's motives had driven him to murder, or if a combination of them both had pushed him past the point of being able to stop himself from killing Cam.

CHAPTER 15

The first thing I noticed when we drove up was the lack of cars at the arcade. Every time I'd been by before during William's business hours, there had been a healthy number of spaces filled in the parking lot, but that wasn't the case now. We pulled up by the main door, and that's when I saw a sign that said, SORRY FOR THE INCONVENIENCE. WE WILL BE CLOSED UNTIL FURTHER NOTICE.

What happened to William? Was there a legitimate reason he'd shut the place down, or was he planning his escape?

"What's going on?" Grace asked. "George just left here and he didn't say a word about William shutting the place down."

"I don't know, but I need to call Jake and see if he knows anything about this. William may be on the run, and if he is, Jake needs to hear about it ASAP." The last thing I wanted was for William to escape if he was the murderer.

My boyfriend's phone went straight to voice mail, though. I had a feeling he was talking to someone and didn't want to be disturbed. In the past, that had been the only reason he ever turned his phone off.

As soon as I got the beep, I said, "Jake, call me as soon as you get this. It's important. William closed the arcade, and I think he might be on the run."

After I ended the message, Grace said, "You're not having a very good day, are you?"

I nodded and said with more than a hint of sadness in my voice, "Some days are like that."

Grace nudged me, clearly trying to cheer me up. "Hey, we've hit brick walls before when we've been snooping. Don't let it get you down."

"That's not it," I said. "At least not all of it." I'd put off telling her the worst news I'd heard that day, but it was time to tell her. "Emma turned in her notice today at the donut shop. She's finally going off to school to get a taste of the world outside of April Springs," I said.

"You knew this day was coming," Grace said softly.

"That doesn't make it any easier. But I

need to stop feeling sorry for myself and start interviewing replacements."

"Good luck with that," Grace said, and then she must have realized how it had sounded to me. In a gentle voice, she added, "Suzanne, all I meant was that it might not be easy getting someone willing to work the hours you're there. You were lucky with Emma, but it could happen again."

"I hope so," I said, not wanting to talk about having to hire someone to take Emma's place.

"Where to now?" she asked.

I was about to answer when my cell phone rang. It was Momma, not Jake. "Hey there," I said.

"Hello yourself. Suzanne, do I detect a note of disappointment in your voice?"

"I was hoping Jake would call me back," I admitted.

"Then I understand. Will you be okay on your own this evening? I've got a date."

"With Chief Martin?" I asked.

"Of course it's with Phillip. Who else might it be?"

I laughed a little. "I don't know, I'd have to imagine there are dozens of men in the five-county area who might enjoy taking you out for a meal."

"There may be at that," she said a little

abruptly, "but none of them have stepped forward. I thought you were fine with my relationship with Phillip."

"I am," I said, letting out a deep breath. "I'm sorry, Momma. I've just had a bad day, and I keep taking it out on the world."

After a brief pause she said, "I could always cancel if you'd like me to stay home so we could talk."

The idea of my mother breaking a date because I was having a rough day was out of the question. "No, I'm fine, truly. Go and have fun."

"If you're certain," she said.

"I'm dead sure," I said, regretting my choice of words.

"Well, I'm here if you need me, any time, day or night. You know that, don't you?"

"I do. Thanks, Momma. I love you."

"I love you, too, Suzanne, forever and ever."

After we hung up, Grace said, "This really has thrown you for a loop, hasn't it?"

"More than I want to admit," I said. "Listen, I think I'm going to just go home. I'm lousy company today."

"I don't mind," she said. "We can wallow in our pity together."

"Thanks for the offer, but actually I'm in a solo kind of mood. I think the best thing I can do is go home, make a sandwich, watch a little television, and then call it an early night."

"I'll tell George, if you're sure," Grace said as we got back to the donut shop.

"I'm positive," I said.

"Then I'll see you tomorrow. Call me if you change your mind."

"I will, but I won't," I said, and then chuckled a little. "You know what I mean."

Grace laughed. "Don't worry, I speak Suzanne, and I've been fluent in it for years."

I was driving up to my cottage when my phone rang. I pulled over to the side of the road and dug it out of my pocket.

It was my boyfriend, at last. "Jake! Thanks for calling me back."

"It sounded urgent," he said. "Suzanne, I don't mean to be rude, but I'm in the middle of something. What's going on?"

"William wasn't at the arcade today, and he's got a sign up that says he's going to be closed until further notice. I just thought you'd like to know."

"Got it. Thanks."

I heard someone calling Jake in the background, and Jake said hurriedly, "Sorry. Gotta go."

He hung up before I had a chance to say good-bye myself, but I knew that my boyfriend wasn't like everyone else. When he was on a case, he was the most single-minded and narrow-focused person I knew, and that was saying a lot. Whether my hot tip helped or not, I couldn't say, but I'd tried.

He had to give me credit for that.

Momma was still at home, getting ready for her date. I walked into her room and watched as she brushed her hair, and a thought suddenly occurred to me. "Momma, don't get me wrong, I'm happy you have a date, but isn't the chief worried about being seen out in public with a murder suspect?"

I hadn't told Momma about her boyfriend's argument with the murder victim just before he died. I had to have more than Max's word before I brought that subject up. Even if I did, I wasn't entirely sure that my mother would believe me, given my tumultuous history with the police chief.

Momma shook her head and frowned. "I tried to tell him the same thing, but he wouldn't listen to me. The man is determined to save my reputation, even though, in my opinion, he's just jeopardizing his own. He has to run for office, after all."

"Hey, don't forget, you're running, too," I

said with a smile.

"Honestly, if it were anyone but Evelyn I was running against, I'd pull my name from contention in a heartbeat. All in all, I'm not sure either one of us should be mayor."

"There really isn't any other choice, is there?"

She got a sudden gleam in her eye, something I'd seen before. An idea had just occurred to her, but I had no idea what it might be. As she tried to choose earrings, she didn't seem to be satisfied with any of her options. "How's George, by the way? Is his leg fully healed? How are his spirits?"

"If you didn't know what to look for, you'd never know he'd been through such an ordeal. I still feel responsible for what happened to him."

"He forgave you long ago. It's time you let yourself off the hook," Momma said. "Suzanne, I hate to ask, but may I borrow a pair of your hoop earrings? I feel a little festive tonight."

"Absolutely. Gold or silver? Small, medium, large, or outrageously big?" While I rarely wore anything but simple studs, I liked to shop for earrings, and had accumulated quite a collection over the years.

She frowned again. "Just bring me a few choices in gold," she said.

"Can do."

I went up to my room, grabbed five pairs, and headed back downstairs. When I got to her door, Momma was just hanging up the phone.

"Sorry, I didn't mean to interrupt," I said as I handed her my choices.

As she took them, Momma said, "You didn't. I just finished."

"The chief didn't have a change of heart, did he?"

"What, the telephone call? No, that was William Benson."

I couldn't believe that. "William just called you? Why? I thought he skipped town," I said.

"Whatever gave you that idea?" Momma asked, clearly perplexed.

"I saw a sign on his door that the arcade has been closed until further notice."

Momma shook her head. "Suzanne, what did I tell you about jumping to conclusions? William's gout flared up and he's taking a week off. The poor man can't even walk, his foot's bothering him so much. Gout is nothing to take lightly, and I've had friends who have been nearly crippled temporarily by it."

I felt a little deflated that my tip to Jake had turned out to be such a dud. "Why did

302

he call you with the news?"

"He didn't. William insisted I let him donate to my campaign when I was running against Cam, but since the mayor's out of the race, he tried to delicately withdraw his financial support. I told him that wasn't necessary, since I had no plans to campaign in the first place. Honestly, the poor man sounded relieved." Her telephone rang again, and I offered to step out of the bedroom. She waved a hand at me to stay right where I was, so I sat in the chair near her bed.

"Hello, Phillip," she said, and I started to get up.

Momma shook her head curtly, and I settled back down. I'd been known to defy that shake in the past, but only with good reason and the full understanding that I was putting myself in mortal jeopardy by doing it.

"Yes. I see. Very well."

"He's standing you up, isn't he?" I asked. "Of all the nerve. The man asked you out on a date, and now he's got cold feet."

Momma laughed at my outburst. "That's not it at all. He feels that going to Union Square sends the wrong message, as though he were ashamed of me. Instead of going to

Napoli's, we're going out to the Boxcar Grill."

"That means you're way overdressed," I said.

She looked at her suit and shook her head. "No, I believe it's perfectly fitting for a date. If the rest of Trish's patrons are underdressed, that's their choice."

The doorbell rang, and I jumped up from the chair. "I'll get it."

"It's most likely just Phillip," Momma said.

I grinned at her. "I'm going to tell him you called him 'just Phillip,' " I said.

She shook her head. "Suzanne, your humor eludes me sometimes."

"Don't feel bad. There aren't many people who get me completely."

"And is Jake one of them?" she asked, ignoring the doorbell.

"He's getting there," I said. "Don't keep your fella waiting."

"I doubt he'll ring the bell again," she said. "Phillip knows how much I dislike that."

"Then you're managing to train him a little."

She laughed openly at that remark. "He would deny it, but perhaps it's true."

She walked out of her room, and I followed.

When Momma answered the door, the chief of police was indeed standing outside, waiting patiently on her. "You look lovely, Dorothy," he said.

"That suit is becoming on you as well," she said.

"You two kids have fun tonight," I said, enjoying tweaking them both.

"Don't wait up," Momma said, and then left. I heard her stop and lock the door behind her, and I had to wonder if she didn't think I was capable of locking up myself.

I'd just made my sandwich and was turning on the television when there was a knock at the front door. "Who is it?" I called as I looked out the peephole.

"Hopefully, the guy who is still your boyfriend," Jake said sheepishly.

"Why wouldn't you be?" I asked as I opened the door to let him in.

"Well, I was kind of abrupt with you earlier, and I felt bad about it."

"Enough to risk being spotted here?" I asked as I stepped aside to let him in.

"I'll take the chance," he said as I wrapped him up in my arms.

After a long and quite thorough kiss, I said, "There should be a reward for being so brave."

"I thought you'd be mad," he said, clearly confused.

"Jake, I know how you are when you're on a case, remember? Honestly, I'm not all that high-maintenance. I appreciate the gesture, though. It was sweet of you to come by. Have you had dinner yet?"

"No," he said as he looked toward the kitchen. In a lower voice he asked, "Your mother is gone, right?"

I nodded. "The good news is that no one can accuse you of fraternizing with a suspect. The bad news is that all I've got to offer you is a sandwich, unless you'd like eggs. I could probably whip those up if you're in a hurry."

He looked at my sandwich sitting on a plate on the coffee table.

I smiled at him. "Go ahead. I'll make myself another one."

"Thanks," he said as he grabbed it and took a large bite. "I only have a minute, but I just had to see you. Suzanne, I'm not a big fan of this arrangement. I miss you."

"I miss you, too," I said as I moved into the kitchen. Jake stopped long enough to grab his sandwich, and then followed me.

"I'm afraid I gave you a bad tip about William," I said as I started pulling out the materials to construct another sandwich.

Jake smiled as he nodded. "I already knew what was going on, but I didn't have the time to tell you. He had to use a cane to answer the door, his gout was so bad. My uncle Timothy had the same problem, and there were weeks at a time where he could barely walk."

"It explains shutting the arcade down," I said. "Is there anything else going on with the investigation?"

He just shrugged, and after he took another bite of the sandwich, he said, "I'm still collecting information and impressions."

As he said it, I watched his eyes, and saw them go down to the floor quickly, and then back up again. Was he lying to me? "Jake, there's something you're not telling me."

"What?" he asked. "What makes you say that?"

"I just have a hunch," I said. I wasn't about to tell him how I'd known. It might come in handy in the future knowing when he was stretching the truth.

"Yes, well, we're on the edge of a pretty big knot, and as soon as I can figure out how to undo it, we're going to catch a killer."

"You're that sure?" I asked.

He finished the last bite, and then nodded. "I'm pretty sure."

"That's a relief," I said.

Jake looked at me carefully. "You're not going to grill me until I tell you who I suspect?"

"Not this time," I said with a slight smile. "Getting my mother off the hook is all I can ask. That *is* what you're doing, right?"

For a flash, I thought Jake might be getting ready to accuse my mother of murder, but I knew better than that. Still, it was a relief when I heard him say, "As far as I'm concerned, your mother is in the clear, unless some new evidence comes to light."

"I'll take that stipulation," I said.

Though he'd just polished off the original sandwich, he stared at the one I had just finished making. With a smile, I shoved it to him and said, "Go ahead and take it."

"I shouldn't," Jake answered. "I really need to get going. To be honest with you, I shouldn't have come at all, but I couldn't stand the thought of upsetting you."

"I can make myself another one once you're gone." I wrapped the sandwich up in a paper towel, gave him a quick kiss, and then sent him on his way.

Once I was alone again, I started to make a third sandwich, only to realize that there was just one piece of bread left, and the ham I'd used before was now gone. It wouldn't be much, but I made myself a peanut butter and jelly sandwich, or a half of one, and ate it happily in front of the television.

It was amazing how much Jake's quick visit had done to lighten the weariness and tensions in my shoulder.

It was early, even for me, when I went to bed, but I had no trouble going to sleep. I'd been living on borrowed hours for too long, and I slept soundly until my alarm went off way too early the next morning.

As always, it was time once again to make the donuts.

CHAPTER 16

When I got to the donut shop the next morning, I was pleased that the new window was still intact, but I knew that I had to call my friend, Annabeth Kline, to paint another sign there for me. Annabeth and I had gone to high school together, but we'd drifted apart when we'd gone to distant colleges. I was delighted when she'd moved back to town just as I was opening Donut Hearts. Her degree had been in graphic design, and I was her first client upon her return to April Springs. I'd barely been able to afford to pay her, bartering some donuts to make up the difference. While my income had stayed the same, Annabeth had clients all over the world now, and was doing quite a bit better than I was. I just hoped I could still afford her.

I flipped on the fryer as I came in, and as a matter of habit I checked the answering machine.

I was glad I remembered when I heard the message.

It was from Elise Black, and she wanted six dozen of my cake donuts for eight a.m. on the twenty-second. That was today. I wasn't sure I'd be able to do it with the ingredients I had on hand, but she was a friend, and if I could manage it, I was going to deliver.

When Emma walked in a little later, she looked at the donuts already glazed, and the batter and dough for more. "Are we having a sale today that I didn't know about?" she asked as she exchanged her jacket for an apron.

"No, but Elise called and placed a pretty big order."

"For today?" Emma asked incredulously.

"That's what the message said," I answered. "I'm dropping donuts, so you might want to retreat."

Emma ducked into my office, and I finished the last of the batter in my dropper.

"All clear," I called out, and as she came in, I saw that Emma wasn't happy.

"What's wrong?" I asked. "Did something else happen?"

"Suzanne, do you know what day it is?"

I nodded my head, told her, and wondered

if she'd hit her head while she'd been in there.

"No, I mean the date."

Why was she playing this game? We had donuts to make. "It's the twenty-second," I said.

"Actually, it's the twenty-first," she answered.

"Are you sure?" I replayed the message in my mind, sure that I'd heard it right the first time. Only I wasn't sure. "Let me check the machine again."

I left Emma to flip and pull the donuts while I went into my office and hit the replay button. It said the twenty-second, so I glanced at my calendar and saw that it was indeed the twenty-first.

I'd made six dozen too many donuts today, and there was no way I could do any less now. We'd have to have a sale after all, but that wasn't the worst part of it.

Tomorrow, I was going to have to do exactly the same thing.

I came back out and Emma was applying the last touches of glaze to the donuts.

"You were right," I said simply.

"Trust me, I don't take any joy from it," she said. "What are we going to do?"

"I think we need to make a sign. How about 'BUY ONE DONUT, GET A CAKE

312

DONUT FREE, WHILE SUPPLIES LAST'?"

"We could do that, but why don't we have a little fun?" Emma asked.

Her days at the shop were numbered, so if she could think of a way for us to amuse ourselves with the time she had left, I was all for it.

"What did you have in mind?"

She thought about it, and then said, "I need a little time, but I'll be able to come up with something before we open."

"Okay, it's a deal. I'm leaving it in your hands." I wouldn't be able to say that much longer.

After all of the cake donuts were finished and the cooling racks were filled to overflowing, Emma and I stepped outside for our break. We always took it between making the cake donuts and waiting while the raised ones went through their first rest, and it was a nice time to chat and catch up.

"How's your dad's investigation going?" I asked. "Is he having any luck on his end of things?"

Emma shrugged. "You know Dad. He thinks he's right, until you or the police prove that he was off base all along. I'm sure he has a suspect in mind, but if he does, he's not sharing it with me."

"It wasn't because you've been feeding

me information, is it?" I asked. I would hate it if my investigation had come between father and daughter.

"No, you're in the clear. As a matter of fact, he just assumes that I'll tell you everything. No, Dad doesn't want his theory to leak to anyone. I know he's serious, because he hasn't even told Mom, and you know how those two are. If I had to guess, though, tomorrow's paper is going to have his theory in it."

"How can he do that without being sued?" I asked.

"Dad won't print anything unless he has evidence to back it up. The funny thing is, I heard him talking to someone on the phone last night, and for a split second I thought I could hear Jake on the other end of the line. I'm crazy, right?"

"You might be in general, but not necessarily about that," I said with a smile. "I know the two of them have spoken from time to time in the past. It would be smart of your dad not to tackle a killer on his own. I bet Jake would give him first shot at a scoop if your father provided him with any valuable information that led to an arrest."

"I don't know. That sounds kind of timid for Dad. He's the kind of guy who rushes into the burning building when everyone with any sense is running the other way."

I shrugged. "I don't know, then. It was just a theory."

We were quiet for a bit, and just before we were due to go back in, Emma said, "I'm going to miss this time most of all."

"It is lovely how quiet it is," I said, taking in the early-morning silence. Despite the frigid temperature, or maybe because of it, I felt more alive when the thermometer dropped.

"I'm talking about our chats," Emma said.

"Don't worry. Anytime you're home from break, you can come by and we'll hang out. It'll be just like old times."

"I'll be here," she said.

I had to laugh. "I won't hold it against you if you don't," I said. "This is still pretty early for a college student."

She grinned. "Maybe I'll swing by before I go to bed, then."

"Either way, you're always welcome," I said. "This is your home, too, and I couldn't have done it these past few years without you."

We stood and hugged, then my timer went off.

"Sorry about that," I said as we headed back inside.

"Are you kidding? I couldn't imagine a

more fitting end to this conversation."

It was nearly time to open, and Emma had stepped up front for a minute.

"What's up?"

"Give me a second," she said with a mischievous grin on her face. "I want to try something out on you."

Two minutes later she called out, "Come on up. I'm ready for you."

I walked into the dining area and saw her sign.

It read: *special onetime offer only: two donuts for a dollar, or three for two bucks.*

"You'd better check your math," I said.

"It's intentional," she said. "Don't you think it's a riot?"

"What I think is that you may be sleep deprived. Nobody in their right mind is going to buy three donuts for two bucks when they can get two of them for a dollar."

"Wanna bet?" she asked me.

I nodded. "If you sell more than three of the two-dollar specials, you can come in an hour late tomorrow morning."

"What if I sell more than that? Is it an hour extra for each special?"

"Not a chance," I said with a smile. "And you can't call anyone or tell anyone at all about our bet. Deal?"

She nodded and stuck out her hand. "Deal."

"I've got a feeling I'm going to get a lot of questions about this sign," I said as I put it in the new window.

"Hey, if it gets folks talking and coming in, that's not a bad thing, is it?"

"I hope not," I said, matching Emma's smile with one of my own. "But I'm not about to rule it out."

"Suzanne, your sign is wrong," James Settle said when he walked into the donut shop a little after nine.

I had explained it two dozen times, and I was tired of going through the same thing over and over. Just as I'd expected, everyone had a comment about it. What had caught me by surprise was how many folks had taken advantage of the two-dollar "bargain." I'd sold seven so far, and several singles beyond it, so that my extra stock was nearly gone.

"You're right," I said as I took a clean towel and wiped the board clean. "Better?"

"Hey, I didn't mean anything by it," the blacksmith said. "I thought it was kind of funny, that's all."

"No worries, James. It was meant as a

joke, but you'd be amazed how many we sold."

He laughed. "It doesn't surprise me a bit. That's why I'm so glad I moved here. This town is full of quirky people."

"You fit right in then, don't you?"

"I hope so," he said seriously. "I've volunteered for everything I can think of. It's a great way to meet people."

"I hear the ladies of the Ruffle and Raffle Society were particularly pleased with your presence."

James shook his head. "I thought it meant something else," he explained. "I know, it doesn't make much sense, either, but what could I do?"

The society was dedicated to making quilts, one every six months, and gossiping about what was going on in April Springs behind the scenes.

"You could always quit," I said. "I can't imagine it's much fun for you."

"Are you kidding? The ladies are teaching me how to sew, and I'm doing any heavy lifting they need taken care of. Besides that," he added with a wink, "they've decided that I'm underweight, so they take turns baking me cakes, cookies, and pies. Trust me, I'm getting the best end of that deal." He waved the bag of donuts at me,

318

smiled broadly, and then left.

James and I had started off on opposite sides of the same issue, but since it had been resolved, we'd formed an odd kind of friendship. Most days I enjoyed seeing the blacksmith, though there were times when we still butted heads. That was okay. Not everyone had to agree with everything I thought. It would be a pretty bland world if that were the case, not that there was any danger of that ever happening.

With the board now blank, it was business as usual. Emma had been banished to the kitchen, lest she give away our competition, but when she finally walked out front near eleven, she looked at the board and asked, "What happened?"

"You won hours ago," I said. "I don't know how you did it, but you nailed it. Enjoy your extra hour tomorrow."

She shrugged. "That's okay. I was just teasing you."

"A deal is a deal," I said. "You earned it. I don't know how we would have unloaded all of those donuts if you hadn't stepped up."

Emma shook her head. "They would have sold. Suzanne, if it's all the same to you, I'll be in at my regular time tomorrow. After all, we only have a few weeks left together."

"It's your choice," I said, touched that she honestly cared that much. "I'd love to have you here, but you had a great idea, and you deserve a reward for it." As I said it, I decided what might be fitting. I reached into the till and took out a twenty-dollar bill. "If you want to work, I insist on giving you an employee bonus for a great idea."

"I shouldn't," she said.

"Nonsense. We had a good day because of you. Tell me you can't use it."

"I would, but I hate to lie to you." She took the bill with a grin and tucked it into her apron. "Thanks. I'll just finish up with the dishes and the racks, and then I'll be on my way. I've got a lunch date."

Emma was known for her joy of dating, but I hadn't heard about anyone new in the past few weeks, a definite change of pace for her. "Anybody I know?"

"It's my dad," she said. "Now that I'm leaving, he suddenly wants to bond with me. Can you believe that?"

"I think it's sweet," I said. "Your dad loves you."

"I know, but I keep telling him that just because I'm moving way doesn't mean that I'm going to change. It's college; it's not like I'm going to the moon."

"What can I say, you are just a lovable

gal," I said with a smile. "Tell you what. At least take off now. I'll wash up, and you can go home and shower before your lunch."

"If you wouldn't mind, that would be great."

I let her out, and then locked the door behind her. Donut Hearts was officially closed for another day, and the donut part of my life was over. That didn't mean I could just go home and relax, though.

I'd already worked a full day, but now it was time to continue investigating Cam Hamilton's murder.

I got a call on my cell phone when my hands were buried in the soapy water, and I couldn't dry them fast enough to answer in time. I waited for a message, but whoever called didn't leave one. I dried my hands and checked to see who the missed call was from. It was Grace, and the impatience she'd shown had been a little out of character for her.

I called her back, and she picked up on the first ring. "Hey. What's up?" I asked.

"I tried calling you, but you didn't answer."

"I'm doing dishes. Where are you?"

"Out front. Any chance there's any coffee left, and maybe a donut or two?"

"Hang on," I said as I walked out into the dining area. I waved to her, hung up my phone, and unlocked the door.

"Hey," she said, "you hung up on me."

"I didn't think there was any need to stay on the phone with you standing right in front of me," I said with a smile.

"Why are you doing dishes and not Emma?" she asked.

"I let her take off early," I explained. "Care to join me?"

"First the coffee, then the treat, and then maybe I'll be decent company."

I studied her a moment, and then asked, "Grace, did you just get up?"

"Hey, I'm on vacation, remember? I'm entitled to sleep in a little." She took a bite of one of the donuts I had left, a peanut-coated cake that I loved myself. I'd saved it for a snack for later, but I could always make more tomorrow, and Grace looked as though she needed it right now.

As I finished drying the last rack, I asked, "Any thoughts on what we should do to-day?"

"I'd like to focus on Hannah and Evelyn," she said.

"Okay, that sounds good," I said. "Why don't we talk to their neighbors first and see if they have any thoughts about Cam's

322

murder. Who knows? Maybe someone can give us a reason we should look at one of them harder than the other."

"I like it," Grace said. "Do you have any more donuts left?"

I scanned the counter and saw three boxes. After peeking under each lid, I said, "We've got thirty-one."

"Box them in half-dozen lots, and we'll use them as bribes."

"What should we do with the odd one that's left?" I asked as I did as she suggested.

The lone holdout was a plain cake donut with no icing or glaze. I made a handful every day, knowing that some of my customers loved them. Grace looked at it for a second, and then shook her head. "No, one is all I can eat. You can have it."

I laughed. "Trust me, I eat enough over the course of the day. Let's give someone a bonus," I proposed, slipping it into one of the boxes. It was a tight fit, but I had a feeling that whoever got it wouldn't mind a spare.

I couldn't figure out why the register wouldn't balance, and then I remembered the twenty I'd given Emma. I marked it as "employee bonus," made out my deposit slip, and then we were ready to go.

As Grace and I loaded the boxes into my Jeep, I wondered if we were getting any closer to figuring out who had killed Cam, and why. Jake had a hunch he was on the right trail, but I was nowhere near as confident myself.

Maybe today would offer a clue we hadn't been able to discover yet.

I could only hope. I wanted to be back with my boyfriend without hiding like a couple of teenagers afraid they might get caught.

Evelyn's place was closer, but I knew I was in no hurry to question her neighbors, so I started to drive past her house. The odd thing was, though, there was a patrol car parked in front as we approached it. Were they making an arrest already? I was about to pull in when I saw her front door open and Chief Martin stepped outside. He looked embarrassed to be caught leaving his former abode, something that made me wonder what exactly he was up to. When he saw us, he blushed as he hurried to his patrol car.

I decided I didn't know how to deal with it, so I kept driving toward Hannah's place.

"Is the police chief actually cheating on your mother?" Grace asked. "With his ex-wife, of all people?"

I didn't want to go where she was thinking. "What are you talking about?"

"Come on, Suzanne. He's sneaking out of her house. Did you see how guilty he just looked when we caught him?"

"Grace, your imagination is on overtime right now. I may not be the police chief's biggest fan, but I can't imagine he'd ever step out on Momma. Think about it. Would you trade my mother for ten Evelyns?"

"No, of course not, but men have been known to do stupid things in the past."

I nodded. "And even a few women, too."

"You know what I mean," she said.

"I do."

As I drove on, Grace asked, "Aren't you at least going to call your mother and tell her what we just saw?"

I shook my head. "It's none of my business."

"Even if it means she's going to be hurt by this?"

I thought about it and realized that it was fine line I was dancing. If I didn't call Momma and it turned out that Grace's suspicions were true, I'd feel like a fool. Then again, if I called and it turned out to be innocent, or nothing at all, Momma would be upset because I was meddling.

I decided to take a chance on getting her mad, and reached for my phone.

"Momma, it's me. Got a second?"

"Just that," she said. "I'm on my way to meet Phillip for lunch."

It was an opening I couldn't resist. "I just saw him, as a matter of fact. He was leaving Evelyn's place."

Momma sighed. "Yes, she's been badgering him to come over, and he decided to go now so he could use his lunch with me as an excuse to get away."

"And you don't mind?" I asked.

"Mind? Why would I mind? I encouraged it. Evelyn has to learn that they aren't together anymore. She's having a more difficult time understanding that than I ever would have imagined. Now, what is it you wanted?"

I had to come up with a lie, and it had to be good, and fast. "I've got extra donuts, and I was wondering if you'd like any."

"Thank you for the offer, but I'm afraid I have to pass. Is that it?"

"That's it," I said. "Have a good lunch."

"I intend to," she said, and then hung up.

Grace was incredulous. "Donuts? You offered your mother, the best cook and baker in the county, *donuts?*"

"What else was I supposed to do? Not

only did she know about the chief seeing his ex-wife, she actually encouraged it. I'm just glad I could come up with something on the spot."

"Thinking of donuts must have been quite a reach for you," she said with a smile.

"What can I say? I'm a woman with a one-track mind."

APPLE YEAST DONUTS

I like to try variations of favorite donuts from time to time, and I'm quite pleased most of the time with the results, like this one. This recipe incorporates a Granny Smith apple, a tart and sweet apple I like to use for baking and donut making. This donut is delicious!

Ingredients

Wet
- 1 cup warm water
- 1 packet active dry yeast (1/4 oz.)
- 1 tablespoon granulated white sugar
- 2 eggs, beaten slightly
- 1/2 cup granulated white sugar
- 1/4 cup canola oil
- 1 teaspoon vanilla extract
- 1 teaspoon grated lemon peel
- Enough canola oil to fry donuts

Dry
- 3 cups all-purpose flour (I prefer unbleached, but bleached is fine, and so is bread flour)
- 1/2 cup finely diced apple (Granny Smith for its tartness)

Directions

Combine the water, yeast, and sugar in a small bowl and set aside.

Combine everything (eggs, sugar, oil, vanilla extract, lemon peel, finely diced apple) in another bowl EXCEPT the yeast mix (water, yeast, sugar) and the flour.

Add the yeast mix, stir, and then begin adding flour. The dough will be a little sticky, so don't worry about it. Turn out on a floured surface and knead the dough a few minutes, then cover and let rise in a warm place for about an hour and a half. I like to cover the bowl with Saran Wrap while it's rising, too.

Heat canola oil to 365 degrees before you roll out the dough.

After the dough has doubled in size, roll it out to 1/2–1/4 inch thick, then cut with a donut cutter.

Fry the donuts, not crowding the oil, flipping them when one side is brown.

Once the donuts are finished, remove them to a cooling rack and drain on paper towels.

These donuts can be dusted with cinnamon sugar (1 tablespoon granulated white sugar mixed with 1 teaspoon cinnamon).

Makes 6–10 donuts, depending on the size of your cutter

CHAPTER 17

"Mr. Yeats, could we have a moment of your time?" I asked as we found Garrett Yeats working in his backyard. Cam's newly purchased land was on one side of Hannah's property, and Garrett's was on the other. He hadn't answered the door when we'd rung the bell, so Grace and I had gone around back to see if we could find him there.

"That depends. Are you paying for it with donuts?" He eyed the box as though it contained gold instead of my treats.

"That's the deal," I said as I offered him the box.

He opened the lid like a kid at Christmas. "I shouldn't," he said as he surveyed my offering, "but I will." Garrett was a spry, older man who clearly loved to garden. All around us was a lovely landscape, and though it was February, it must have all been spectacular when it bloomed. Even in winter, the terracing, fountains, and arbors made it look as though it had been ripped from the pages of a horticultural magazine.

"Your garden is breathtaking," I said.

"This? You should see it when it's in full bloom. Glenda started it, and she poured so much of herself into it that when she died, I decided I had to keep it going. It's all for her."

"How long has it been?" Grace asked quietly.

"She passed away four years ago tomorrow, as a matter of fact. I'm taking some greenery to her grave, but on the half-year anniversary of her passing, I take her the loveliest bouquets so I can show her how everything is doing."

"I'm so sorry for your loss," I said. I knew they'd been together forever, and I couldn't imagine the hole his wife's departure must have left in his heart. Then again, Momma had had a hole herself for the longest time, and it was just now beginning to heal.

"Don't be," he said with a sad smile. "We had more time together than most, and I feel closest to her when I'm out here working."

He must have heard something that Grace and I had missed, because he suddenly stopped talking and shushed us.

I finally heard someone singing off-key, mangling the words to a song I loved. It was Hannah, and I suddenly understood Garrett's desire not to be spotted.

After she was safely past us, Garrett shook his head. "You can set your watch by that woman. From ten o'clock to eleven fifteen every morning, rain or shine, she's walking her property, singing in the worst way, and generally upsetting the wildlife around here. I duck her every chance I get, but sometimes I can't get away in time, and she chews my ear off."

"Did you happen to see her the day Cam Hamilton was murdered?" I asked.

"Oh, yes," Garrett said. "That was one of the bad days."

"Because of his murder?" Grace asked.

Garrett actually blushed a little. "It should have been because of that, but I meant it was one of the times Hannah caught me. She must have blabbered on for forty-five minutes about Cam and how he was going to destroy our neighborhood."

"Any idea when you two finished talking?" I asked.

"It was around eleven-thirty," he said. "My stomach was grumbling and groaning the whole time."

"Why wouldn't she admit that to us?" I

asked. "It gives her a perfect alibi."

Garrett chuckled softly. "That I can guess. Hannah is trying to lose weight, and this walking routine around her property is the way she's chosen to do it. If she admits to being out walking for so long, she has to admit why she's doing it, and that woman has become as vain as they come. When she had her shop, she was too busy to stop to eat much, but since she closed her business and sold the building, she's been slowly putting on the pounds." He winked at us and said, "Do me a favor and don't tell her I said that."

"Thanks, Mr. Yeats" I said.

"Is that all you wanted? And I get six donuts for it?"

"Actually, there are seven in there," I said, "and you earned every bite."

"Come back anytime," he said. "And you don't have to bring donuts next time, either. I just wish I had flowers to share with you that come close to matching how lovely you two ladies are this fine, brisk day."

As we walked back to the Jeep, Grace said, "He's a real charmer, isn't he?"

"From what I've heard, he always has been," I said. "I can't believe that Hannah is so vain that she wouldn't use an alibi that clears her of murder just because she doesn't want anyone to know that she was exercising."

"Funny, I have no problem believing it at all," Grace said.

After we drove for a few minutes, I said, "I suppose we have to tackle Evelyn now."

"Well, her neighbors, at any rate," Grace said. "Sorry, there's no way around it."

"At least we're all set with bribes," I said as I glanced in the back where the donuts were safely resting.

"There aren't many folks who can say no to them, are there?"

I laughed. "There are a few holdouts, but not that many."

I parked down the block so that Evelyn wouldn't see us as we got out.

At least that was my theory.

It was just too bad that she came out her front door the second I parked.

"Duck," I told Grace, who did it without being asked.

I peeked over the dash and saw Evelyn getting into her car, a brand-new blue Toyota Yaris that I had to wonder if she'd paid for with money from the divorce settlement.

"What are we doing?" Grace asked.

"There's a change of plans. We're going to

follow Evelyn and see where she's going."

"Isn't this the perfect time to talk to her neighbors?" Grace asked. "At least then we know there's no way she's going to just pop up."

"We'll come back if there's time, but I've got a hunch this is more important."

"Then let's follow her," Grace suggested. She was easy to get on board any plan I came up with, supporting it as strongly as though she'd developed it herself.

As Evelyn drove on ahead of us, I tried to stay back far enough so she wouldn't spot me, but close enough so that I wouldn't lose her. It was harder than it sounded, complicated by the fact that there were only a handful of Jeeps the color of mine in the county. If she spotted us on her tail, I had a feeling there was going to be a scene, and a bad one at that.

"Why is she going there?" Grace asked as we saw Evelyn head toward the hospital.

"I haven't a clue. Could she be visiting someone?" I asked.

But Evelyn didn't turn off when we got to the hospital. Instead, she kept driving toward Maple Hollow.

I had a feeling in my gut that I knew exactly where she was headed.

I just didn't know why.

When she turned off two miles later, I knew I had to be right. "This is the way to Harvey Hunt's place."

"Why would Evelyn go see Harvey?" Grace asked.

"I wish I knew, but this is too big a coincidence to write off."

Sure enough, Evelyn pulled into Harvey's driveway, and I managed to hide the Jeep twenty feet down the road behind a stand of white pines. It gave us enough cover to be out of sight, but we could still see Harvey's front door. Evelyn got out of her car and walked up the front steps. After ringing the bell half a dozen times, she looked as though she were about to explode.

Even at the distance Grace and I were watching from, we could hear her pounding on the door with her fist. "Harvey, open this door this instant, you big coward. The money I loaned you may not mean much to you, but it's just about all I have in the world, and I want it back right now, one way or the other. Either you give me my cash, or I'll take it out of your hide!"

There was still no response, and Evelyn left the porch and walked around to the back of the house. I had to give her chops: she was persistent. As soon as she disappeared, I opened the Jeep door and

337

started to get out.

"Where are you going?" Grace asked, whispering for some odd reason.

"We need to see what she does next," I answered.

"How are we going to explain being here if she catches us?"

I grabbed a box of donuts, not at all sure how I was going to use them, but glad I had them with me.

Grace looked at me with open wonder. "Donuts? Seriously?"

"Come on," I said as I headed toward the house. "Where's your sense of adventure?"

"Just being your friend is an adventure most of the time," she said with a low laugh.

We got around the house just in time to see Evelyn start pounding on the back door.

The response was the same, and I had to wonder if Harvey was even there. I wasn't sure what Evelyn was going to do next, but if she threw a brick through Harvey's window, it wouldn't have surprised me in the least.

There was nothing that dramatic, though. She finally gave up, and as she walked back to her car, Grace and I cut through a neighbor's yard and raced for my Jeep.

Only to find Jake already standing there, as though he'd been waiting for the two of us all along.

"Care to explain yourselves?" Jake asked with a smile.

"Would you believe we're having a fund-raiser for charity?" I asked as I held the box of donuts in my hand out to him. "Care to buy a half dozen?"

Jake shook his head. "Sorry, I'm not buying it. What's going on?"

I thought about a thousand lies I could tell him but finally settled on the truth. "We were following Evelyn Martin, and to our surprise, she led us straight here."

"Do I even want to know why you were tailing the police chief's ex-wife?"

"She's on our suspect list," I admitted. "Hey, I've got some good news. We came up with an alibi for Hannah."

Jake looked surprised to hear it. "Go on, I'm listening."

"She was walking her land for exercise when Cam was murdered."

My boyfriend frowned at the news. "How could you possibly know that?"

"Go talk to Garrett Yeats," I said. "He's her alibi. Ironically enough, she talked the entire time about how they had to do something to stop Cam from clear-cutting the lot beside her."

"Good work. I'll talk to him," Jake said.

"We gave you something," Grace said. "It's only fair that you tell us something. We told you why we're here, but how about you? I refuse to believe that we all just randomly showed up at the same place."

I could have strangled Grace, but Jake didn't seem to mind. "I'm looking for Harvey Hunt. It seems that he's the one missing now."

I let that go. "Do you think he killed Cam?"

Jake just shrugged. "I can't say for sure, but I would love to find him and ask him a few questions. You don't have any idea where he might be, do you?"

I looked at Grace, and we both shook our heads.

"We don't have a clue," I said.

"Don't worry. We'll find him, one way or another," Jake answered.

"Good luck with that," I said as I got into the Jeep. "Let me know, okay?"

He didn't answer my request, but he asked something himself: "Where are you two troublemakers headed off to now?"

I shrugged. "Hey, we've got to get busy. After all, these donuts aren't going to sell themselves."

As we drove away, I could see Jake in my

rearview mirror, and if I wasn't mistaken, he was gently laughing as he watched us leave.

Harvey Hunt's disappearance was no laughing matter, though. Had he run when he believed that the police were closing in on him, or was it something more chilling? Was it possible that the real murderer had claimed another victim, and Harvey was inside his house right now, sharing the same fate that had struck Cam Hamilton?

"Who's next on our list? We'd better ask any questions we can, if folks are going to start disappearing on us," I said after we stopped twenty minutes for two Pepsis.

"We're closer to Kelly, and after we talk to her, we can tackle William again. At least we know he's not running, not with his gout."

We got to Kelly's place, but she wasn't home, either.

"This is so frustrating," I told Grace. "Why can't people hold still so we can question them?"

"In a perfect world, we could lock them all in the same room and grill them until we were ready to unmask the killer."

"Unfortunately, we don't have that option. I think we should —"

341

My sentence was interrupted when Grace's cell phone rang.

"You're what?" she asked excitedly. "I'll be there in ten minutes."

"Take me home," she said the second she hung up.

"Yes, ma'am. Right away, ma'am."

"Sorry, I didn't mean for that to sound like an order," Grace said with a broad smile. "Peter got back early, and he's sitting on my front porch waiting for me. Do you mind?"

"Not one bit," I said as I turned the Jeep around and headed back to Grace's house. I tried my best to be a part of her excitement. "That's a nice surprise, isn't it?"

"Suzanne, I don't know how you do it," she said.

"What's that?"

"Spend so much time away from Jake. I think it would kill me to do that with Peter."

I shrugged. "It's amazing what you can deal with in the name of love."

"Isn't it?" she asked.

I wasn't about to go down that road with Grace. As we neared her car back in town, she barely waited for me to slow down before she jumped out of the Jeep. "Call me later," she said.

"Sure thing," I said, absolutely knowing that there was no way I was going to interrupt her reunion with her boyfriend.

I thought about driving the last quarter mile home and calling it a day myself, but just because Grace was playing hooky from our investigation didn't mean that I could. I knew that every moment I wasted was another minute that Momma stayed a suspect in the mayor's murder. I also realized that Jake was on the case, and I had full confidence in my boyfriend, but there was a little stirring I could do behind the scenes that he couldn't do.

My phone rang, and it was George.

"Hey, where are you?" I asked as I turned around.

"I have one more stop to make before I'm on my way back to my place," he said. "I talked to Evelyn again," he added softly.

"When did this happen?"

"As a matter of fact, I just left her."

"Is she okay?" I wasn't suddenly concerned for her, but more for my mother's sake. If Evelyn could make trouble for Momma, then she was making trouble for me, too.

"She finally broke down and told me her secret," George said. "It's an alibi that I'm going to confirm right now, and if it holds up, which I'm willing to bet it will, she's in the clear."

"What has she been hiding?" I asked, barely able to contain my excitement.

"I can't tell you that, but it didn't involve Cam, at least not directly."

"Are you saying that she didn't have a motive for murder?"

George answered, "Suzanne, you can cross her off of your list; Evelyn didn't kill Cam. She just told me so herself."

"And you believed her?" I couldn't believe that George, a seasoned ex-cop, could buy her story that easily.

"I'm a good judge of character. I saw the look on Evelyn's face when she told me where she was when Cam was murdered, and there was certainly a lot of shame there, but not an ounce of guilt, at least about what happened to Cam. The guy she was with is married, but if you breathe a word of that to anyone, we're through. That avenue is a dead end."

How was I going to handle this without alienating a dear friend? "George, I appreciate your loyalty to her, but I have to know. What did she tell you? Who exactly was she with?" I asked. I knew that it was none of my business, or anyone else's, except the wife of the man she'd been cheating with.

344

Evelyn was as free as the chief was to see other people.

He blew out a huff of air, and then said, "I forgot how clever you were, but you're not getting anything else out of me. That part of our investigation is over."

"Fine," I said. I wasn't as accepting of Evelyn's story to George as he had clearly been, but I would put her on the back burner, at least for now. If her alibi checked out, I would trust George to tell me the truth. While he was following up on that, I had three other good suspects to consider at the moment myself. Harvey Hunt had owed Cam a great deal of money, and we only had his word that he'd paid the debt off before the murder. Too, Harvey had lost a big contract to Cam, something that had to be a blow to his financial status as well as his pride. There was a possibility that both situations had worked out for him with the mayor's murder. William Benson had a pair of reasons to want the mayor dead as well. Not only had he lost a permit he'd been counting on to expand his business, but he'd also developed a crush on Kelly Davis, a woman who admitted that Cam had her heart. Kelly herself had a motive, too, being dumped unceremoniously after believing that Cam was going to marry her. She had a temper too, I'd seen that myself, and I had no problem believing that Kelly could have killed Cam in a fit of rage.

I had three suspects, most likely just one killer, and no idea about how to prove who, exactly, had killed the mayor.

It was time to stir the pot again, and William was next on my list.

As I drove up to his house, I saw Kelly's black Trans Am parked in front. How odd. I didn't think Kelly wanted to have anything to do with William, but had she changed her mind now that Cam was dead? Or was there something more sinister going on inside? I would have loved to hear what they were saying. It would even be worth the chance that they'd catch me doing it.

Maybe, if I got lucky, I could sneak up without them knowing I was there.

I tried the front door, but it was no real surprise when I discovered that it was locked. The next step was to test the windows on the front porch, though I wasn't sure I could crawl through one without anyone noticing.

Maybe I wouldn't have to, though.

I pushed at one of the windows, and was delighted when it opened slightly. I hadn't heard any voices before, but now I could make out two: Kelly and William were discussing something, and it was pretty clear that neither one was very happy about it.

CHAPTER 18

"I don't care how much you say you love me," I heard Kelly say loudly. "I'm not interested, William, so stop pursuing me. Trust me. It's never going to happen."

I couldn't see them, but from their voices, I guessed they were in William's living room. I felt like a Peeping Tom standing there listening, but I couldn't pass up a chance to get more information from the two of them.

William's voice was raw as he answered her, as though he'd been crying. "You can't do this to me, Kelly. You told me a month ago that if Cam weren't around, you might decide to be with me."

"I said it to get you to leave me alone, you idiot," she said, the scorn in her voice coming through clearly. "Why would I be interested in you? You're too old for me, and you own an arcade, for goodness' sake. I used to call you Uncle William when I was a kid.

The idea of being with you now just creeps me out."

"Why didn't you tell me the truth before?" he asked, his voice nearly weeping again.

"It wasn't worth the effort," Kelly said.

"There's so much I can never take back, things I've done that can't be undone. I did so much for you," William said, and I watched as he hurried toward her.

"You're nothing but an old fool. Stop that. Let go of my arm," Kelly said loudly, and I leaned forward to see if there was any way I could see them better.

That was a mistake.

"Suzanne?" William asked, his voice shaking with anger. "How long have you been standing there?"

"I just got here," I said.

"You might as well come in," he said. "You've heard enough already."

"That's okay. I can come back later," I said. There was something about the way they'd been talking that unsettled me. William's last comment in particular sent my mind racing. He'd said, "I did so much for you." It could mean only one thing. He must have killed Cam to get Kelly. Only, after William had done the deed, he found out that Kelly didn't want him after all. I'd been looking at the denied permit as William's most likely motive, but it seemed that Kelly was the real reason he'd committed murder.

"You two can do what you want," Kelly said, "but I'm leaving. Let go of my arm, William."

He shook his head, and I saw his grip tighten on her as he pulled a gun from his pocket. "Suzanne, get in here, or you're going to have Kelly's blood on your hands."

I thought about running then and there, but if I did that, Kelly was dead. I couldn't have that on my conscience for the rest of my life.

"The door's locked," I said as I tried to put a hand in my pocket so I could take out my cell phone.

"Climb in through the window, then," William said. All traces of friendly Uncle William were gone.

A murderer was talking now.

I flipped the phone open and managed to hit a speed dial button, hoping I'd dialed Jake's number. I didn't want Grace or Momma to rush over there, as much as I loved them. I was in enough trouble as it was without having to worry about them.

As I climbed in through the window, the first thing William said was "Give me your cell phone. Now!"

I'd tried to let someone know that I was in serious trouble, but there was one more thing I might be able to do.

"Here, William," I said as I handed it to him.

He saw that it was on when he took it, and before I could say another word, he threw my phone down on the floor with such force that it broke and scattered into a dozen pieces.

"Why did you have to come here?" William asked. "Your nosing around is going to cost you big-time."

"You're hurting me," Kelly said, the sting out of her voice now. She was clearly afraid, and from the way William was looking at her, I didn't blame her one bit.

"You deserve it, and more," William said. "You can't treat people that way and get away with it." He shoved her as he released her arm, and Kelly stumbled toward me.

I steadied her as she neared me, and we both faced William together. "I see your gout's better. It's a real miracle, isn't it?"

"I had to move quickly, so I figured if folks around town thought I couldn't walk, it might be to my advantage."

"Is that how you got Cam to come to Hannah's to meet you?" I asked, hoping to stall him long enough to figure out a way to stop him. Kelly was not going to be any help. I glanced over at her and saw that she was staring at him, nearly catatonic with fear. Unfortunately, this wasn't the first time someone had pointed a gun at me. Instead of petrifying me, it sharpened my senses and put my mind into some kind of accelerated state. I tried to take in every detail around us, searching for something I could use as a weapon.

The only thing I could see was William's cane. Unfortunately, it was two steps closer to the man with the gun, and if I reached for it, I'd be dead before my hand ever touched the handle. There had to be some way to distract him, but I didn't have the slightest clue what it might be.

"Cam was an arrogant fool," William said, "and a greedy pig. He underestimated me, especially when I showed up at the empty shop with my cane, looking like a doddering old man. I told him I'd had a change of heart about the bribe he'd required to stop blocking my permit and that I had the cash in my pocket. It was almost amusing to see how eager he was to get the graft."

"Why Hannah's old business, though?" I asked as I used one arm to nudge Kelly forward. She hadn't been expecting it, and she nearly stumbled from the force of my shove. I was hoping William hadn't seen it as I stepped forward twice as I steadied her.

"What's wrong with her?" William asked, though there was no tenderness in his voice now. He was being the stern taskmaster, the benevolent uncle long gone.

"Can't you see that she's scared out of her mind?" I asked. "I think she's in shock."

William shook his head in disgust as I looked at the cane. One lunge would get me to it, and if I could swing it at his gun, I might just be able to knock it out of his hand. I needed a big distraction, though, and I wasn't sure that I could shove Kelly again without him noticing it. "You never answered my question. Why Hannah's?"

"I had a key from when Amanda worked there," he said. "That fool Hannah never took it back, and to my surprise, the new owner didn't change the lock either. It seemed to be fated when I found that out."

"So you killed Cam to get Kelly," I said.

William looked at the object of his unrequited love with open contempt. "It might not have worked out the way I'd hoped it would, but he deserved it. Cam Hamilton was a bad man, and an even worse mayor. We're all well rid of him."

William's phone rang at that moment, and he glanced at it for a split second to see who was calling, taking his eyes off us in the process. I shoved Kelly down as I reached for the cane, and as William whirled back toward us, I scooped it up and threw it at William with as much force as I could muster.

We were close enough to each other that, though I missed the gun, I did manage to hit his arm instead. The result was nearly the same as I'd hoped, with the weapon clattering to the floor out of his grip. William dove for it, but I was a little faster, and I got it in my hands, at least for a second or two.

Then he grabbed both of my hands, and we wrestled for the weapon as we fought on the floor for control.

I knew if I lost this battle, he'd kill Kelly and me.

But though William was quite a bit older than me, his grip was stronger, and I felt myself slowly losing control. Nothing else mattered, and I blocked the world around us out of my mind as we grappled together for control of our destinies.

I nearly had it, at least I thought I did, but then my grip started to fade.

It was starting to feel like he was going to get control.

William might win, but not before I used

my last ounce of power to stop him.

He was just about to wrestle the gun away from me when I saw that Kelly had somehow managed to shake at least some of the cobwebs from her mind and stand up. She was still mostly in her trance-like state, though, and I knew she wouldn't be able to help me beat William.

Or could she? "Go on, hit him. What are you waiting for?" I asked, staring at her as though she were holding a club over his head.

William's grip eased as he looked back toward her and flinched from the imagined upcoming impact, and I gave one last push, spending the last bit of my strength, but managing to finally get the gun away from him.

I stood and backed away from him, keeping the gun on him at all times, but William just laughed as he stood as well.

"Come on, Suzanne, who are you kidding? You wouldn't shoot Uncle William, now, would you?"

I put a bullet between his feet, and he stopped laughing.

It also managed to snap Kelly out of her trance. "What happened?"

"Uncle William just punched his last ticket for the arcade," I said. "Call the police, would you? My cell phone doesn't look as though it's going to do me much good."

Kelly did as I asked, though I never saw it. The gun in my hands never wavered from William's heart, and it was only after the police chief got there that I relinquished it.

"He killed Cam to get to Kelly," I said simply.

"Harvey didn't do it?" Chief Martin asked, clearly having a hard time believing it.

"No, though he had reason himself. I heard the complete confession."

"Can you back it up?" Chief Martin asked Kelly.

"I heard it all, too," she said, with more conviction than I could ever believe she could muster, given her recent state.

As the chief cuffed William, I asked Kelly softly, "Did you really hear him?"

"I lost it, I know, but I remember that part of it. You saved me, Suzanne."

"I saved us both," I said as I found myself in her embrace. My arms were worn-out, but it was my legs that deserted me then. My body had stayed hopped-up on adrenaline long enough to get me out of a jam, but after that, it clearly decided that its work was done for now. Kelly held me up for a few seconds, and then I recovered enough to stand upright on my own.

Jake came rushing in and took over, a situation I much preferred. He hugged me, gave me a quick kiss, and then brushed the hair off my face. "Are you okay?"

"I'm good now," I said. "Thanks for coming."

He grinned. "Thanks for calling."

"You actually got that?"

Jake nodded. "I heard you say William's name before the call went dead."

"And that was enough of a clue for you?"

"Hey, we're in sync, what can I say? Not that you needed me," he said. "It seems you took care of it on your own."

"I had a little help from a friend," I said, glancing at Kelly.

Kelly heard it and wouldn't let it stand. "Don't kid yourself, I was worthless."

"I don't know about that," I said, remembering how I'd used her twice as a distraction to take William down.

"I do." She looked at Jake and said, "You've got yourself one brave woman there."

"Don't I know it," he said.

An hour later, we were in Chief Martin's office, just the chief, Jake, and me. I asked, "What ever happened with Harvey? Did you

357

find him?"

Jake grinned. "Oh, I found him, all right."

"Did he say why he ran?" I hadn't been able to figure that part out.

"He told me, but I didn't believe him until I got your call. He thought Vern Yancey was trying to kill him."

"Vern, from Hudson Creek? Why would Vern want to kill Harvey?" I'd had my own share of run-ins with the man in the past, but I couldn't imagine how his name came up in all of this.

"Vern was the third bidder on the sewage treatment plant," Jake explained. "Harvey figured that with Cam out of the way, Vern would come after him next, since he was the third-highest bidder on the contract, and Harvey knew that he hadn't killed the mayor himself."

"Wow, talk about your rampant paranoia," I said.

"From Harvey's perspective, it made perfect sense," Jake said with a wry smile. "I figure he just projected how he'd react if he was desperate enough onto how Vern might behave."

We'd both met Vern, and the man was indeed a weasel in his own right, but I didn't think he'd kill for another job. From what I'd heard, he was already rich enough, if there really was such a thing for some people.

"What about the money he owed Cam? Did you ever find it?"

"I'm guessing it never got paid back," Chief Martin said. "I can't prove it, though."

"Are you saying that Harvey would actually lie to us?" I asked, with a grin of my own.

"With every breath he takes," the chief said. "We'll probably never really know."

Something had been bothering me for some time, and I had to know the answer, no matter what the consequences.

I looked at my boyfriend and asked, "Jake, would you give us a second alone?"

Jake looked surprised by the request, but he started to stand when the chief asked, "Is this about the case, or your mother?"

"The case," I said.

"Then Jake can stay."

"Are you sure?"

"There aren't any secrets here anymore, Suzanne," the chief said earnestly.

"Okay. Then why were you arguing with the mayor in your car just before he was murdered, and why didn't you tell Jake about it when he asked you?"

Jake nodded, looked at the chief for a second, and then said, "I'd like to know that myself. You've been guarded with me about your behavior from the start, and it's only served to make you look more and more suspicious in my mind. The first time we spoke, you were evasive about everything; and during our second conversation you tried to deny what I'd heard, remember?"

"It's not something I'm going to ever forget. You came as close to accusing me of murder as you could have without just coming out and saying it," the chief said. "I wanted to tell you, every last bit of it, but I was afraid how it would look."

"So you just decided to keep digging the hole you were in deeper and deeper," Jake said.

"It wasn't my intention, but I know that you both have a right to know those answers," he said. "I just hope that what I'm about to tell you doesn't go beyond this room."

I agreed readily, but Jake answered gravely, "That all depends on what you're about to say."

The chief thought about it for a few seconds and then nodded. "Fair enough. I've long had a suspicion that Cam was taking money for rigging bids, but I never had any proof. Finally, I couldn't take it anymore. He was a disgrace to this town, and I

360

decided it was time to have it out with him. I confronted him, and he demanded to know what evidence I had. I ended up bluffing him. I told him that if he didn't drop out of the mayor's race, I'd go to you, Jake, and tell you everything I knew about his illegal actions. He started yelling at me, and I yelled right back. Cam stormed out of the car then, and I never saw him alive again."

"Why didn't you come to me with this in the first place?" Jake asked in a cool, hard voice. "Don't you think that would have made more sense than keeping all of this to yourself?"

The police chief looked frustrated. "I was going to if he filed again, but I didn't have a thing on him that I could prove. You would have been just as helpless as I was. I figured getting him out of office was the best result I could hope for, since I couldn't just lock him up." He hesitated for a moment and then looked my boyfriend straight in the eye. "I'm sorry I didn't tell you about the argument. I guess I just didn't want to look bad in your eyes, but I know now that it was my pride holding me back."

We both waited for Jake to speak next, but when I saw my boyfriend nod once, I knew that the sheriff was going to be okay.

"Given the circumstances, you most likely

did the best you could," Jake said. "No one else needs to know about it."

Chief Martin was noticeably relieved.

I asked Jake, "So, what happens now?"

"There are no worries about William. He told me everything, and it backs up your story. He was so obsessed with Kelly, I'm not even sure that he knew what he was doing."

That surprised me, hearing Jake say that. "You think he was insane?"

My boyfriend just shrugged. "He thought he was in love. How much crazier can anybody get than feeling that way?"

"Hey, you're still talking about William, right?"

Jake squeezed my hand. "Don't worry. I don't mind being crazy about you."

"Right back at you," I said, and then turned to the police chief. "Have you told Momma yet that she's in the clear?"

"I thought I'd let you do it, since you solved the case," he said sheepishly.

I frowned. "I didn't solve it as much as I stumbled into the solution. It wasn't through some act of mental power that I uncovered what really happened."

"Don't sell yourself short," Chief Martin said. "You were in the right place at the right time, but you were in a bad situation, and you managed to get everyone out alive."

Compliments from him were rare indeed, so I decided not to dispute this one. "Why don't you go ahead and tell her?"

"Really? You wouldn't mind?" He looked as eager as a puppy striving to please.

"Go on," I said.

"Thanks, I appreciate that. I'll call her at the front desk," he said.

After he was gone, I asked Jake, "Did he just leave his own office for us? I thought for sure he was going to throw us out."

"You're in his good graces, but I wouldn't bank on it lasting very long," Jake said.

"Hey, I'll take whatever I can get. You're not mad, are you?"

My boyfriend looked puzzled by the question. "Why should I be mad?"

"I ended up stumbling upon the answer," I said. "You're a trained investigator, and I know that you would have arrested William sooner rather than later. I just got lucky, that's all."

Jake shook his head. "The chief was right. You had William pegged as a suspect before I did, and you were the one there following up on a lead. My definition of luck is being prepared when an opportunity presents itself."

"I just don't want this to come between us."

He took my hands as he stood, and I joined him.

After a long and lingering embrace, Jake said, "I don't know what you're talking about. I'm proud of you."

He kissed me then, and I felt my knees going weak again.

At least this time it was all for a good reason.

OLD-FASHIONED
CORNBREAD DROP DONUTS

Growing up, the cornbread my mother made was dense and more savory than the cornbread my family loves now. Our version is quite a bit lighter in texture and sweeter in taste. I love both versions, and this donut combines the best of both worlds. It's worth a try if you've ever been a fan of cornbread in your life.

Ingredients

Wet
- 1 egg, beaten slightly
- 1/2 cup granulated white sugar
- 1/2 cup whole milk (2% can be substituted.)
- 1/2 cup buttermilk
- 3 tablespoons butter, melted (I use unsalted; salted can be used, but cut the added salt by half.)
- 1/2 teaspoon vanilla extract

Dry
- 1 cup all-purpose flour (I prefer unbleached, but bleached is fine, and so is bread flour.)
- 1/2 cup cornmeal, self-rising (or regular cornmeal with 1 teaspoon baking powder)

- 1/4 teaspoon salt
- 1/4 teaspoon nutmeg

Directions

Heat canola oil to 365 degrees.

Combine the dry ingredients (flour, corn-meal, salt, and nutmeg) in a bowl and sift together. In another bowl, combine the wet ingredients (beaten egg, sugar, milk, but-termilk, butter, and vanilla extract). Slowly add the wet mix to the dry mix, stirring until it's incorporated. Don't overmix.

Drop teaspoon-size balls of batter into the oil, turning as they brown.

Remove and drain on a paper towel, then enjoy. We don't add any sweetness to these, but powdered sugar would be fine if you'd like something a little sweeter.

Makes 5–9 drop donuts, depending on bak-ing method

CHAPTER 19

A few weeks later at nine in the morning, I came over to the cottage Momma and I shared. I hadn't been there at that hour in more months than I could name, but this was a special occasion. Not only was Emma working her last day at Donut Hearts, but it was Election Day, and unless I missed my guess, my mother was about to become mayor of April Springs.

She was sitting at the table, reading the paper quietly and drinking a cup of coffee as I walked in.

A look of immediate concern spread over her face. "Suzanne, what are you doing here? Is something wrong?"

"You haven't voted yet, have you?" I asked. "Emma's working the front so we can go together."

"I thought I'd go sometime this afternoon," she said.

I took the newspaper from her and said

firmly, "I've got a better idea. Let's go now."

"Is it really necessary?" she asked.

"Oh, yes."

"Very well. We might as well get it over with."

"Aren't you excited?" I asked as I drove her to city hall where we always voted.

"I am, actually," she said with that secret grin of hers.

"Momma, what's going on? Have you done something?"

"Whatever do you mean?" she asked, her smile now even more prominent.

"You didn't throw the election, did you?" The last thing I wanted was Evelyn Martin as our new mayor.

"Suzanne, your imagination is much too active. I wouldn't even know how to go about such a thing."

"Come on, remember who you're talking to? You could overthrow a third world government if you set your mind to it. A small-town election would be a piece of cake for you."

"Let's just vote, shall we?"

We did that indeed, and a few folks wished Momma good luck as we left the polling place. While there were no signs at all for my mother, Evelyn had bought quite a few. I wondered if it might be enough to sway the election in her favor, but I had to rely on the good sense of my fellow townsfolk not to elect the woman.

As I headed for my Jeep, Momma didn't join me. "Get in. I have time to take you back home."

"Thanks, but it's such a lovely day, I think I'll walk," she said.

"Good luck," I said as she strolled casually away.

"Thank you, but I have a feeling luck won't have anything to do with the outcome."

Her smile was back again, but I had no idea what it was about.

"I'm back," I said as I walked into the donut shop. "Anything exciting happen while I was gone?"

Emma shook her head. "It's just been business as usual," she said. "Do you have the front now?"

"I've got it. Thanks. I can't believe this is it. Our last day together."

"Don't say anything," Emma said. "I don't want to start crying again."

During our early morning break, we'd both gotten maudlin, and it was all we could do to manage to produce the donuts together without ruining the batters and doughs with the added moisture from our tears.

"I'm okay now, but there are no promises for later."

"But not until we close," she said.

"Agreed."

Once Emma was safely in back, I motioned to the crowd waiting outside: George, Sandi, Emily, Grace, my favorite two snow-plow operators, Emma's mother and father, and even Jake were all there. They came in as a group, with balloons, flowers, banners, and even a cake. Once they had things set up, I opened the kitchen door and called out, "Emma, I need a hand for a second."

"I've just about got this load of dishes finished," she said. "Can it wait?"

"Sorry, no," I said, having a hard time keeping the grin off my face. "This is too important."

Emma came up front, wiping her hands on her apron, and with a curious expression on her face. "What's so important that it can't wait a second, Suzanne?"

Then she spotted everything, the crowd, the decorations, the cake, the entire celebration set up in her honor.

"Surprise!" everyone shouted in unison.

"I don't know what to say," Emma exclaimed.

"Wow, I never thought I'd ever hear you say that," I answered with a grin. "We're all going to miss you."

She started crying then, and I joined her as we hugged. I wasn't just losing my only employee; one of my best friends was leaving as well.

After the party broke up and everyone had pitched in to help clean up before leaving, only Emma and I were left in Donut Hearts.

"I guess this is it, then," she said as she handed me her apron.

"You're coming to the victory party in city hall, aren't you?" I asked. A great many of us had decided to have another party, two in one day. This one was for election night results. It wouldn't be on television, announced breathlessly to a waiting world. Marybeth Jenkins would walk down the steps with the results, and we'd know who our new mayor was, hopefully Momma.

"Don't worry. I'll be there."

I took her apron from her, gave her another hug, and then said, "I'm really going to miss you."

"Nan will be fine," Emma said. I'd hired a middle-aged woman to work with me, and she'd spent the last three days training with us. Nan had skipped the farewell party, though. She'd gone out of town while she

371

still could get away, and she wouldn't be back for several days. In the meantime I'd run Donut Hearts by myself, a fitting transition.

The party at the city hall wasn't anything like the farewell to Emma. There were no banners, though there were plenty of balloons. There was a punch bowl and a cake, but everyone was waiting to eat until we found out the results. Even Evelyn was there, though she stayed in one corner with her pack of friends.

Emma was standing with her folks to one side, and I asked her if I could have a moment of her time.

"I wanted to give you something before you left," I said as I reached into my jeans and pulled out an envelope.

"You already gave me a bonus," she said. "What's this?"

"Just open it," I urged her.

She did, and then saw the size of the check. It wasn't much from most people's standards, but it was all I could afford.

"Suzanne, I can't accept this," she said.

"You'd better. I've been saving it for nearly a month. Good luck, Emma. I'll miss you."

"I'll miss you, too," she said. "No matter

where I am, you'll always be in my heart." As Emma started to cry again, she headed for the bathroom to wipe away her tears.

When Marybeth finally tottered down the steps with the results, she had a confused expression on her face.

She faced us from the third step, and the room quieted instantly.

"I'm not sure how to say this, but something has happened that is unprecedented in town history."

"Was there a tie?" someone asked from the back.

"No, the results were absolutely conclusive, and I've just certified them, so the election is official."

"Who won, then?" another woman asked.

"Yes, I should get on with the announcement, shouldn't I," Marybeth said. She cleared her voice, and then read from the sheet of paper in her hands. "In an overwhelming majority vote, our new mayor is . . . a write-in candidate."

"What?" a dozen of us asked at the same time. I was standing beside Momma, ready to congratulate her, when I saw the broad smile on her face.

"What did you do? You never wanted the job, did you?"

"Neither did Evelyn," Momma said. "We

were both motivated for the wrong reasons."

"Who won, then?"

"Shhh," she said as she pointed to Marybeth. "Listen and you'll find out along with the rest of us."

"Quiet down, folks. If you give me the chance, I'll tell you the name of our new mayor."

For a brief second, I was horrified by the thought that Marybeth was about to read my name. I could never be mayor, and it wasn't just because of my business hours. I didn't have the temperament to do it.

When Marybeth finally did read the winner's name, it took me a second to realize who had won, I was so relieved that she hadn't called my name.

And then it sank in.

My dear friend George was the new mayor of April Springs.

And he looked as surprised to hear the news as everyone else.

It was indeed a new day in my hometown, some good, some bad, and some just different, but I loved living there, and couldn't imagine myself being anyplace else.

As we all congratulated George, he looked shell-shocked by the announcement, but he didn't say he was turning it down.

I smiled for a moment, realizing that I now

had a very important friend in city hall.

It might just help keep me out of trouble in the future, but somehow, I doubted it.

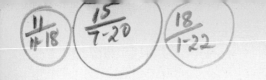

11
4-18

15
7-20

18
1-22

The employees of Thorndike Press hope you have enjoyed this Large Print book. All our Thorndike, Wheeler, and Kennebec Large Print titles are designed for easy reading, and all our books are made to last. Other Thorndike Press Large Print books are available at your library, through selected bookstores, or directly from us.

For information about titles, please call:
(800) 223-1244

or visit our Web site at:
http://gale.cengage.com/thorndike

To share your comments, please write:
Publisher
Thorndike Press
10 Water St., Suite 310
Waterville, ME 04901

JAN 0 3 2013

$\frac{3}{8-13}$ $\frac{7}{10-15}$ $\frac{18}{4-24}$

5-14   1-16

CPSIA information can be obtained
at www.ICGtesting.com
Printed in the USA
FFOW042038101212
458FF

9 781410 452658